EXCLUSIVE OFFER

Look out for the link at the end of this book or visit my website at **www.jmdalgliesh.com** to sign up to my no-spam VIP Club and receive a FREE Hidden Norfolk novella plus news and previews of forthcoming works.

Never miss a new release.

No spam, ever, guaranteed. You can unsubscribe at any time.

BURY YOUR PAST

HIDDEN NORFOLK BOOK 2

J M DALGLIESH

First published by Hamilton Press in 2019

Copyright © J M Dalgliesh, 2019

BURY YOUR PAST

PROLOGUE

THE EASTERLY WIND whipped sand into his face. The clouds parted momentarily revealing the new moon and a brief glance to the horizon saw the shifting light of the coming dawn. Time was limited. The fallen trees, a result of the violence of the previous night, left many local roads impassable with residents hunkering down in their homes to wait out the storm. Many heeded the warnings and travelled inland away from the coast, thereby avoiding the worst of the damage and disruption. Others, however, didn't fare as well. Coastal flooding struck several communities overnight according to the news report he heard on the radio. The power was out across much of the region with no indication of when things would return to normal, Norfolk's eastern coast battered back to the stone age in the space of a few hours.

Now amongst the dunes, he caught sight of another soul braving the lull that followed the previous night's events, walking their dog along the deserted beach. Dropping down he found some shelter from the elements with the dunes acting as a natural windbreak and the relative calm allowed him to hear the sounds of the nearby breakers crashing onto the beach. Reaching into his knapsack, he took out his small bundle tightly wrapped in linen. Laying it on the ground, he carefully unfurled the material to reveal the contents. A small circular mirror, slightly smaller than the palm of an adult hand, was put to one side. Alongside this he placed a black candle, a length of string and a piece of cinnamon bark. Lastly, he set down a smooth oval rock the size of a closed fist that he'd collected from the shoreline.

Taking a marker pen from his jacket, he picked up the mirror and scribbled a word upon it. Laying it in the centre of the linen he retrieved a cigarette lighter from his pocket and, protecting the wick from the breeze with his body, lit the candle. Once the wax began to melt, he angled the candle in order to allow three drops of wax to splash down onto the surface of the mirror. Then he allowed the breeze to extinguish the flame. Nervously casting his eyes to the east, the sun threatened to breach the horizon at any moment. The reddish backdrop to the tumbling angry clouds promised yet another day of turbulence. Putting the candle aside he reached for the cinnamon. Snapping the bark into smaller pieces in the palm of his hand, he closed his eyes and sprinkled it over the mirror whilst softly mouthing an incantation long committed to memory. Taking each corner of the linen in turn, he folded them into the centre creating a pouch of sorts and tied the corners together with the string. Working with more haste now, he used both hands to dig in and push the sand aside in order to fashion a hole roughly six inches deep at its centre. Then, he lifted the pouch and laid it carefully inside.

Picking up the rock, he hefted it above his head and looked out to sea once more. As the first glimpse of the sun crested the horizon, he brought his arm down as fast as he could, hurling the rock into the hole. The muted sound of the mirror smashing under the impact carried and without a moment to lose he refilled the hole as fast he could, smoothing over the topmost layer of sand with the palms of both hands. He left them flat against the ground, stretching out his fingers into the sand and feeling the slight warmth of the rising sun on his skin. Closing his eyes, in that very moment, he was certain the elemental power of the earth coursed through him.

The sound of a dog barking came to him on the wind, erratic and shrill. Something about the animal's intensity piqued his interest and he stood, slowly clambering up to the crest of the dune and looking down along the beach. Barely forty yards away, the dog, a black Labrador, was standing as if on point barking to alert its owner, occasionally stopping and leaning into the ground, pawing at the sand and tugging on something at the base of the dunes. Curious, he moved closer, watching as the dog's owner, an elderly man, drew near, pulling the animal away by its collar. For its part, the dog continued to bark excitedly.

Making his way toward them, he watched as the man knelt and appeared to be trying to retrieve something from the ground. Approaching, he saw whatever it was, it was wrapped in a piece of material and apparently well buried in the sand. The receding water lapped at their feet leaving a frothy residue as it dragged sand away from their discovery with each tidal sway. The dog came over to inspect the newcomer and he held out the back of his hand to allow the animal to smell him. The creature became rapidly disinterested and returned to its owner. Coming to stand alongside, he watched him recoil from the discovery before rising and backing away. They hadn't met before. The old man's face was ashen and pale, his eyes haunted. Looking past him, he wondered what he'd found.

"I… I better call the police," the man said, fumbling for his mobile phone. Intrigued, he stepped past and dropped to his haunches to inspect the find. Once white, the material was now heavily stained and discoloured by exposure to the elements. "Damn it. I haven't got a signal." That wasn't a surprise. The storm had brought down both trees as well as power lines and there was no reason the cell towers wouldn't also have been disrupted. Meeting the old man's eye, he recognised the expression. Not merely apprehension but true fear invoked by the discovery. *People are so scared of what they don't understand.*

Returning his gaze to the ground, he lifted the material to reveal what lay beneath. Folding it back he drew a hand across his mouth. The skull and a portion of the neck were given up from its sandy grave. The eye sockets stared up at him, empty and lifeless and the dawn sunlight glinted from a silver necklace hanging between the vertebrae. He leaned closer, lifting the pendant for a better look. "Do you think you should be doing that?" A nervous voice said from behind. He ignored him, inclining his head sideways and trying to imagine the face of the person buried in the sand. He pursed his lips. "I'm going back to my house. Maybe the landline will work from there. I really don't think you should be touching that." Summoning his dog, the man set off without another word.

Looking over his shoulder, he watched the retreating figure as he walked away. Once he was out of earshot, he returned his focus to the human remains once more and smiled, releasing his hold on the chain and allowing the necklace to drop. "I always knew one day you would be returned to us."

CHAPTER ONE

HAMMERING the pin into the bank, Tom Janssen tethered the bow of the boat to its mooring once again. Ensuring the rope was neither too loose nor too tight, thereby avoiding the mistake during the early hours when the boat slipped its mooring, he stepped away and decided to revisit the other pins just to be sure. He was disappointed with himself for making such a schoolboy error. Had he not returned when he had Alice would have been left in something of a predicament while he assisted with the evacuations. The previous night was one that would live long in the memory.

Satisfied with the handiwork of the remaining knots and the mooring pins they were tied to, he relaxed a little. Looking along the line of boats, none of the other owners were present. Many of them were weekend cruisers or used for short holidays across the water network, easily accessible by a trip along the coast, and very few were permanently occupied such as his. That suited him. The whole point was to offer respite from the constant barrage of the modern world, a place of calm where he could live a simpler existence. It might not last for more than another year or two, although that was what he said when he bought *The Moody Cow* four years ago. The name, painted on both sides of the hull and embossed on a plate hanging alongside the door at the stern, still brought a smile to his face. The man he bought it from didn't know from where the name originated, admitting he lacked the nerve to ask at the point of purchase. Often, he'd thought about changing it but nothing he could think of seemed right and besides, the boat held a charm of its own and the name seemed to fit.

"Tom! Coffee," Alice called, appearing from the cabin and stepping out onto the deck at the stern with a steaming mug in hand. She wore one of his jumpers over her own and ran her free hand through her hair. Clutching the hammer in one hand, he used the other to steady himself as he stepped aboard, placing the tool aside and gratefully accepting the drink. His eyes felt gritty and he lacked his usual energy off the back of three hours' sleep. "Breakfast's nearly ready. Do you want to eat out here?" He nodded and she disappeared below. Clearing space on the seats he also brushed some fallen leaves from the table and sat down. He admired how Alice took to spending time on the boat. The novelty factor, probably. Although adamant there was no better place to be in the spring and summer months, he accepted now autumn was upon them the best of the weather had passed. Even with the wood burner, a diesel generator and the pitiful insulation lining the cabin walls there was little escape from the reality that life aboard was tougher and far removed from the creature comforts of dry land.

This week turned out far different than intended. The plan was to take the boat down the coast, a break from the pressures of work and also giving the boat a much-needed run out. The last thing he needed was the engine seizing over the winter and he had been remiss with the maintenance during a much-troubled summer period. The office was still without a resident detective sergeant and central were debating the need for a permanent DCI. Until these decisions were made, they would continue on. Not that the indecision was causing him any concern. He was handling his caseload, just about. The superintendent even took him aside to sound him out about taking on the role himself. With the appointment of an experienced DS there was no reason why that couldn't work out.

This break was the last opportunity before the expected changes would no doubt be announced. After that there would be precious little time available. The complexity of combining his leave with Alice's, at a time when her estranged husband was available to take their daughter was also a challenge. Particularly once he found out Tom was on the scene. Last minute cancellations and changes to drop off and collections had become too frequent to be a coincidence. The desire to have a private word was tempting but not his place, he understood that. Alice needed to work it through with him but for someone as proactive and organised as she was, her ex appeared to have the measure of her and he couldn't quite understand why.

The double beep of his radio sounded below and descending the first couple of steps into the cabin, he reached across onto the nearby shelf to retrieve the unit. Catching sight of Alice frowning in the galley a few feet away, he depressed the call button and responded with his police ID before heading back up on deck. The unit crackled as he adjusted the volume.

"Tom, it's Eric." The detective constable sounded unsure of himself despite finally accepting they could be on first name terms. The formality required in the ranks seemed somewhat unnecessary in the size of the team they worked in and Tom pushed for CID to be as tight as possible. He spent more time with these officers than with his own family, or, as it recently transpired catching sight of Alice coming up the steps bearing a tray of food, his partner.

"What is it Eric?" His tone was firm but that was for Alice's benefit rather than through genuine irritation.

"We've had a call from a member of the public out at Wells. He says he's found a body on the beach... sort of... towards the Wells end of Holkham beach."

"Say again, Eric. Did you say *sort of*? Either he has or he hasn't." The reception was poor and he took out his mobile, glancing at the coverage indicator and seeing it crossed out indicating the network was still down. Seeing Alice in the corner of his eye setting out their food he knew she was upset. He understood why.

"Possibly brought ashore by the storm overnight but to be honest the details got to me second hand so I'm guessing. I'm heading over now but what with the road closures and everything it might take me some time to get there. The chief wants the scene contained just in case and the on call FME is as close as you are and... well..."

"Don't worry, I'll check it out and get back to you." He signed off and pulled out his chair. Alice was already eating, chewing slowly, her body shape rigid. You didn't need to be an expert to read the body language. "I'm sorry, love but I'm—"

"On call," she finished for him. She was curt, unforgiving. Had it not been for the arrival of the storm front and the region's emergency evacuation plan being put into action they would have been far from here by now, well removed from the impact of the tidal surge. He reached over and placed a hand on the back of hers, relieved it wasn't immediately batted away. She met his eye. "Go and do your thing, Tom. I'll be here when you get back."

"Thanks. I'll be as quick as I can. It's probably nothing anyway, a seal carcass got washed up or something and one of the locals got carried away. I'll get it squared away and be back as soon as I can." He leaned over and she turned her face to his, allowing him to kiss her briefly on the lips. "I'll make it up to you."

"Yes, you will, Tom Janssen. You most definitely will," she replied with a hint of a smile. "Now make sure you take your breakfast with you. I didn't spend the morning figuring out how to use your mini grill for you to clear off without eating it."

He grinned as he picked up the breakfast bap she'd assembled for him, taking a healthy bite from it as he descended below. Reappearing moments later in his waterproof jacket with car keys and radio in hand, he kissed her cheek and stepped off the boat and onto the bank. Today was their last day together before Saffy would be dropped home by her father and now it looked like he'd be working much of it. The drive out to Wells would take a while. The mooring was on his patch but what with the disruption wrought by the storm it would take longer than usual to reach the coastal town. Thinking on Alice's frustration, he understood completely. Eric would have let him be if at all possible but services in the region were stretched and in this job he was always on call.

REACHING the town half an hour later, he skirted the edge of the seafront of the town and continued on up Beach Road. To the right were the salt marshes and the entrance to the harbour front itself with a camp site for permanent holiday homes over the raised embankment off to his left. A thriving location for tourism, the sea front was dominated by signs of its traditional past. Warehouses, now converted into accommodation, lined the harbour walls and a mix of fishing vessels and pleasure boats lay at anchor. The impact of the tidal surge was apparent as he came upon the purpose-built dock set aside for the unloading of commercial vessels near to the harbour mouth. Several of the smaller vessels were either upended or lifted out of the water and deposited on the quay. Even the built-up protections were not enough to shelter them from the might of the North Sea on this occasion. Many of the locals responded to the threat and drew their smaller boats out of the water as far as possible. Those who didn't, gambled. Looking along the line back towards Wells itself, many appeared to have lost out. There were a few people around but far fewer than normal. Those keen to inspect the damage to property alongside others voyeuristically taking in the unusual events of the night were the only ones to venture out with the majority keen to remain where they were.

Coming to the gated end of the road within sight of the lifeboat station, he parked his car alongside a liveried police vehicle, no doubt the first responder sent to secure the scene if necessary. The exact position of the discovery was far too vague to pinpoint but he was sure it would become apparent the further he went. The beach café was locked up and the holiday park looked deserted. Even this late in the season it would usually be almost at capacity. From a cursory examination it appeared to have weathered the elements reasonably well. Signage was down and strewn across the car park in front of the café but the windows were either shuttered or boarded up and the damage was only superficial.

Passing through the gate he climbed the incline to the top of the embankment and looked down onto the beach. It was a well-trodden path and he made his way down. The high tide may have receded but the evidence of the night's events was all around with fresh seaweed deposited far higher than was normal such was the intensity of the swell. The breakers still hammered the shoreline and the forecast indicated much of the same was to come albeit not hitting the ferocity of the previous night. Even so, emergency plans remained in place for the coming days. Descending the wooden path bearing left around the headland and onto the sand, he was met by a scene of devastation.

Hugging the line of the coastal headland were the beach huts Wells was known for. Numbering around a hundred or so, the brightly coloured prized wooden huts, sitting directly on the sands, were famous in north Norfolk. Built on stilts to keep them safe above the tideline, they were not immune to the effects of the near-perfect storm surge. The sand was strewn with material from the huts. Splintered wood lay amongst chairs and equipment usually kept safely under lock and key but were now reminiscent of scattered matchsticks, some parts brightly coloured and identifiable whereas others were unrecognisable. Many of the huts survived intact with barely visible damage, aside from the likely water ingress, alongside others which were largely obliterated. In the distance a small group of people were gathered and he caught a glimpse of a high visibility jacket among them.

Arriving at the group, the constable spotted his approach and ushered him beyond the makeshift cordon, little more than two points marked out by the policeman and ostensibly being used as a point from which onlookers could observe. Word must have already spread and the level of interest told him the find was likely to be more than a dead seal carcass. He was led a further twenty yards to where the dunes began. Here he was greeted by Fiona Williams, the on call forensic medical examiner whom he knew well, an accomplished and diligent practitioner. She was kneeling as he greeted her and she rose, removing a latex glove and taking his offered hand.

"Tom. Good to see you." She indicated the ground at her feet. "You are going to find this one interesting, I can assure you."

CHAPTER TWO

DR WILLIAMS STEPPED ASIDE and Janssen moved closer. A discoloured material protruded from the sand with the remainder buried beneath perhaps two feet of sand although it was hard to tell. Dropping to his haunches and donning a pair of gloves, he gripped the edge of the material between thumb and forefinger lifting it to reveal what lay beneath. Easily identifiable as a human skull, he looked beyond the obvious in search of greater detail. The skull appeared to be remarkably well preserved and other than being buried in the sand, he could see no indication of damage to the face or jaw. The neck was also partly revealed and he was drawn to a silver necklace pendant hanging around it. The pendant itself was roughly an inch in diameter and consisted of a thin silver circle at the centre with two more crescents attached to either side.

"What are we potentially looking at here?" he asked over his shoulder before turning to Williams. She knelt alongside him bearing an expression of concentration. "I mean, is this recent or could we be looking at a site of archaeological interest?" Norfolk, as well as Suffolk further south, had a long history entwined with occupation by the Vikings and subsequently settled by the Saxons and notable finds were commonplace. Janssen was well aware of those people's connections with the sea and could countenance a burial on the coast.

"It's hard to be definitive but I think we're looking at something far more recent than that," she explained. "The fact the body has lain in the sand helps significantly. The lack of any stone or rock that could unsettle the pattern of the bone structure means the skeleton has remained intact and pretty well preserved. However, the bone is not as discoloured as I would expect were it to have been lying here for centuries. Not to mention this material that the body seems to have been wrapped in is a blend of cotton and something else. Otherwise it would have long since rotted away. Without wishing to damage your crime scene, I think we can see some of her clothing is still attached to her as well. That could help with dating when she went into the sand as well. Regarding the death, I think we can rule out natural causes." She pointed to an area on the right side of the skull, tracing several lines spreading out in different directions with her forefinger. "You can see these fractures emanating from this impact point. Obviously, it is too early to attribute that as the cause of death but I imagine it likely. What may have been used to do it is open to debate, arguably something with a flat edge and probably weighty."

Janssen took that on board, now gazing upon the remains as a definite crime scene. If she was correct, then they were probably looking at a murder. "There's always the possibility she was buried whilst still alive rather than dying from the blow." Dr Williams agreed with a brief nod of affirmation. "Early days but any idea if the victim is male or female?"

"Looking at the size and formation of the bone structure to the forehead, I would say it's most likely female." She leaned in closer and indicated the line of the forehead with her index finger. "You see here, the rounded shape of the bone and the smoothness of the supraorbital brow?" Janssen nodded. "That's indicative of a female, particularly when you take into account the round orbits of the eyes along with the obtuse angle of the jaw. Male jawlines are usually set at a more acute angle than this."

"Any idea of age?"

"The condition of the teeth, lack of fillings and the cosmetic dentistry imply she was young. Perhaps in her teens or early twenties."

"Cosmetic dentistry?" he asked, angling his head for a better view. Williams nodded.

"As adults we should have thirty-two teeth but this skull only has twenty-four," she explained. "Now, they are in great condition with none having been broken out prior to or displaced in burial so I should imagine she had her four wisdom teeth removed, as many of us do, and a further four to make room for straightening. Most likely through fitted braces. Rarely do humans generate such good alignment without help. If you look closely at the second to last molars, particularly on the upper track, you'll see discolouration of the enamel. That's probably down to the glue used to affix the blocks in place."

"If we find no other identifying marks that should give us some records to follow up on," he said, sounding hopeful.

"Bear in mind, though, this is still very much supposition until we can reveal the pelvic bone. I'll be far more confident then, provided we are dealing with a more or less complete skeleton of course. Once the lab techs can get involved, they will be able to do some chemical analysis of DNA extracted from the bone to determine how old she was and most likely her country or region of origin."

"Presupposing you are right how long would she have to have lain here for her to decompose this far?"

Dr Williams thought on it before answering. As Janssen suspected, she was trying to be as accurate as possible. "To be fully skeletonised such as she is… five, maybe six years. Perhaps a little longer. I'd need to consult a forensic osteo-archaeologist to be sure but that's certainly in the ball park. Do you have any outstanding disappearances from back then that spring to mind?"

Janssen shook his head, running a hand across his chin and feeling both the stubble and every bit of his fatigue. "Before my time here, Fiona. Besides, even if she turns out to be a late-teen runaway it wouldn't raise much of an alarm these days, less so if she's in her twenties. And, as you rightly point out, she could just as easily be transient, a migrant worker or backpacker. No one may have known to report her to us as missing in the first place."

"She'll be missed by someone. Isn't everyone?"

Janssen blew out his cheeks. "Not always." Looking out at the sea and then above at the storm clouds passing overhead, he realised they were in a race against time. A quick glance at his watch and Dr Williams must have guessed what he was thinking.

"High tide tonight will be around 9 PM, possibly a bit earlier."

Janssen met her eye. On a normal day they would be hard pressed to process a crime scene to satisfactory completion in around ten hours. To do so with the transport and communication networks in disarray and resources stretched as they were would be nigh on impossible. "That's pretty tight." After such time buried in the sands there would be little trace evidence remaining and every scrap of forensic detail, they could document would be precious. Despite the worst of the storm surge having struck, the coast was braced for yet more turmoil in the coming hours. The battering the dunes took overnight to reveal the body would most likely be repeated and when the sea returned later it would decimate anything that remained here. "I'd better make some calls."

First, he instructed the constable to ensure no one breached the cordon. The mobile network was still not functioning and he also found his radio struggling to connect to the network, so he climbed to the top of the dunes in the hope of getting a better signal. From there he contacted the control room and advised they had an active crime scene and requested a full forensic unit be assigned, stressing the curtailed timescale involved. Looking down upon where the body lay, he knew that even if everything went as well as could be hoped they would still be up against it.

From his vantage point he scanned the area. Beyond the dunes lay an established pine forest. It was not particularly thick and was easily passable on foot. Similarly, the nearby holiday park was a short walk away and anyone could make it out to this point and back again under the cover of darkness. The beach huts also offered an opportunity to give people cause to be out here, many would use them during the day and for barbecues in the evening. They also provided the advantage of concealment. A body could be hidden there and then removed and buried once everyone else locked up and went home. The body being wrapped in material gave rise to that consideration. Possibly the only reason for this would be to enable transportation, to avoid anyone seeing what was happening as well as to minimise the chance of leaving any forensic clues behind to the killer's identity.

For a moment he thought he was possibly getting ahead of himself but dismissed the notion almost immediately. There was no other logical reason that came to mind why anyone would bury a young woman out here unless there was foul play. Why would you need to? The crowd of onlookers was growing and his eyes drifted across them. If the killer was local could they resist the draw of coming back to view the discovery or would they stay away for fear someone might link their involvement? Making his way back down to the cordon he asked who found the body and was directed to a man sitting nearby. As he approached, Janssen judged the man was a little shell-shocked by his discovery. A dog sat beside him, its tongue lolling to one side as it panted away.

"Mr Curtis?" he asked, coming to stand before him. "I'm Detective Janssen. I understand you found the body this morning?" The man stood, slowly and with some difficulty, using a stick to aid him. Janssen reached out to help but his offer was waved away.

"It was more Petra here, my dog who found it. She's always had a nose for things." He looked past him and back to where Dr Williams was making notes. She glanced in their direction. "Never thought she'd find something like this. Who is it, do you know?"

Janssen shook his head. "Too early to say, I'm afraid."

"Is it... you know... a murder?" His voice tailed off as if fearful of the answer.

"Can't say at the moment," he replied. "Tell me, did your dog interfere with the body or did you touch anything?"

Curtis straightened himself upright, mumbling something inaudible in defence of his dog but Janssen reassured him it was just so they were clear from the outset. "She was pawing at the sand around it but I don't think she disturbed anything."

"And you?"

"No! I didn't want anything to do with it. I tried to call your lot immediately but the phones were down. I had to walk home, back into Wells, before I could get you out."

"You did the right thing, Mr Curtis. Thank you. I'll have someone call by later to take a formal statement—"

"That other bloke did, though." Janssen raised an eyebrow in query. "The other chap who was here just after we found it... the body, I mean. He touched it."

"Someone else was with you?"

"No, not with me but he appeared around the same time. I assumed he was out walking like I was. I don't think he had a dog or anything but he was out early. I often walk the dog at dawn. Best time of the day. I don't sleep too well these days, what with the arthritis and all."

"Who was it? Do you know him?"

Curtis shook his head. "Nah. Never seen him before. Curious-looking chap though. One of these new age types, long hair and earrings. All dishevelled. Could do with a good scrub, if you ask me."

"You said he touched something?" Janssen was seeking facts rather than a judgement on personal hygiene.

"Yeah, he lifted the necklace and seemed quite taken with it. I was a bit worried he was going to lift it once my back was turned."

"Is he still around?" He looked around at the people nearby. Curtis followed his gaze and also eyed the onlookers for a moment before shaking his head.

"By the time I got back with your constable there was no sign of him. Is the necklace still there? Your man wouldn't let me near it again."

"Yes, it's still there." Janssen saw no need to facilitate an opportunity for rumours to start.

"I guess he just didn't want to get involved. Can't blame him really."

"No," Janssen replied, looking back at the grave site. "I guess you can't."

CHAPTER THREE

DC ERIC COLLET sat back in his seat and lifted the mug of tea to his lips, frowning as he tasted it. It was cold. Vowing to drink it anyway, he glanced at the clock and couldn't believe how quickly the day was passing. Surveying his desk, it looked a mess but he was satisfied there was nothing else he could do with the limited information he'd been given. Janssen chose to remain at the crime scene and delegated the background searches to him and he was keen to demonstrate his ability. Without even a year under his belt in CID, he felt like an established member of the team. Initially, he thought Janssen was breaking him in gently by not passing any of the major cases in his direction, but, as the months rolled by, he found out that most crimes afflicting the rural community were not very exciting. The discovery of a body, one buried for years, was altogether different. The problem might be identification.

In his twenties, Eric's knowledge of the area and those who lived amongst the community was second to none and he couldn't recall a fuss being made surrounding the disappearance of any teenager in the recent past. That sort of thing would make news, certainly when it came to the tongue wagging of the local gossips. Often there was little requirement for facts in order to get a rumour doing the rounds. Even so, he diligently delved into the missing person reports held on file. As a starting point, he chose seven years ago. If they managed to rule those out then he would work backwards. There was the hope that unearthing the remainder of the body might produce something else that would narrow their search, a link to a place or a specific person with the most optimistic outcome being an ID. That was unlikely but still possible, often dependent on whether the murderer felt the need to strip the victim of their identity or not. In the meantime, the files sitting in front of him on the desk were all he had to go with and their limitations were obvious. The victim needed to be reported missing in the first place for her to be one of them.

Janssen said the victim was most likely female, so he disregarded any of the males but left them in a separate stack just in case the initial assessment was inaccurate. He was surprised by the number of cases that left him with. Despite a familiarity with the statistics, several hundred thousand people going missing annually, there still seemed to be an inordinate number for him to sift through. Missing children numbered one in every two hundred nationally with adults that rose to five hundred but that statistic was not an accurate reflection in north Norfolk. A smaller population with rural communities and towns saw that gap widen in stark contrast to those located in cities. Less attention was paid to adults and if the victim turned out to be in her twenties, then there was every chance it wasn't investigated at all.

Setting aside any of the reported women who were over the age of twenty-five was next. That reduced the number to a manageable four MisPers that were still considered as active and under investigation. These were the ones sitting on his desk, freshly retrieved from the archives. Looking at the case notes, however, they hadn't been visited in several years. The sobering thought that one of these names might presently be in the process of being exhumed came to mind. Suddenly, his cold tea seemed less significant.

Stifling a yawn, he leaned back and stretched. Movement in the corner of his eye saw Tom Janssen enter the room and he threw himself forward instinctively. If his detective inspector noticed or was in any way bothered, he didn't comment. The DI placed a brown evidence bag on the table at the centre of the room and turned to him.

"Eric, how did you get on?" As always once they were into the throes of a case, he was direct. The switch was incredible to see. Tom Janssen was witty, charming and yet his focus was such that all of that persona could be cast aside in an instant.

"I've brought it down to an initial four possibilities," Eric said, tapping his desk and bringing the folders together. Rising, he took them over to the table and laid them out. Janssen came to stand alongside. "I'll run you through them. The first is Tracy Bartlett. She was twenty-five, involved with a local man, no children. She worked part time at a supermarket in nearby Hunstanton and finished her shift on a Thursday lunchtime, in August five years ago, and that was the last reported time she was seen."

"Who reported her missing?" Janssen said as he passed him a picture of the young woman.

"Her boyfriend, Lee Taylor, later that night," he explained, glancing through the case notes. "He worked shifts at a food processing facility and returned home from work to find the house in darkness and no sign of her. He was concerned, so he called around their friends but no one had seen her. Then he called us."

"Any activity around her bank accounts, credit cards or mobile phone use? That type of thing."

Eric shook his head. "No hits recorded to any of them. The investigating officer spoke to a few friends who knew nothing of any plan to leave either the boyfriend or the area. Similarly, co-workers were informally interviewed and none of them shed any light on her personal life. As far as they knew she had no plans to leave, or if she did, they weren't made aware of them. She vanished."

"What about the boyfriend, what do we know about him?"

"There is a report on file of a uniform call-out to a domestic violence incident," Eric flicked his eyebrows up. To him, that was significant. "Although, no arrests were made and the attending officers recorded that the situation was calm when they left. There was no further follow up. The boyfriend has a number of arrests for affray and another for handling, but nothing recent."

"Is he still in the area?"

"I believe so. No longer at the same address but still local."

"Any distinguishing personal effects listed in the file that we might find on the body?" Eric scanned the contents. Nothing leapt from memory and confident there was nothing specific described, he shook his head. "Okay, who's next?"

"The next one I have for you is Sophie Maddox." Eric glanced at the picture as he took it out of the file before passing it to Janssen. "Classic MisPer, if I had to label her," he said, inclining his head to one side. "Troubled background, raised in a single parent family after her father skipped out on her and her mother when Sophie was barely three years old. The mother suffered from alcoholism, couldn't cope and her daughter was eventually made a ward of the state at the age of fifteen. Sophie bounced around foster homes but what with her age, and apparent mental health problems, the file says she suffered from schizophrenia, they never placed her in a permanent home."

"How old was she and where was she living when she disappeared?" Janssen was staring intently at the girl's picture.

"With a foster mother, alongside three other kids who were of a similar age and situation. It was the carer who reported her missing." Eric read down, searching for the conclusion of the investigation. "There was no evidence of foul play..." he read aloud, "the possibility of a boyfriend was present but no one confirmed as such or obviously identified... at the end of the day, by the time she disappeared she was seventeen and virtually a grown adult. Notwithstanding at that time, the law was such that in a few months she would no longer have been considered a ward of the state."

"So, they let it slide." Janssen's tone was disapproving. "Another teen runaway that no one followed up. Did she have any relatives elsewhere she may have gone to?"

"No one besides the mother is listed here, no," he replied. "Sad really, that someone so young has no one else to turn to."

"And the mother, where is she now?"

"I'll need to check. There are no details on the file." Janssen's eyes lingered on the photograph of Sophie for a few moments before he handed it back. Eric closed the file, placed it on the table and picked up the third. "Clare Hardy, went missing six years ago," he said, opening it and passing the top sheet over to Janssen. "Twenty-two years old and at the time of her disappearance she was a sex worker and a known addict. This one is interesting because the alarm was only raised when her landlord went to her flat to chase up her rent arrears. The place was turned over and he called us." Janssen was concentrating hard, reading down the page he had given him cataloguing her various arrests for solicitation alongside multiple arrests for petty theft, shoplifting and the like. He knew all of this would have been necessitated by the need to fulfil her habit. Eventually, Janssen glanced up at him.

"Was the burglary of her home linked to her disappearance?"

"Clare hadn't been seen for almost a week by the time we were called and it took a little time to track down the circle she moved in."

"She was an independent worker then?"

"Presumably, yeah," he confirmed. "Had she been working with a pimp something would have been said earlier."

"Unless it was the pimp who killed her," Janssen countered. "Although, were that the case, they like to make it common knowledge what happened in order to deter others from transgressing. If she worked alone, it stands to reason no one reported her missing. She'll know other working girls but they just might not have seen her around for a bit and let's face it until a few go missing no one really says much do they?"

"Going back to the state of her flat. It was considered at the time that she wasn't present when it was ransacked; that she upped and left to avoid paying the rent arrears and was quite possibly indebted to a local dealer. The flat appeared to have been broken into and it's conceivable they may have been looking for items of value in lieu of payment."

"It also gives us plenty of motive as well as lines of inquiry," Janssen concluded. "Run a check on her and see if she's been picked up anywhere else in the country. She may have taken off to start again and cleaned up her life but if not, it's more than likely she'd return to old habits. If so, she'll be on file and we'll be able to chalk her off." Janssen sat back and blew out his cheeks, casting his eye across the folders on the table. Eric knew what he was thinking. All of them had merit. "You said there were four."

"Yes, the last one is Lesley Abbott. Now she's interesting to me for a number of reasons. She went missing around the same time as Sophie Maddox, shortly after actually. It was a friend who reported her missing."

"What about her do you find particularly interesting?" Janssen replied, narrowing his eyes.

"She doesn't fit the usual profile. No criminal record and comes from an upper middle-class background." He turned to his notebook to re-familiarise himself with the details. "She was orphaned at an early age, raised by an uncle and aunt, but left home when she went to university. Cambridge no less! Dropped out and drifted around. For a time, she lodged with acquaintances locally. It was one of these who reported her missing."

"What made them think she was in trouble?"

"Apparently, she was mixing with some oddballs and when she vanished without a word, they thought it unusual. Nothing turned up in the subsequent investigation. With no evidence of a crime taking place, no further action was taken. It was left open as an active missing person's case."

"Define *oddballs* for me, would you?"

"Knew you'd ask." Eric smiled, returning to Lesley Abbott's file. "The friend said she was starting to show an interest in the occult, hanging out with some locals who she reckoned were practitioners of all things magic." He twiddled his fingers in the air, circling his hands for dramatic effect. Janssen's expression didn't crack. If anything, his brow furrowed deeper. Eric dropped the action, clearing his throat. "By all accounts, Lesley was really getting into it. She was talking about spells and pagan gods and the like. It started to creep her housemates right out. They had words about it and shortly after, Lesley disappeared."

"So, she could just as easily have moved on?" Janssen queried.

"That's exactly what our colleagues thought at the time."

"We'll need to speak to the investigating officers."

"I anticipated that as well," Eric replied. "One of them is still serving but moved south. Two are now retired and one has passed away."

"The retirees shouldn't be too hard to track down," Janssen said with confidence. "I doubt they went far. Many people retire to Norfolk, not away from it. When I left the forensics team at the scene, the body wasn't fully uncovered. There were signs some clothing may have survived attached to the body but they hadn't revealed any identification as yet. In this day and age, everyone carries something that can identify them, either a cashpoint card, student ID, driving licence. If we don't turn anything up, what does that suggest to you?"

Janssen was testing his analytical skills, seeing what he'd learned in the job. "If the victim has no ID, it probably indicates one of two things. Either the killer and the victim know each other and that means one will most likely lead to the other or, alternatively, they don't know each other but the killer could be placed with the victim at or around the time or location of death." He looked to Janssen to assess whether the answer was suitable. Janssen remained impassive. Eric continued. "By removing any identification, it provides ambiguity to the investigating officers and gives the killer more time to put distance between themselves and the crime scene."

Janssen smiled. Eric breathed a silent sigh of relief. "Correct, on all counts, Eric. The location of burial is also interesting to me. It's very brazen. The beach is often busy, used throughout the year and where the body was found is close to the holiday camp. The risk for the killer, at both the time of burying the body and the chance of its subsequent discovery, suggests it's a local to me. If not a permanent resident, certainly someone with intimate local knowledge. He felt comfortable. I think it quite likely the killer is still walking among us."

CHAPTER FOUR

JANSSEN TURNED and stretched out for the brown evidence envelope he'd brought with him and left on a nearby desk. Sitting forward in his chair, he opened it and withdrew a smaller transparent evidence bag. Laying that on the table, he inclined his head indicating for Eric to take a closer look.

"At the time I left the team, this was the only distinguishing item on the body. What do you make of it?"

Eric could see it contained a necklace. The chain was silver and of a ringlet design with very fine links. The chain met at either end of a pendant, both connected to a crescent set either side of a larger circle. "A triple moon would be my guess," he said, glancing at Janssen. "Depicting the three phases of the moon, waxing, full and waning. May I?" Reaching for the bag, Janssen nodded. Flipping it over so that he could look at the reverse of the pendant, he found himself admiring the craftmanship of the item. "You know, I don't think this is mass produced. The chain, definitely, but not the pendant."

"You think it's valuable?"

Eric shrugged. Placing any kind of a valuation on the item was well beyond his limited knowledge. "My sister makes her own jewellery. She's studied the process as part of her design course at… never mind." He waved away the comment. "Sarah's quite skilled, she can do the simple metalwork and such. However, this is far beyond what she would produce. You can see here," he pointed to the reverse where one of the crescents joined the full circle, "where the join has been soldered. Obviously, it has then been worked and buffed to smooth it out but if this were a mass-produced item then it would be heated before being poured into moulds and cast in batches, probably hundreds at a time. You can see the handiwork here, it's quite remarkable."

"It might well be bespoke, which could help in identifying the owner but the design itself is common enough," Janssen said, inspecting the join Eric was pointing to.

"It might still be significant to the wearer, though," Eric argued. "She may have been religious. Sometimes, this design is used by Christians to reflect the Holy Trinity. I know that's a long shot but it's a starting point. There are also a number of arts and crafts places around here. If the victim is local, there is always the possibility she bought it at one of the gift shops, craft stalls or at the folk festival. The maker would recognise their own work. If it's a one-off, maybe they'd also even recollect the purchaser." The last suggestion suddenly made him feel foolish. Expecting someone to remember a trinket sold at least five years previously, if not longer, and to what could have been a passing tourist sounded daft in his head. He was relieved to see Janssen accept the point.

"Definitely worth asking the question. Let's put a list together of local possibilities and take it from there," Janssen said. "In the meantime, until we have anything more substantial to go on, I want you to revisit each of these MisPers you have there. If they haven't been reviewed recently, follow up on them and see if they've subsequently reappeared. Take a look at electoral rolls, birth, marriage and death records and you can throw in the police national database as well. Some of these women have been known to the police in the past and old habits die hard. They may have resurfaced and it hasn't been updated in the files. It's possible we can rule them out pretty quickly, avoid us wasting time looking at them. Any idea where would be a good place to start with the hunt for the maker of this?" Janssen picked up the evidence bag, holding it up as he inspected the necklace again.

"I'll give Sarah a quick call. I know she doesn't live around here anymore but she's pretty friendly with everyone who would know."

A SMALL BELL hanging above the door announced his entrance as Janssen opened it and passed through. There were a handful of people inside, browsing the displays. Items were arranged either behind secure glass cabinets or dotted around on display tables and shelving. The products available ranged from intricate wood carvings to jewellery and ceramics, along with artworks hanging on the walls presumably painted by local artists. Some of these were abstract contemporary pieces but the majority were landscapes, predominantly depicting the Norfolk coastline or rural scenery. He waited for an elderly couple to conclude their purchase before approaching the counter. The lady smiled as he greeted her, offering up his identification.

"I'm looking for Margo Wilson, the owner."

"Look no further," she beamed at him as she spoke. "Sarah said someone would be calling by."

Janssen was slightly perturbed that Eric's sister called ahead, not that it really mattered. "I was hoping you might be able to help us identify the maker of this." He took out the necklace from his pocket and handed it over, still inside the transparent bag. Another customer came to the counter and Margo called another member of staff over to serve them and ushered him away to another counter nearby, alongside a display case containing Celtic style jewellery.

"Now, let me take a proper look at this," she said, lifting and putting on the glasses suspended by a cord around her neck. The woman carried herself with a somewhat jovial demeanour, apparently enthusiastic and interested in whatever came her way. Some people were naturally pleasant and upbeat. "Ah, yes. If I'm not mistaken, and I rarely am," she said with a smile and an accompanying wink, "this is Beatrice's handiwork. I'm almost positive it is."

"Beatrice?" he confirmed. "Is she local?"

"Absolutely, yes. She's been producing jewellery around here for years. She's very well regarded. Not commercially valuable as such but her work sells well with the tourists. It's most certainly a living." Margo waved him in the direction of a glass case, coming alongside him and guiding him across the room with a gentle touch to his forearm. There were six shelves behind the locked glass with a mixture of rings, necklaces and earrings, in various styles. Janssen found his eye drawn to the third shelf down and a pendant reminiscent of the one found around the victim's neck. Only this time, the two crescents overlapped the full circle making the piece a lot smaller than the one he had with him. He pointed to it.

Margo produced a bunch of keys from beneath the counter and after a few moments of hunting found the right one, unlocking the door to the case. Removing the pendant, she handed it to him and he examined it. In all honesty, he couldn't tell if it was made by the same person but Margo flipped the pendant over and pointed out a small trademark on the reverse. It was an imprint that he struggled to make out. "This isn't on the necklace I have."

"No. Beatty… sorry, Beatrice only started applying a mark to her pieces when she began to sell them in significant numbers a few years back. Prior to that I think it was more of a hobby, selling to family and friends. Once her work started to gain in popularity, she was keen to put her mark to it just in case her profile continued on its upward course."

"And did it? Continue, I mean." Margo shook her head.

"No, it was short-lived. A few people showed an interest in taking her work and making them into a marketable product line but as far as I know it didn't come to anything. It's a shame really but…"

Janssen sensed she was going to allow the comment to tail off. "But?"

"Well… Beatty is a bit of an old kook, if you know what I mean? Tends to rub people up the wrong way for no other reason than because she seems to enjoy it." Margo lowered her voice so they couldn't be overheard. "I wouldn't be surprised if they just thought she wasn't worth the maintenance."

"She's difficult?" he asked.

"Oh, yes. That would be putting it mildly. We've had a few run-ins ourselves. Mind you, aren't many of these creative types a little bit off-the-wall? That's how they come up with the things they do."

Janssen politely agreed, returning to his inspection of the pendant and the other pieces on display. The price tags looked to be substantial. If she was selling a number of these at this price, then she was doing well. "Do you sell many works on behalf of a lot of people?" He looked around, roughly assessing how many people were represented in the sales area.

"I have twelve to fifteen at any given time. Each with their own pitch where they can display whatever they like. I take a cut of any sales."

"Out of interest, how does Beatrice get on?"

"Very well. Not as well as she used to, though. Beatty went from producing trinkets as something to make a few extra pounds while her daughter was young, to making a decent living from it. Less so now but still one of my better sellers. She started out with a small section in the corner and it grew there."

"And the imprint, roughly when would you say she started to stamp her pieces?"

"Must be five years or thereabouts," Margo said, thinking

hard. "Certainly no later. That was when things really happened for her but it only lasted a couple of years."

"Why, what happened?"

"She went off the boil. Talk was she got distracted by her personal life. Can't be easy being a single mum, not on a fixed income, and that daughter of hers caused her all manner of problems." A customer came near, hovering around the next display and Margo appeared reluctant to say any more. Janssen let it go. Gossip was of limited use to him. He could always check out her background for himself.

"Do you have an address for her?" he asked.

"Of course. Hold on here and I'll be right back." Margo headed towards the rear of the shop and disappeared through a door marked private. It looked like her office. When she returned a few minutes later, she passed him a slip of paper with a handwritten address on it. Then she replaced the pendant he was holding back in its place and secured the door closed, ensuring it was properly locked. Janssen eyed the pieces again.

"Is she known for religious pieces as well as the Celtic ones?"

"What makes you ask?" Margo appeared curious. "When you say *religious,* do you mean in a Christian sense?"

He nodded. "Doesn't this have Christian religious connotations? Symbolising the Holy Trinity." He glanced at the one in the evidence bag in his hand.

"As far as I know, Beatty has never been a religiously inspired person. Not in that sense, at least. The Celtic symbolism is rooted in pagan gods. The triple moon represents the sacred number three, which I guess is also sacred in Christianity but in Celtic traditions it symbolises the three elements that can be seen, the sky, the sea and the land."

"I see," he replied, inclining his head to one side.

"Then there's the other stuff that she likes to produce." Margo looked around nervously. It was the first time she appeared reticent. "The pieces I'm not so keen to stock."

"Such as?"

"There's been a rising interest in this sort of thing in recent years," Margo said, guiding him to the lower shelf and pointing out several star-shaped pieces. "That one is a septagram. It's linked to the fairy realm. Then you have the pentagrams. People like them and... I guess it's harmless enough but then... some people follow these beliefs. I'm not so keen to promote them."

"What type of thing are you referring to?"

"The occult. Paganism is all right up to a point. Many people celebrate the solstices and so on and I have no problem with it as such but... there's the darker side of it and... well, I'm not so keen. You understand? I mean, that pendant you have there has several meanings."

He glanced at it. "Does it?"

"Yes, it can not only represent the three earthly elements but also the three phases of the goddess, in her maiden, mother and crone aspects. Not to mention the Wiccan symbol of the sacred feminine. As I say, it's all a bit odd to me but it seems fashionable these days so I have to stock at least some of it."

"I know teenagers are often curious about the occult but I wasn't aware it was a thing amongst adults. Not many at least."

Margo let out a short laugh as a retort. Not in itself a dismissive gesture but it seemed to be slightly mocking. "I think you would be surprised, Inspector, I really do. There's a neo-pagan group that meet up every week, at a pub here in the town. They even put flyers up to advertise it. I've no idea what they get up to but I assure you they're not discussing baptisms and church fetes."

Janssen raised his eyebrows in response. "In a pub? Hardly clandestine."

"Strange people, if you ask me." Janssen smiled. He hadn't asked and the conversation was taking a slightly odd turn. Margo must have interpreted his tone a negative judgement on her for she excused herself citing customers she needed to attend to. There was only one person in the shop and he was being helped by her assistant. Thanking her for her time and the information, he said goodbye and left.

Stepping out into the street, he was buffeted by the wind. A timely reminder that the stormy weather of the last twenty-four hours was yet to pass. The overcast sky made it seem darker than it should be and glancing at his watch, he calculated the forensic team had only a couple of hours remaining before the sea would reclaim their crime scene. Taking out his mobile, he saw there was still no signal. He needed to confirm whether Beatrice made the necklace and if so, they could attach a rough date to the length of time the body had been buried in the dunes. More than five years. It wasn't conclusive but it could help to narrow the timeframe.

Doing a quick calculation, he thought if he set off now, then he had every chance of being there for the last hour or so of the excavation. Although there would be nothing he could add, it felt necessary for him to be present as the body was finally unearthed. Whoever she was, she had a story to tell and he intended to hear it.

CHAPTER FIVE

JANSSEN ARRIVED at the beach to find the forensics team working hard under portable floodlights. A uniformed presence maintained the cordon, keeping back the curious bystanders as well as the local press. Word must have got around regarding the discovery in the dunes. With the onslaught and destruction wrought by the storm, the media were out and about in force so it was only a matter of time before they appeared. A journalist was recording a piece to camera as he approached and she tried to attract his attention and pull him into shot but he expected it, ducking under the cordon and walking away without a backward glance. He heard her return to her pre-scripted patter, raising her voice to be heard above the sound of the wind and the breakers.

Fiona Williams saw his approach and rose from her kneeling position alongside the grave site. "It's a full skeleton," she advised him as he greeted her. "I'm pretty confident my initial assessment is accurate. A young woman and in quite a well-preserved condition."

"Any indication of significant injuries, broken bones, cuts or anything to indicate a cause of death?" he asked, glancing past her to where the body was discovered. The photographer was packing up and the team were making ready to lift the remains for transport.

"Other than the blow to the head, no. There was also no sign of anything buried with the body or nearby to indicate she hit her head as she was placed in the grave. That indicates to me she most likely suffered the damage to the skull prior to death. I think it will be almost impossible to confirm beyond a strong suspicion that the blow was the cause of death. There appears to be some staining to the material she was wrapped in around the head. I imagine the lab tests will come back with a conclusion that it's blood."

"Killed elsewhere and dumped in the dunes," he replied pursing his lips.

"There's always the possibility she was alive when she was buried and merely unconscious but we'll never know for certain."

"Did we get lucky regarding identification, can we put a name to her?" He was hopeful but the feeling was soon extinguished.

"No such luck, I'm afraid. You're going to have to earn your money, Detective," Fiona replied. "However, I believe the team did uncover some useful finds."

Janssen thanked her and attracted the attention of the lead CSI. He recognised him, Terry Manafort, an experienced investigator. They'd met several times before. The water was lapping at the edge of the crime scene and the team were hastily cataloguing the elements of the skeleton before carefully wrapping them and placing them into waiting containers. Once satisfied the team could manage without him, he led Janssen over to a sheet of plastic laid out for them to place items prior to closing down the scene. Usually these would be in a secure van by now but time constraints, as well as being unable to get a vehicle far enough up the beach and away from the encroaching sea, meant everything had a makeshift approach to it.

Janssen knelt, scanning the collection of evidence bags in

front of him. There weren't many. The scene hadn't given him much to work with. "There were some surviving fragments of clothing around the body. She must have been wearing a denim jacket or shirt. The hard-wearing material has survived," Manafort explained. Janssen examined it without opening the bag. In the descending darkness it looked black but that could have been the dampness of the material, it was most likely blue. Moving to the next, it looked like a shoulder or clutch bag with a long-corded strap.

"Leather," he asked, looking up over his shoulder.

Manafort shook his head. "Doubtful. I think we'll find that is a leather lookalike fashioned from manmade materials. It's too well preserved to be natural. I reckon it's a mass-produced item, so you'll find no help there. The contents, however, are much more enlightening." Pointing at a collection of bags, separated from the others, Janssen leaned in to examine them, struggling in the failing light. The first looked to contain a small cylinder-shaped item which he assumed was a lipstick or mascara tube and the other two contained similar cosmetic items. "They are all from a brand quite well known for its strongest selling point, ethical testing. Again, quite commonly found in most major shops. What you'll find in the one on the right makes it quite intriguing though." Janssen picked it up. The contents appeared to be suffering from a degree of water damage that made it hard to read the print. It looked to him to be a business card.

"Is this what I think it is?" he asked expectantly.

Manafort nodded. "The lab should be able to clean that up for you. What you have there was inside the shoulder bag. The lining protected it a little and I think there would have been a number of paper items in there, probably receipts, perhaps paper money or other items that deteriorated beyond recognition as a result of being exposed to the sea water. However, that is laminated card which is why it's partially survived."

Janssen angled the card towards the floodlights, seeking to read the company name. "Norfolk… something… I can't quite make it out," he read aloud. The surname was obscured by water damage but the first name, Darren, was still distinguishable as was the mobile phone number printed in the bottom left corner. The remains of a logo were also partly visible. "Any ideas which firm we're talking about?" He was calling on Manafort's local knowledge.

"If I'm not mistaken, that's the logo of what was once *Norfolk Reactive Sciences* but they've rebranded since then and are now better known as *Norfolk Labtech.*"

"I've heard of them. They carry out experimental research, don't they? Quite a big player if memory serves." Pleased to have a proper lead to follow up on, Janssen noted a couple of evidence bags containing more jewellery. Looking closer, he found two rings. One was silver with a black stone at the centre with what looked like Celtic patterns around the outer rim, whereas the other, also fashioned from silver, was shaped in a starburst pattern.

"They were found one on each hand, still present on the fingers," Manafort told him. "And you're right about the company. They carry out research for pharmaceutical firms, testing medical products by running human trials. They used to be a big player in cosmetic testing… on animals. It had quite a negative press for a while. Hence the rebranding and change of direction I should imagine."

That struck a chord with him, vaguely recollecting something about the press stories. However, the details escaped him. "There were a number of protests against them, is that right? Years ago."

"Yes. They were targeted by animal rights protestors for a number of years. It all got a bit nasty. For a while there was speculation the company might fold under the pressure. Weren't you working on those cases?"

Janssen shook his head. "All before my time but I recall it made national news."

"All the more curious to find the contact card of an employee of that company in the possession of a woman who apparently had an ethical approach to her cosmetics."

"Interesting angle. Unless she liked the brand, irrespective of their ethos," he theorised. "Worth looking into. When was all the drama around the business taking place?"

"Six… maybe seven years ago," Manafort replied without conviction. "I'd have to check."

Janssen took out his phone and placed the two bags containing the rings back down alongside one another. First illuminating them with the torch on his phone, he took a couple of photographs before doing the same with the necklace and pendant. Satisfied there was nothing else for him to learn, he left the team to close off the crime scene and headed back to where he'd parked his car. Opening the door, he heard movement behind him. It was the journalist who'd been standing alongside the cordon when he arrived. The associated cameraman was nowhere to be seen.

"Hi, are you on the investigation team," she asked him, smiling warmly.

"Yes, but I'm afraid I have no information for you at this time."

"Don't worry, I'm not going to put you on the spot. We were just packing up for the night and I saw you walking back," she indicated over her shoulder, down towards the car park of the beach café where her colleague was loading cases into the rear of a van. "Can you at least confirm it's a dead body? Everyone's talking about it anyway." He didn't reply, merely smiling politely. "It's quite a scoop. I was sent out to get shots of fallen trees and to interview residents worrying about flooding."

"You never know when a story is going to break," he replied, staring past her and back towards the scene beyond the dunes. Just the glow of the floodlights was visible from where they were.

"My name's Kelly. Kelly Donovan," she said, offering him her hand. He shook it.

"Tom Janssen. Detective Inspector," he added, reading her inquiring look. "It's a pleasure to meet you, Kelly. You'll still have to wait for an official statement, though." She grinned and he winked as he slid into the driver's seat. She passed him a contact card and he glanced at it briefly before putting it in his pocket.

"Just in case you want to offer me an exclusive at some point," she said it with such confidence that it made him laugh.

"I'll bear it in mind." She turned and he watched her walk away. A double notification sounded from his phone. The networks must be back up and running. Glancing at the screen, he saw a text from Alice and a missed call from the station. Opening the text, it simply read *Gone home see you tomorrow*. He swore under his breath. He'd completely lost track of time. Hitting call back, he waited but the call diverted straight to voicemail. The status bar on the screen showed he had full service. Either Alice didn't have decent coverage where she was or she'd switched her phone off. Suspecting the latter, he hung up without leaving a message. It was almost nine o'clock. Despite the lateness of the hour, he decided to pay one more person a visit before calling it a day.

CHAPTER SIX

RAIN WAS FALLING STEADILY when Janssen arrived at the address. The promised second storm front that'd been brewing all day was about to make landfall, coupled with a high tide. Knowing the military engineers had been monitoring the flood defences filled him with some confidence but the area wasn't out of danger yet. Those naïve enough to think the worst was behind them could be in for a surprise. The address was situated at the end of a lane, flanked on all sides by mature trees offering a break to the wind that rattled across these flat lands. He looked around. Once part of a small holding, or leased to tenant farmers, the ancillary buildings looked as if their usage had fallen by the wayside with scant attention paid to their maintenance. The only exception to this was a small barn attached to the main house, itself a modest farmworkers' cottage, thatched roof and small windows.

No lights were visible inside the main house but the barn was illuminated from within and movement passed by an interior light casting a momentary shadow. Fastening his coat, he got out of the car and trotted the short distance across the yard. What previously would have been a wagon access, it was now converted into the entrance door and in the absence of a bell or a knocker, he hammered on the wood with his fist. Moments passed without reply and he turned his collar to the rain which grew in intensity. Repeating his efforts and knocking harder, he hoped he would be heard over the noise of the wind and the driving rain. The sound of a bar being dislodged came to him and the door creaked open to reveal a set of suspicious eyes assessing him.

"Beatrice Malloy?" he asked, brandishing his warrant card. She bobbed her head but didn't speak. "Detective Inspector Janssen. May I have a word?" For a moment she stared at him before standing aside and ushering him in. The door was closed and he stood in relative calm in stark contrast to the outside. Doing his best not to shake his coat off inside her property, he took in her appearance. He judged she was in her early seventies but figured she might be younger. Her hair was a mix of different shades of grey, pulled back from her face and tied at the base of her head with a rainbow hairband that matched the tattered jumper she currently wore. She was thin, ascetic looking with a wary expression that revealed her discomfort at his presence. What he couldn't tell was whether that was her normal demeanour or if it was the police which made her uncomfortable. Perhaps it was him.

"What can I do for the police at this hour, Inspector? Is everything all right with my daughter?"

"I'm sorry for the lateness of the hour and I'm sure your daughter is well, Mrs Malloy."

"Well, I wouldn't leap to that conclusion if I were you but don't worry about the hour." She walked past him as he wiped the rainwater from his eyes with the flat of his hand. "As you can see, I tend to work late most nights." Janssen looked around. The barn was a workshop. There were several workbenches around the exterior walls. All were littered with materials, plastic tubs, trays and bottles all set alongside tools and other equipment. In one corner was a large piece of apparatus, dominating the area with nothing else nearby.

"Is that a kiln?"

Beatrice looked up from where she'd seated herself, at a bench with a large magnifying glass attached to the edge, allowing her to keep both hands free to work with. "Of sorts, yes," she replied, returning to what she was doing. He came across and saw she was working on a silver bracelet, apparently in the process of setting stones into it. They were a mix of green, red and blue gems.

"Are they as valuable as they look?" he asked, indicating what was in front of her.

She shook her head. "Polished crystals but they certainly look the part. I admire your interest, Inspector but how may I help you?"

Taking the bag containing the necklace found on the body at the beach, he offered it to her. "I was hoping you could help me identify this." She accepted the bag, lowering her half-rim glasses from atop her head and leaning closer to inspect the item.

"Hmm… I guess it could be one of mine…" she said quietly before sitting upright, glancing in his direction and exhaling. "One from some years ago, if it is."

"When was it made?"

"That's an early one, as I said. Probably before I was selling into shops or soon after. I couldn't really say with any accuracy. Anywhere between six to eight years ago, I guess, but I wasn't really keeping track."

"Any idea when or where you may have sold it?"

Beatrice shrugged, accompanied by a brief shake of the head.

"It would help if you could narrow it down a little."

She made to fold her arms across her chest but before completing the action, she reached up and rubbed the side of her neck with her palm. "Sorry, I wasn't keeping records in the early days. I used to have stalls at small fairs and boot sales, that type of thing. Why? What's all this about anyway?" She slid off the stool and stood, leaning back against the workbench, slipping her arms behind her back. Janssen ignored the question for the time being.

"What about these?" He took out his mobile and brought up the photos he took of the rings found at the crime scene. Beatrice angled her head slightly, narrowing her eyes.

"Ah… not so sure about those. They might be mine but I make a lot of jewellery. Sorry."

"Have you always made pieces themed in the occult?"

"I make whatever sells," she replied with a straight face. "I'm not an arty type, never have been, which may or may not surprise you, Inspector. If there is an interest there, I'm happy to supply it. The themes I use are heavily influenced by traditional Celtic art, Norse as well as other pagan traditions. The occult theme is one that has seen something of a resurgence in recent years."

"Why is that do you think? Are we living in a darker society now?"

She laughed at the notion. "I think the prevalence of witchcraft and vampires in film and television in recent times plays a greater role, seeing as you're asking. The occult has become… cool and not only with your goths."

The latch on an interior door clacked as someone opened it from inside the main house and both of them turned as a young woman entered. "Mum, I was—" she stopped talking the moment she realised he was there, her eyes narrowing as they fell upon him. "Sorry, I didn't know you had company." She was in her late twenties or early thirties, he guessed. Despite having removed her coat, her hair was wet through which gave away she must have recently returned home. Her hair lay to her shoulders, straight and far too black not to be dyed. A black jumper and matching eyeliner, to both top and bottom, completed quite a striking look.

"That's okay, dear," Beatrice said. "This is a policeman. They've come across a piece of my jewellery and he has come to ask me about it."

"Oh… I'll leave you to it." She averted her eyes, turned and left the same way she arrived closing the door behind her. Not once did she make eye contact with him. That struck him as odd but not necessarily unusual. It came with the job. Beatrice watched her daughter leave, absently fiddling with the chain around her own neck.

"You'll have to forgive, River, Inspector. She's not very comfortable around men… or police officers, if I'm honest."

"I'm sorry to hear that. Any particular reason?" He was curious.

"Too many to go into. You'll be here all night. Was there anything else you wanted to ask me about the necklace? As I said, I've no memory of selling it or who to."

Janssen scanned through the notes in his pocket book. "She would have been a similar age to your daughter. How old is River now, thirty, thirty-two?"

"She's twenty-eight," Beatrice replied, somewhat curt, almost irritated. "But looks much older, I'll grant you." Janssen was surprised by the response but he didn't show it. He would also have placed River as much older than her years. Usually, he was a far better judge of these things. Perhaps it was the make-up and clothing that threw him off. "I'm sorry, Inspector but what is the point of all this?"

"I understand before you sold your work in the local gift shops you used to make and sell pieces to family and friends. Is that correct?" She nodded. "Presumably you were making fewer pieces and operating on a much smaller scale than you are now."

"Yes, that's true."

"In which case, if this is one of your earlier works then it stands to reason you will either know the person who owns this necklace or whoever bought it for her as a gift."

"I can't recall a girl buying anything from me in this case, I'm sorry."

"Are you any better with names?" he asked, remembering the business card retrieved from the victim's bag. He looked up the name, choosing not to mention the source of where it came from.

"What about a man, perhaps that stands out? Someone by the name of Darren? Perhaps it was a boyfriend purchasing a gift for a loved one?" Without a flicker of recognition, she shook her head. Feeling he'd reached the end of the conversation, he closed his pocket book and retrieved the evidence bag containing the necklace from the workbench, securing both in his coat. "Okay, I think that'll be all for now. I appreciate your time. As I said, I know it's late."

"I'm sorry I couldn't help you more."

Janssen turned and made his way to the door. Fastening up his coat, he braced himself for a dash back to the car. Taking a contact card from his wallet, he handed it to Beatrice. "If anything comes to mind, please can you give me a call?" She indicated she would and then opened the door for him. Glancing outside, the rain was practically horizontal.

Slipping out into the darkness, he heard the door close behind him before he'd managed a couple of steps. Reaching the relative sanctuary of his car, he got in as fast as he could and slammed the door. Looking back at the main house, he was almost certain he saw a curtain twitch but there were still no lights visible in any of the rooms. River could have gone straight to bed or be in one of the rooms to the rear. He thought about her reaction to his presence and why she might not like policemen. There were countless reasons as to why she might not take to men in general but most found security or reassurance in the presence of the law. Those who didn't were often keeping secrets or masking a guilty conscience. *Which is it with you, River?*

Remembering the missed call from the station, he checked the time. It was too late to call now. Everyone would have gone home and the station was unmanned overnight. A call at this time would be passed through to the area control room and would serve no purpose. He could catch up with Eric in the morning. Typing out a brief apologetic text message to Alice, he clicked send and waited for the confirmation it had actually gone. Starting the car, the headlights illuminated the house through the driving rain and he realised the workshop in the old barn was now in darkness as well. There was an inescapable feeling that Beatrice was somewhat reticent in their conversation but perhaps he was reading too much into it. After all, Margo described her as a bit of a kook and on first impressions, he had to agree. She also implied River was a disruptive child. Maybe she had a history with the local police he was unaware of. Making a mental note to look her up in the morning, he set off for home.

CHAPTER SEVEN

THE POLICEMAN LOOKED DIRECTLY at her, she was certain. Instinctively stepping back from the window, the familiar tightening in her chest returned as she stared out into the rain. Once again, playing the conversation over and over in her mind, seeing the two of them talking with one another as she entered, he knew. Whether it was how he looked at her with those dark, piercing eyes, or doubts about how she carried herself she was unsure but this man was to be feared. The headlights came on, illuminating the interior for a fraction of a second casting a shadow from the curtains on the wall beyond but she was out of sight now.

Sitting on her bed, River recognised the change of gear as the driver turned the car around. Chancing another look out through the window, she saw the car heading down the narrow lane away from the house and she exhaled deeply. She was safe. So, why didn't she feel it? The tell-tale creaks announcing someone was climbing the stairs to the landing outside her room could be heard, and she turned to face the door. A gentle knock followed before her mother's face appeared, leaning around and scanning the room in search of her.

"River, are you in here?" Her voice was soft and kindly, far removed from the woman who'd raised her all these years. She wanted to run to her, throw herself into her mother's arms and be comforted. She didn't. Instead, her senses were overwhelmed. She could feel her face flush and her thoughts were jumbled, muscles tightening. Opening her mouth to speak, words wouldn't come and instead tears fell. Someone was close, putting a comforting arm around her shoulder. River felt her mother pull her in close, hugging her tightly. She responded, gripping her mother's jumper as would a child having woken from an intense nightmare.

"I... I... can't go back, Mum," she stammered in between sobs. "I won't go back." Her mother pushed the hair away from her face, whispering soothing words and rocking them gently backwards and forwards.

"You won't have to, sweetheart. You won't have to."

She pulled away from her mother slightly, looking up in an attempt to read her expression. The available light coming in from the outside was minimal, allowing only the briefest detail to be visible. So strong. So able. If only she could have half the strength and courage of her mother, then she would have coped with all of this. But she wasn't her mother, and never could be.

"Why did he have to come here? What if... what if they start looking—"

"They won't, love," her mother said, cupping the side of her face in the palm of her hand. The skin felt rough to the touch, hardened by years of craftwork. Stroking the side of her cheek, she stopped, lifting River's chin with a smooth movement of her forefinger forcing her to meet her eye. "Nothing is going to happen to you. I'll take care of it. You know I will."

"Do you promise?" she heard herself say. The tone of her voice sounded weak, pathetic. That hadn't always been the case but five years of hell had changed her, altered her perception of the world and there was no going back to how things once were.

"I'll not let you down again," her mother replied. The assuredness with which the commitment was made offered comfort and her breathing softened, no longer was it coming in short, rapid gasps. The trembling of her hands subsided and a feeling of safety, of having someone beside her who was both willing and able to bear the strain returned. She was home and nothing was going to take her away again.

CHAPTER EIGHT

PLACING the final photograph on the board, Tamara Greave stepped back and scanned the four women. Each picture was one supplied by family or loved ones. The four faces were happy, smiling. They were snapshots of moments in time radiating the joy of their particular lives but as was often the way in these cases, they belied the reality of their daily lives. Certainly at the point where they disappeared without a trace at any rate. There was no outward indication of Clare Hardy's drug and alcohol dependency as she cuddled up with her mother's golden retriever, a brief time in between rehabilitation and relapse. Nor were there signs of a fraught relationship within Tracy Bartlett's picture, taken at a beach party on a summer's day. Nothing in that carefree expression to suggest she was under threat or to herald a desire to run away. Lesley Abbott's preoccupation with all things of the occult was curious but not as alarming in the modern era as it might have been for the peer group of her own parents.

Recollecting the fuss made at her grammar school when a small section of the year group was found to be exploring the use of a Ouija board, it was easy to jump to conclusions. A number of the parents contacted the school, fearing a cult was corrupting their offspring. In reality, it was a childish fascination with something different to the norm. A challenge to the established traditions, morning assembly hymns and religious studies classes focussing primarily on Christianity. All of those kids grew out of it, never descending into the depths of darkness their parents feared. Lesley was older when she disappeared though. A fascination beyond a teenager's enquiring mind. A girl with a preponderance to drift, without any apparent focus in her life. Such a personality was quite capable of disappearing of her own accord without it being the result of anything sinister.

All the potential names offered for their victim were, to some degree, associated with a tragic background. Sophie Maddox, however, was the one name leaping out at her. Not necessarily due to a stronger likelihood that it was her buried in the dunes but more a result of her back story. The others had someone, a loved one or a family. Sophie was a product of the system. To all intents and purposes, she was orphaned, raised in different homes and moved from place to place without any true security. She was of an age where she would soon be heading out into the world alone. Was she prepared for that? Everyone finds their way in life. You have to. It isn't a choice. How a child is raised to adulthood shapes the possibility of success whichever way you choose to define that success. Some lives are planned, mapped out, whereas others fall into place along the way. Hopefully. Who shaped Sophie's approach to life, guided her world view and where did she want to go? None of the answers to these questions would be found in the scribbled notes of a social worker's case file.

Hearing someone entering behind her, she turned expecting to see Eric with the coffees she sent him out to collect. It wasn't Eric. Tom Janssen stood before her with his mouth slightly open. He appeared to be caught momentarily off guard, as was she. A flutter rose in her chest, passing off almost as quickly as it had come. They faced each other in a moment of silence before both tried speaking at once.

"I'm sorry," Janssen said, raising his hands in supplication. "You go."

"I came across last night." Assessing him as she spoke, he looked tired. More so than the last time they worked together. Apart from that, he was still Tom, with the same striking appearance. His broad frame, chiselled bone structure and shock of blonde hair, with just a hint of ruggedness threatening to take the edge off his presentation, but only serving to understate his handsome features. There was something else though, something she hadn't seen before whenever he looked at her. Realisation dawned. He didn't know. "The super wants me on this case. You weren't told, were you?" He bit his lower lip before rolling his tongue along the inside of his cheek. Tom Janssen should never play poker with her.

"I was out late at the scene and… comms were down much of the day." That was the Tom she remembered. Measured, calm.

"It's not a problem is it, me being here?" She heard the doubt creeping into her voice. Eric's arrival cut through the awkward moment. He must have caught wind of the atmosphere because he pulled up, eyes flitting between the two of them.

"Ah… I called you last night to let you know DCI Greave would be here this morning," Eric said, putting the carry tray holding the coffees down on the nearest desk before passing Tamara her cup. She accepted it with a smile. "I got you the usual." He handed one to Janssen, who thanked him with a half-smile.

"What is the usual?" she asked, removing the lid of her own. "Just so I know for future reference."

"Black, no sugar," Janssen replied, crossing the ops room and putting his cup down on the desk. Tamara watched as he turned his back to her, taking off his coat. *Black coffee.* That wasn't a surprise. It suited him. No nonsense. Returning, coffee in hand, it was like the awkward moment never happened. He indicated in Lesley Abbott's direction. "I paid Beatrice Malloy a visit last night."

"She makes jewellery similar to that found on the victim, right?"

"Yes. She more or less confirmed she made the necklace but was less certain about the rings."

"Was she able to shed any light on who she sold the necklace to?"

Janssen shook his head but his eyes drifted back to Lesley Abbott.

"You're leaning towards her?"

Janssen nodded. "Only because of her interest in the occult and that matches the pendant found on the body. Eric, did you have any luck tracking down the housemates she was living with or the one who reported her missing."

"I did. One of those living with her is still resident locally. She has a flat in Wells. That's a short walk from where the body was found." Eric directed the last at Tamara, knowing she was less familiar with the area.

"Presumably, you were following up on all of those listed in the original missing person reports and not just this one?" she said aloud, looking at Lesley's picture. In the corner of her eye, Tom Janssen shifted his weight slightly and exhaled.

"I've found the current address for Tracy Bartlett's boyfriend, he's still in Norfolk. Clare Hardy's mother passed away last year and her father wasn't in her life, so as far as we can tell there are no living relatives."

"What about the girl in care, Sophie Maddox?" Tamara, glanced at him. Janssen was sipping in his coffee, his eyes drifting from board to board, reading through the information already listed.

"She was living with a foster mother. I have the address here," Eric said, waving his pocket book in the air.

"Okay, here's what I think we should do. The remains of the victim have been shipped down to Norwich for a full forensic analysis. After speaking with the team who processed the scene this morning, the autopsy is unlikely to give us an actual cause of death and certainly no date. After this length of time in the sand, it'll be more of a list of probabilities. However, they are going to fast track the chemical analysis of the bones. That will give us a wealth of detail to try and help narrow down the list of likely names we currently have. Apart from giving us a probable age, they'll also be able to tell us whether the victim grew up here or elsewhere, which region she spent time in or hopefully which country she originated from. If she's a backpacker from abroad or a migrant worker, we'll have somewhere to go to for leads on identification. Putting a name to the victim is priority number one." She looked to Eric, who was listening intently, and then to Janssen who maintained his focus on the information boards, rubbing absently at his chin. "We have three victims with next of kin to speak to. If Beatrice was little help in identifying who bought the necklace or the rings, let's see if those closest to the missing girls recognise them. Eric, can you pay a visit to Tracy's boyfriend? Tom, you're already leaning towards Lesley Abbott, so how about you call on the housemate and I'll pay the foster mother a visit. We can regroup after that, maybe we'll get a positive ID. Whoever gets through and back here first can follow up on Clare Hardy, the missing sex worker. Agreed?"

Eric nodded, "I'll head off now."

"Be sure to remember what you're there for, though, Eric," she said as the constable turned away. "You're not only talking to a loved one but also a potential suspect. You may well be opening old wounds that probably haven't healed yet but gauge the reaction. The guilty person will probably spend their life waiting for that knock on the door. Be mindful of it." Eric took his coat from the back of his chair and made for the door, before returning for his coffee and scurrying out of the room. She waited until sure they were alone before speaking. "He's come a long way in a short time."

Janssen looked past her in the direction of where Eric had been, now an empty corridor. "Yes, he's coming on well. Better than I anticipated. Not that he was falling short but you never quite know."

"True. Listen," she said, taking a deep breath. "I don't think you should take it personally that they called me in—"

"I'm not," Janssen cut in, meeting her eye. She was unconvinced.

"I can see I'm treading on your toes."

"It's a bit early to call in the big guns," Janssen replied with a sideways smile. Tamara hardly considered herself as such.

"I worked a similar case back in Bristol. My guess is the brass want both my experience as well as to make a statement, appear to be taking it seriously. Having a murderer at large can negatively affect an area and let's be honest, bearing in mind how important tourism is to this part of the country, they want to make an impression." She watched him intently, trying to figure him out. However, the mask had dropped. To really get a handle on what Tom Janssen thought, you needed to catch him in the moment. After that, once he'd deliberated it with his analytical mind, there would be little opportunity to learn what he thought unless he chose to share. "Are we okay?" He smiled. The warm expression was reassuring. He didn't strike her as one to bear a grudge.

"Of course. Where are you staying?"

"Same place as last time. How are things anyway?"

"Yeah, good. Right, I'll chase up this housemate," Janssen said, finishing his coffee and scooping up the name and address Eric left for him. Scanning the note, he met her eye. "Catch up with you later?"

"Absolutely."

Watching him go, she considered the polite brush-off. The expectation compared to the reality left a bitter taste. Driving up from Norwich last night, excited by the prospect of seeing and working with Tom again, today she had to consider how reality bites.

Glancing at the pictures of the jewellery pinned to the board, the occult theme was obvious but was it a reflection of a fashion trend or representative of a lead as to how she died? In her own youth, they'd dabbled in such things over a few cans of cider on quiet nights hanging out in the park with her mates. Sure that her parents wouldn't have been overly alarmed for they were arguably more liberal than most of their peers at that time, she was confident what they would have said about it. Far from approving, however, they associated pagan worship, gathering at ancient sites at the time of the equinoxes, as leftovers from the sixties counter culture and freedom of expression. Not something to be concerned with, but then again, at her school nobody disappeared or turned up dead.

Making a note of the address she was heading to, she left ops finding herself preoccupied with Tom's reaction to her presence and hoping he would move quickly past it.

CHAPTER NINE

TOM JANSSEN FOUND his route to Wells-next-the-sea passable without event. The much feared second night's storm surge failed to match the anticipated heights and everyone breathed a sigh of relief as the night passed without more damage. Today, people were out taking stock. Pulling onto the quay, he found an available space in the harbour car park. From here, he glanced up the East Fleet in the direction of where the body was discovered the previous day. Figures could be seen in the distance walking the length of Beach Road in the morning sun. The beach itself was fully open again, the crime scene catalogued and cleared before the tide washed over it once again.

He waited as a lorry passed by and darted between oncoming vehicles to cross the road. Life was starting to return to normal. Walking down Tunns Lane, a narrow street between an old dockside warehouse and a café, he eyed the buildings looking for house numbers. There was a number of flint clad new builds, in traditional Norfolk style, and the further he retreated from the harbour front the less traditional in appearance the buildings became. Coming upon the ground floor flat, he pressed the doorbell and waited. A few moments later he heard the key turn in the lock and a bleary-eyed woman cracked open the door, peering out through the gap. He brandished his warrant card. "Kelly Parsons?" he asked. She eyed his identification but whether she actually read it he didn't know.

The door closed and he heard the security chain detach before it reopened fully and she beckoned him in, drawing her dressing gown about her and pulling it tight. The interior was gloomy. It was a small flat with few windows and what natural light there was available was obscured by a mixture of shades and curtains.

"Is this about Les?" she asked, drawing back the curtains in the living room. She blinked at the brightness of the sunlight streaming in. Janssen looked around. There were a number of empty beer cans and wine bottles scattered around the room. Kelly seemed to notice. "The pubs closed early last couple of nights, so a few of us hung out here."

"Must have been quite a party," he said, smiling.

"Saturday night," she replied, dropping onto the sofa. Reaching forward to the table, she hunted around for a packet of cigarettes. Lighting one, she coughed on the first draw.

"What makes you think I'm here about Lesley?"

"Stands to reason, doesn't it?" she countered, blowing out smoke off to her right. "Everyone's talking about how you've found a body at the beach."

"You think it's Lesley?" She shrugged. "Do you think it might be?"

He was interested to know whether she'd considered her friend's disappearance to be the result of foul play or not.

"I've no idea. Maybe. I've thought about it on and off over the years. Did she say anything that might have told me where she was going? Have I missed something that might help to find her?" She took another steep draw. "To be honest, I reckon I hardly knew the girl."

"You shared a house with her. You must have known her a little."

"True. We hung out but there were four of us in that house, each renting rooms. You must have had that happen yourself, making friends and associating with people because you happen upon one another not because you choose to. Be it work or cohabiting. That was Lesley and me. Lesley and the rest of us."

"Were you surprised when she disappeared?"

Kelly sat back, thinking about it before answering.

"Yeah, I was… at the time."

"What's changed now?"

"I'm not so sure. Like I said, I don't think I really knew her. Les moved in a couple of months before she vanished. She was a scatty mare, as I recall. Always losing stuff, you know. It drove us all mad. Borrowing stuff and forgetting where she left it. Keys, cash card… whatever. Then you wouldn't see her for a few days and you'd start to worry and then… bang, up she pops like she never left."

Janssen smiled. "Did you ever ask where she'd been?"

"Yeah, course we did. You care about people you hang out with. She never said though. *Just around.* That's what she'd say."

"What did she used to do for money? She'd dropped out of university and her family were estranged."

"She didn't talk about her family much. Money never seemed to be a problem for her, she was quite free with it to be fair. Didn't have a job as far as I knew, so we figured she had a trust fund or something like that. She was posh, Les. No airs and graces but you could tell she'd been brought up right."

"Accent, do you mean?" Janssen was taking notes. Very little of this was in the missing person's file.

"Yeah, she spoke properly. Like I said, posh but manners as well. She might have been off the wall in many, many ways but she treated people right. I've no idea why she mixed with the likes of us."

"The file says she was mixing with other people. Some of whom you disapproved of." Kelly laughed at that comment. "Sorry, what's so funny?"

"Nothing, just the way you describe it. Look around, who am I to disapprove of anyone? No, they were just odd. Not my sort of people *at all*."

"You're talking about the pagan worshippers?"

"That's a fancy title, yeah. All black magic, spells and stuff like that. I mean, don't get me wrong. Back in the day when I left school... even beforehand, while I was at school, I did the whole Goth thing, you know. I went everywhere dressed head to toe in black, listening to thrash and dismissing *the mainstream* and that but... Les took this witchcraft thing to a new level."

"How so?"

"Oh, I don't know. It was years back. We'd come home to find candles lit everywhere, sheets on the floor and hanging on the walls with weird symbols drawn on them... chanting at odd hours, stuff like that. It got really weird when we were finding unidentifiable things in the fridge. She said they were bits of dragon or something."

"*Dragon*?" he found it difficult to keep the scepticism from his tone. Kelly bobbed her head.

"Exactly. We figured she was going a bit bonkers. It was too weird."

"And the others? These people you said she was mixing with, there's no record of who they were."

"I didn't know them by name, sorry," she replied, stubbing out her cigarette. "I know they used to meet up at one of the pubs in town. *The Black Dog*, I think. I met one of them once, though. A guy. Les brought him back here. He was in his late thirties I reckon."

"Can you describe him to me?"

She screwed up her face, clearly struggling to remember. "Presented himself like a wannabe rock star but came across more like a pound shop Bob Dylan. Grunge-type hair, a little gold hoop earring. Really rated himself too. The rest of us didn't. Kind of intense and a bit creepy."

"How often did she see him? Any idea?"

She shook her head. "I only met him the once. Never saw him again but he was very familiar with her, Les, I mean. I reckon they were an item or at least, he thought they might be. Is it her then? Have you found Les?"

"The honest answer is I don't know, too early to say. We're trying to identify the person as well as what happened to them. We are looking at a number of possibilities." Taking out his mobile, he opened up the gallery of images. "We found a necklace and some rings on the body. Can you take a look and see if they are familiar to you?" He handed her the phone. She narrowed her eyes as she flicked through the images. After a few passes, she shook her head.

"I'm sorry. They might have been hers. She certainly wore stuff like that, but I've no idea if she would have been wearing them when she left or not. Like I said, it was a long time ago."

Janssen handed her one of his contact cards, just in case she remembered anything else that might be useful. She took it, putting it into her back pocket as she showed him out. Walking back towards the quay, rather than heading towards his car he set off for *The Black Dog* pub. It was further along the waterfront on East Quay. Having grown up a short distance along the coast at Sheringham, he knew this area well.

Tamara Greave drifted into focus as he walked. He realised he'd handled the situation badly. It wasn't that he was disappointed to see her. Quite the opposite in fact. His reaction to her arrival was far from professional, which was the least she could have expected from him. The decision to bring in a DCI was valid. Had the cell tower network been operational he would have known in advance. Was his reaction the result of feeling blindsided? Usually a stranger to affronts to the ego, his response was a personal let down no matter what she thought. He should have greeted her warmly, talked through his thoughts regarding the body and their list of potential names for the victim. He did none of those things, behaving like a petulant child.

Coming upon the pub, he found it closed up. Not a surprise given it was still early on a Sunday morning. Strolling around the outside, he looked at the flyers in the window listing forthcoming events. None of them were of interest to him. Using his phone, he did an internet search for pagan groups and was surprised at the number of returns. Scrolling through, he found a website listing groups across East Anglia. A group based in north Norfolk appeared to hold regular meetings, or *Moots* as they were described, three days prior to every full moon as well as on the third Sunday of each month. The next meeting was scheduled for that night, here at *The Black Dog*.

CHAPTER TEN

THE GRAVEL on the drive announced her arrival long before she got out of the car and was able to knock on the door. Tamara Greave was greeted with a broad welcoming smile from a woman standing beneath the canopy of the porch. She guessed the foster mother to be in her seventies and carried herself with a vibrant energy that Tamara found enviable whilst escorting her into the house.

"Thank you for agreeing to see me on a Sunday morning," she said as the front door closed behind them. They were in the former rectory, a large Victorian property built during the arts and crafts heyday and located adjacent to the village church.

"That's no trouble at all," Ann Grable replied. "It's a good job you called ahead, though. For the first time in months I'm able to attend the Sunday morning service and I wouldn't have been here."

"I'm terribly sorry. You should have said. We could have rescheduled for later." Ann waved away the apology, showing her through to the drawing room.

"No matter," Ann said, offering her a seat on what was a very grand sofa in a room to match. "It's largely an opportunity for a bit of a natter. I'll catch up later. Besides, when you told me what it was regarding, there was no way I'd delay our conversation. I still think a lot about Sophie."

Tamara took out her pocketbook and mobile. "I'd like to take notes as well as record our conversation. Do you mind? It's just that I like to listen back to interviews in case I've missed anything." Again, Ann waved away any concerns. She put the mobile on the coffee table between them and pressed record on the app. "Tell me, do you remember Sophie well, and how long was she with you?"

"Remember her? Of course. Rarely have I had an issue where one of my children runs away never to return. Don't get me wrong, there are often incidences of children running away but they usually return either in a police car or of their own volition. Mind you, I think I would have remembered Sophie, regardless. A troubled girl. Such a shame because she was quite a character and had tremendous spirit. I don't doubt she would have gone far in life if given the right support."

"I understand she came into the system aged fifteen, is that correct?"

Ann nodded. "At least that was when she entered the foster system. Social workers were involved in her life for years prior to that, what with her mother's condition."

"She was an alcoholic," Tamara said, revisiting her own notes.

"Correct. Every endeavour was made to keep the two of them together but, in the end, they felt the best scenario was for Sophie to be brought into a secure environment. At her age, adoption wasn't really a serious option. So, she wound up in permanent foster care."

"With you?" Ann shook her head. "So how long was she with you prior to her disappearance?"

"A good six or seven months, as I recall," Ann replied, thinking hard. "She'd been to several other foster homes before coming to me. Probably, she should have come here first." Ann must have read her inquisitive expression, continuing to explain the run up to Sophie's arrival. "The poor girl suffered from mental health issues, diagnosed schizophrenia. Not anything too debilitating, you understand. Nothing that her medication couldn't manage but she would have episodes on occasion. I usually take older children here, those who can have a degree of responsibility in their lives. It helps to prepare them for after they leave the system. The other homes Sophie stayed in were more suited for younger placings. Her episodes were difficult for children to see and process. Older children can cope better."

Looking around, Tamara considered the size of the house and how well it could cope with a number of children. The grounds were large and well maintained. For a girl like Sophie, this place must have seemed like a different world to the one she lived in. "How many children can you take at any one time?"

"I used to take up to five but these days, I rarely have more than three. I'm not getting any younger."

"And have you always fostered?"

"Since the nineties, yes. It used to be Gerald and myself. Gerald's my late husband." She pointed to a photograph on the mantle depicting a slim, kindly looking man sporting half rim glasses. "Now, it's only me."

"I am sorry," she said, smiling. "You said Sophie was something of a character?" Ann chuckled. It was an infectious laugh and Tamara could see why she would be a good choice for a foster parent. She had a manner that put you at ease.

"Very outgoing and upbeat. Not so much when she first arrived. I think the trauma of her home life knocked much of the stuffing from her but within a fortnight the real Sophie began to emerge. Witty, intelligent and... opinionated. Definitely opinionated. I think she had a great deal of freedom at home due to a lack of care and attention. Some of the curbs placed on her when she came here did not go down well but... we found a balance."

"How did that *freedom* manifest in Sophie's case, if you don't mind me asking?"

"Sophie wanted to keep her own hours. These days, it's the children wanting to stay up using the broadband until all hours, chatting with friends or playing games on their mobiles. Not Sophie. She was used to being *out* until all hours with whoever she chose. That wasn't going to wash with me. I give the older children latitude but they must be home by nine o'clock every night, and the broadband goes off at ten."

"Was there ever a boyfriend on the scene?" For the first time, Ann's demeanour changed taking on a melancholy expression.

"Sophie was far older than her years. It stands to reason after the upbringing she had." As she spoke, she reached for her necklace, fiddling with it while apparently arranging her thoughts. Tamara waited patiently. "I can't say with certainty, and I would be lying if I said I could but I dare say Sophie was close to someone. Perhaps more than one."

There was more to this but she sensed Ann was reticent. Why that would be so, she wasn't sure. Possibly she didn't want to drift into speculation or could the information prove damaging for her in her role as a foster carer?

"Any idea who that may have been?"

"Sophie formed associations… and I choose that term specifically, rather than friends. Some of them I approved of, others less so."

"Why associations? If you don't mind me saying, it seems an odd turn of phrase."

"They were such a disparate bunch, that's why." Ann seemed unable to articulate her words and convey her meaning. "She would bring back a couple of young girls from the school. They were lovely, well mannered. I knew their parents well. Then, once she'd finished her exams and officially left school, she took up with those dreadful activist types who were wreaking havoc around here a few years ago."

"Activists? I'm sorry, I was living in the west until recently."

"Oh, those animal rights campaigners. There was all manner of goings on, disrupting hunts, protesting outside that local pharmaceutical firm… on occasion it all became very heated with some exchanges with the police, vandalism and so on." She reached across, placing a hand on Tamara's knee. "Not that Sophie was involved in any of that. And, let's be honest, the protestors had a very just cause. Morality was on their side, if you ask me but they approached it in such an antagonistic manner."

"And Sophie mixed with these people, hunt saboteurs and activists?"

"Some of them, yes. Not that I'd ever understood her to be interested in the cause before but all of a sudden, she was talking about cruelty and how things should be banned. She became very exercised about it all."

"Was she easily influenced do you think?" Ann shook her head emphatically.

"That's not Sophie. If you knew her, you'd know what I mean. If anything, she would be the one to take the lead. She never struck me as a follower."

"Was there anyone specific that you can recall her mixing with? Teenage girls usually have at least one confidant."

"The only one I knew of was the Malloy girl. Beatty's daughter, River. They live out… towards the coast… I forget exactly where."

"We'll find it, don't worry," Tamara said, scribbling the names in her book. "And would you say they were close?"

"They were quite friendly for a time. Not so much around when she took off, Sophie, but prior to that they used to spend time together."

"That's an interesting choice of phrase, *took off*. You don't think anything untoward happened to her?"

"With Sophie, I imagine she figured she could manage just as well by herself. Being in the system doesn't suit everyone and her personality was fiercely independent. No amount of guidance was going to deter her from doing whatever she set her mind to." Up until that point, Ann appeared very positive and jovial but there was something in the recanting of Sophie's history that seemed to induce a touch of melancholy. She caught Tamara looking at her. "Sophie was one of the few charges I fear I failed with. I did my best by her, I really did."

"I don't think anyone's doubting that, Mrs Grable." Taking a folder from her bag, she pulled out the photographs of the jewellery found at the grave site. "I was wondering if you could take a look at these. Is there any chance they belong to Sophie? Might she have been wearing them at the time of her disappearance?" Ann took the pictures. Reaching across the table she put on her reading glasses and examined them determinedly.

"I'm sorry, my dear. I couldn't say either way." Passing the pictures back, she looked past Tamara furrowing her brow.

"What is it?"

"If I'm not mistaken, I might have some of Sophie's things. There was some costume jewellery in amongst the rest." She smiled, wagging an excited finger in the air. "Yes, I'm certain. Gerald and I placed some of her things in a box and they might still be in the garage. Social services arranged for her clothing and possessions to be removed from the house once we thought she wouldn't be returning, even if she was found. However, we knew they'd most likely donate the clothing and throw the rest away. It seemed like such a shame, so we kept what we thought might have some sentimental associations for her. Just in case she did ever want them back."

"May I see them?"

"Yes, do come with me."

Ann led them out of the room and to their right, passing through the kitchen where she picked up a set of keys hanging on a hook by the door to the garden. Outside, the large double garage stood a short walk away at the end of the driveway. Walking down the length of the building, they came to a side door and she stopped to find the right key. Tamara looked around. This seemed like an idyllic place to live, reminding her very much of where she grew up in the west country. "You said earlier you aren't usually able to make the Sunday service. Why is that?"

Ann looked over her shoulder, sliding the key into the lock.

"If I have mixed gender placements, I'm not allowed to leave them alone in the house. It's a regulatory stipulation. In most cases it wouldn't be necessary but where you are often dealing with vulnerable children, you can't be too careful. Imagine if one of the girls were to get... well, never mind. I'm sure you understand."

Tamara nodded. The safe-guarding of children in care needed to be focussed on. For many years it wasn't the case, leading to disastrous abuses within the system. The door creaked open and they went in. The garage smelt damp and stale. "I'm sure there's a light switch somewhere about. My Gerald used to live out here some days but I rarely come out here anymore."

Tamara located a cord and pulled on it. Seconds later, six fluorescent tubes flickered into life. A car took up half of the space. Despite it being covered, she could tell it was a convertible sports car of some description. Judging by the size, she guessed it was vintage. Ann saw her scanning it as they made their way to the rear where shelving racks were fixed to the walls with gardening tools hanging alongside. "I imagine there's a classic under there."

"That was Gerald's pride and joy. The one thing he loved as much as me... if not more I used to say."

Tamara smiled as the woman reminisced. "I haven't been able to bring myself to get rid of it. I probably should. It's just rotting away sitting in here. I've never been a fan of cars."

"I am," she replied. "May I?"

Ann gestured with an open hand, apparently pleased that someone took an interest in her late husband's hobby. Pulling back the tarpaulin from the corner of the bonnet, back as far as the windscreen, she revealed the two-tone paintwork, Healey blue over ivory. Immediately recognising the marque, she was unable to mask her enthusiasm. "An *Austin Healey 3000*. Your husband had great taste." Even with only half of the car revealed, she could admire the care and attention Gerald Grable must have lavished on the vehicle. Ann chuckled whilst rooting around amongst the boxes stacked on the shelves.

"I'll take your word for it. I always thought it was just an excuse to get out of the house after he retired."

"What did he do?"

"He was an aircraft engineer in the RAF. After that, he used to restore cars. He was close to completing that one when he became ill. Never quite managed to finish it off."

"Looks great to me."

"Here it is," Ann exclaimed, beckoning her over.

Tamara replaced the tarpaulin and crossed to where Ann stood. Picking up the old cardboard shoebox, she transferred it to a nearby workbench. Lifting off the lid, disturbing a cloud of dust in the process, she waved her hand through it in a crude attempt to clear it. At first glance of the contents, there didn't appear to be much to speak of when looking at the sum possessions of a young woman's life. A small zip bag contained various cosmetic items, several shades of lipstick, eye-liner along with foundation and mascara. Putting that aside, she took out a knitted rainbow hat. Ann came alongside her.

"I think a friend made that for her, although I can't remember which one." Placing it down, she lifted out a small metal tin. It was previously a biscuit tin, common around Christmas time. Inside were a collection of envelopes and a few keepsakes. A ticket stub for a cinema visit, a number of hairbands and a small clear plastic sleeve containing a handful of picture postcards depicting Norfolk. There were three letters seemingly written by the same hand. Opening the first, she carefully removed the letter and unfolded it. The paper was discoloured by age, the handwriting childlike and difficult to read.

"That is from her mother," Ann said over her shoulder. "She wrote once while Sophie was with us. She must have kept the previous letters. I gather she was an equally troubled soul but I like to believe she truly loved her daughter, just unable to keep herself right let alone raise a young woman. Such a shame."

The letter was a rambling affair. A lot of apologies along with vague promises about a brighter future. To her it seemed as if it may have been composed whilst under the influence. From what she knew of Sophie's background, that wouldn't be a surprise. Skipping the other letters from her mother, she opened the next. It was addressed to *Dearest Sophie* and signed off by *Kim and Mark*. She glanced to Ann who offered the context.

"Her previous foster family before she came to us. I believe they felt terribly that they couldn't do right by her but with younger children in the home, the disruption was too great. They kept in touch for a while. Probably would have kept it up… well… if she'd stayed."

Returning to the sleeve, Tamara withdrew the postcards and a number of photos tucked in among them fell to the floor. Flipping the cards over in her hand revealed no writing on the reverse and she put them down before kneeling to retrieve the photos. There were three aged pictures and a more recent folded strip produced by a photo booth. One picture was of a square-jawed, stocky man in T-shirt and jeans leaning against a works van. On the reverse was scribbled simply, *Dad.* The next was a picture of a woman holding a baby in her arms. The child was a new born and couldn't have been more than a month old. She figured it was Sophie and her mother but there was nothing to confirm that thought. The third was taken at some kind of a gathering, a party or similar, with many people present in shot. At first glance, none of them were either of her parents. Unfolding the photobooth strip, she easily recognised Sophie, pulling silly faces at the camera much as teenagers do on those occasions. What was intriguing and caused a flicker of excitement was the presence of another alongside her.

It was a young man or a teenage boy, hard to tell as his face was obscured one way or another in most of the shots. In the first, only the side of his head was visible as they embraced. In two of the others, they were both pulling daft facial expressions at the camera. In the last, he was leaning in to kiss Sophie's neck, her head thrown back with a joyous grin on her face. Two lovers sharing a moment of private happiness. Angling the photos towards Ann, she raised an eyebrow. "Have you seen these before?" The foster mother appeared thrown. "Do you know this boy?"

Ann squinted, staring hard at the photographs before frowning and shaking her head. "No! I don't remember seeing those photographs nor that boy before."

"Is this how you remember her looking during her time with you, or could these have been taken prior to her placement here?"

"They must have been taken around the time she was with us. I remember her dyeing her hair and shaping it like that," Ann said, absently rolling her fingers within one another as she spoke. "I don't recall her ever mentioning a young man."

"I think we've answered the question as to whether Sophie had a boyfriend. I take it the investigating officer never saw this at the time of her disappearance."

"He can't have, no. He barely looked into her room, just took her details and left."

Tamara stared at the images of the young couple. In that moment they were focussing on nothing but one another. Attachment such as that was hard to fake. Why wouldn't this young man have come forward when Sophie disappeared? Even if one of them had broken off the relationship prior to her disappearance, he should have at the very least been questioned regarding his knowledge of her whereabouts. Perhaps Sophie's friend, River could put a name to the face.

CHAPTER ELEVEN

WATCHING as the workers stepped out of the warehouse at the end of their nightshift, fanning out and slowly splitting into smaller groups as they said their goodbyes or continued their conversations with one another, Eric got out of his car. He'd been waiting there for three quarters of an hour. He needn't have, if he'd chosen not to. However, marching into a person's place of work unannounced and pulling them from their shift in front of employers and co-workers didn't strike him as fair. Apart from causing Lee Taylor discomfort it would no doubt set the tongues wagging. Potentially they'd found his girlfriend's body and he deserved to learn that away from the watching eyes of the workplace.

Leaning against the side of his car, a few eyes fell upon him as staff got into their vehicles or walked out of the main gate. He stood out. It was Sunday morning and he was a strange face, suited, loitering. Two men approached chatting with one another. One was younger, in his thirties. That was Lee Taylor. His description on file fitted him perfectly, aided by the man's own choices of body art. He sported multiple tattoos across his fingers as well as the backs of his hands. Most distinctive, though, were the tear drops beneath his right eye and lines of stars running up both sides of his neck stopping just short of his jaw. The men said goodbye to each other, the older breaking off and walking to a hatchback, glancing sideways at Eric as he got in. Taylor slowed as he approached and Eric smiled, offering his identification. "Mr Taylor?" The man nodded, coming to stand before him. "Norfolk police."

"Yeah, I guessed who you were." Eric was momentarily thrown. "My line manager told me someone had called to see if I was on shift. Cheers for that. Now everyone thinks I'm getting nicked."

"I'm sorry," he replied, realising the attempt at discretion had proved futile. Taylor shrugged, dismissing the need of an apology.

"Don't worry about it. That guy doesn't like me anyway." He twirled his car keys on his forefinger, biting his lower lip. "What can I do for you?"

Eric could see the man was tired. A gruelling nightshift, at least he always found them so, followed by an unexpected visit from the police was far from ideal. "We've made a discovery along the coast and it may be related to the disappearance of your girlfriend." Taylor stood still, upright and tight-lipped. Rubbing a hand across his mouth, he held it beneath his nose and sniffed loudly before meeting his eye.

"You found a body… on the beach out towards Wells."

"We have, yes." Eric watched him closely, gauging his response. "You've heard about it?"

"Everyone's talking about it," he said, glancing back over his shoulder towards the warehouse. "The most interesting thing to happen around here in ages. What makes you think it's Tracy?" Eric found the offhand reaction disturbing, curt.

"What makes you think it isn't?"

He appeared thoughtful for a moment, staring off into the distance. Suddenly his features looked drawn, emphasising the black circles beneath his eyes. "You know what," he began, "I've played out almost every conceivable idea of what happened to my Tracy, from her taking off with another bloke, killing herself and, yeah… someone… doing her in… and you know where it's got me?" Eric shook his head slightly. "Nowhere! Absolutely nowhere! I went around and around in circles, nearly drove me mad. Our relationship was on the skids, you'll know that already. I decided a few years back that she'd taken off by herself, or with someone else, I didn't know and I figured good riddance."

"It may not have gone down like that," Eric countered. "Surely, you'll want to know either way?" Taylor met his eye, chewing on his lower lip. He nodded almost imperceptibly. Eric retrieved a folder from the passenger seat of his car. Looking around, they were the only ones left in the car park now. Taking out copies of the jewellery found on the body at the grave site, he laid them out on the bonnet of his car. Taylor cleared his throat, appearing to take a deep breath as he scanned them. "Can you tell me if these are what Tracy might have been wearing on the day she went missing?" He stared hard at the images, unblinking. There was a flicker of recognition, Eric was almost certain.

"The necklace looks like one she had."

"She wore one just like this or it was similar?"

Taylor's brow furrowed and he pursed his lips. "It was similar. Maybe not quite the same. She was into all that new age stuff for a while, you know."

"You recognise the symbolism. Was she into pagan spirituality?"

Taylor laughed then, breaking his concentration.

"Man… no!" he said, shaking his head. "She was into smoking weed and having a laugh. Her and her mates used to muck around with fads, veganism, crystal healing and other nonsense were just some of the many back then. Tracy wasn't a believer in anything like that, not really. She'd take them up and go headlong at it for a while and then move onto the next. Always into some new cause or trend."

"I see. What about the rings?"

"She wore more than that on one hand let alone two."

"Could they be hers?" Eric tried to mask his irritation.

"Maybe. She had all kinds of stuff like that," he replied, looking closer at the pictures. "But I don't think it's her. It's not Tracy."

"You sound pretty confident about that." Eric fixed the man with his gaze. He shifted his weight between his feet. What had been a casual demeanour dissipated under the scrutiny and he sought to backtrack.

"Well… I mean… I don't think these are hers, you know."

"But they are similar."

"Yeah… similar."

"What can you remember about the day she disappeared?" Eric took out a pen and his notebook.

Taylor blew out his cheeks. "Man, that was years ago now. Haven't you got it all from the time."

"Often it pays to have a fresh account, straight from the horse's mouth," he countered. "Paperwork can be a bit dry. Just what you can recall will be fine." He stood with the pen poised. Taylor eyed him, letting out an exasperated sigh as he leaned against his car.

"I came home after a few beers with the guys. Tracy wasn't there, which was a surprise as she hadn't said she was off out." He stared off into the distance beyond Eric, appearing thoughtful. "When she didn't show by about ten, I got a bit worried."

"And what did you do then?"

"Texted a few mates of hers, workmates. That type of thing."

"Had they seen her?" Taylor shook his head, sniffing loudly. "When did you decide to call the police?"

"One of her friends suggested I check with the hospital. No one was admitted by her name or description. After that, I figured I should call your lot just in case she'd been in an accident or something."

"And there was no sign of trouble at home. No mess, missing clothes, nothing to imply she had been in an altercation or a rush to leave?"

"No! The house was as it usually is, a right tip. Tracy was rubbish at clearing up." Eric found himself wondering what was wrong with his ability to pick things up but chose not to mention it. "Look, we've been over this so many times. You interviewed me at the time, took a statement. There's not a lot else I can say."

"Fair enough, Mr Taylor. One thing though. You said you'd been out for a few drinks with friends." He nodded. "In your original statement, you said you found your girlfriend missing when you arrived home from work." Eric fixed him with a stare. Taylor's eyes widened and he looked up to his left.

"Yeah, that's right. I went to the pub after my shift with a couple of the guys. After that, I went home and found she wasn't there."

"Which pub?" he asked, looking around. The food processing warehouse was located on a small industrial estate some distance away from any local amenities. To walk to a pub would be some distance.

"I don't remember. We went to several."

"Quite a session then. Not exactly a few drinks. I hope you weren't driving yourself home."

"Hardly a session," Taylor argued, "and no, I wasn't driving."

"What time did you say you returned home?"

"Nine or ten, I think."

"You said you waited for Tracy to come home and became concerned around ten o'clock. You can't have been waiting long if you were contacting friends at ten, if you'd only just got in." Taylor bristled, stepping away from the car and folding his arms across his chest. "I'm just trying to ensure clarity, Mr Taylor."

"Yeah, well... maybe I remembered wrong... I've just come off the back of a twelve-hour shift. I'm knackered and you're asking me what I was up to years ago. Can you remember what you were doing last Tuesday? I doubt it. Is there anything else you want to ask me about or can I go home? I really want to get some sleep."

Eric stepped aside, gesturing that he was finished. Taylor walked past him, unlocked the car and opened the door. "One more thing, if you don't mind?" Eric asked.

"Yeah, sure." He leaned on the open door with his right arm.

"Do you miss her, Tracy?"

"She left. It was her choice," Taylor said, removing his jacket and tossing it into the rear of the car. "Unless you can tell me otherwise."

"That doesn't answer my question."

"Like I said before, it was a long time ago. She was alright, Tracy, but if she don't want to be around then that's up to her. I'm not going to lose sleep over it. Besides, I'm married now. Dragging all this up isn't going to be popular at home, know what I mean? Are we finished?"

Eric nodded and Taylor got into his car, slamming the door. Starting the car and moving off before applying his seat belt, Eric watched, turning over their conversation in his mind. He was quite a character. Broadly speaking, an unpleasant one. It was hard to determine how one might react to the disappearance of a loved one, both at the time and with the application of hindsight. Perhaps it was the nature of the relationship that would determine how it was viewed. No evidence of foul play was uncovered at the time and their relationship could be considered fractious, judging from what Lee told him as well as what was recorded in the file. A plausible argument could be made for her decision to leave. The fact she hadn't resurfaced elsewhere gave rise to a degree of concern but people took off all the time, thousands per year, to start new lives. Considering his own exchange with the man, he understood the appeal.

CHAPTER TWELVE

Tamara Greave returned to the station, finding Tom Janssen hunched over a computer screen in the ops room. He was so focussed on what he was reading that he failed to note her arrival. A fleeting doubt struck her that he was ignoring her. Putting her bag down heavily to ensure her presence was unmistakable, she was pleased to see the noise startled him.

"I didn't hear you come in," he said with a smile, his cheeks flushing with embarrassment. That was the first time she'd ever seen him respond so self-consciously. Usually, he was the implacable rock, fixed and unmovable.

"How did you get on in Wells?" She was pleased there was no sign of the earlier awkwardness.

"Interesting," Tom leaned back in his chair, stretching and extending his arms whilst stifling a yawn. "I get the impression from the housemate Lesley Abbott was quite aloof, somewhat scatty and mixing with colourful characters. She also seemed to be out of place in the circles she moved in. It's pretty tough to get a lead on who she really was. Nothing concrete to put Lesley's name to our victim."

"Can you define *colourful* for me?"

"She became quite taken with all things spiritual, as well as a deepening attraction to the occult. There's a possibility she was seeing someone who her friends disapproved of, or at least, she was knocking around with him for a time. By all accounts he was into this pagan worship too."

"Do we have a name for him?" She wondered if this was what had him so captivated.

"No, sadly not. Lesley's housemate described him as a throwback to Bob Dylan. Presumably from his heyday."

"My mum would have been hanging on his every word if that's the case," she said drawing a smile from Tom. "What have you got there? Are you looking at Clare Hardy?" She looked past him to the screen. He was reviewing someone's arrest record and she presumed it was the missing sex worker.

"Oh, this was something I had left over from yesterday. You know I went out to see Beatrice Malloy, who possibly made the jewellery found on our victim," he said glancing back at the screen. "Well, her daughter came home as we were talking and I got the impression she didn't take to my being there. I was curious."

"And, anything interesting?"

"Turns out she's got a record. She's out on licence, released two months ago which would explain why she didn't take to me."

"I'm surprised your charm couldn't override her distaste for the law." She winked at him. "What was she in for?"

"There was a string of attacks aimed at a local pharmaceutical company, who were specifically a vivisection clinic using live animals for the testing of cosmetics. The premises were broken into several times, vandalised, and on the last occasion the complex was set on fire. One of the activists died in the blaze but was never identified."

"How come they couldn't identify them?"

"The body was burned beyond recognition, too damaged to allow any form of identification. None of those arrested admitted to being present let alone setting the fire. River was one of a number of activists arrested in the subsequent investigation and eventually went to trial. Five were convicted, including a charge of involuntary manslaughter for the death, and given sentences ranging from two to six years inside. It looks like River, who was considered a foremost figure in the activism campaign, was seen as one of the lead perpetrators and got one of the stiffest sentences."

Tamara found her curiosity piqued. "River Malloy?" she asked, leafing back through her notes.

"The very same. You know of her?" Janssen frowned with surprise.

"She was friendly with Sophie Maddox... according to her foster mother at any rate."

"That figures, I suppose. They are around the same age and everyone knows everyone around here."

"I also found these," she said, reaching into her bag and pulling out what she'd taken from Ann Grable's garage. Passing the photos over to him, she indicated the strip from the photo booth. "Any idea who the boy might be?" Janssen pored over the images. It was clear he hadn't seen the face before. She knew of his attention to detail. If he'd come across him already, he would remember.

"A boyfriend was only suspected as being a possibility. How come we have no mention of him in the investigation? These images imply they were pretty tight."

"The foster parents were unaware. It seems like she played her cards close to her chest. Certainly, a question for the investigating officer when we have a word. Likewise, why didn't this boy come forward when she went missing? River Malloy might not have an affinity for the police but let's hope she can point us in his direction. Girls confide in one another. Even if he was off the scene, she should know who he is and the nature of the relationship."

"Speaking of Sophie Maddox, what's your take on her?" Janssen asked.

She thought hard before answering. Sophie ticked so many of the boxes usually filled by teenage runaways. She was older than her years, unsurprising bearing in mind the conditions of her upbringing, apparently strong willed and capable. "Her foster mother thinks she did a moonlit flit of her own accord, describing her as being quite capable of looking after herself and single-minded. Whether that's said to appease her own conscience at losing a child in her care or not, I can't be sure. She seemed genuine enough. But…"

"But?"

"I'm not sure." She sighed, struggling to articulate her thoughts into words. "There's something about her: Sophie. I can't say what it is for sure but she kept everyone who came into contact with her at a distance, running the risk of being seen as a loner. However, she wasn't cut off from her emotions. She's kept letters from her estranged mother, previous foster family as well as these." She passed him the other photographs. Janssen lingered on the picture of her father, then glanced at the mother and baby.

"Her parents. What's this other one?" he asked, pointing at the third aged photograph depicting a party scene, holding it aloft in her direction.

"I don't know. Maybe it's a family gathering. It was in with the others but I don't see either of the parents in it."

"Do you think she may have talked about her past with her friends. With River?"

"Possibly. However, if she had trust issues, it might be understandable if she didn't. That could also explain why no one knows much about what she thought, felt or who she associated with. I was going to swing by and have a word with River this afternoon. Do you want to tag along?"

"Absolutely. There's also a meeting tonight for a local pagan group. I figured I'd go along and see if anyone there remembers this Dylan lookalike who Lesley Abbott was seen with six years ago. If he moves in that circle then he may well still be around. You up for that as well?"

"Full moons and witchcraft on the Sabbath?" she said with a broad smile.

"More like a half of lager and a packet of crisps," Janssen returned hers with a grin of his own, "they're meeting in a local pub in Wells."

"Less interesting but I'm in." She feigned disappointment.

"How are things with you anyway?" Janssen asked. "Set a date for the wedding yet?" Eric's arrival into the ops room avoided her concocting an answer to the question. She could have kissed the young detective constable's unwittingly impeccable sense of timing.

"Sorry I took so long," he said, his eyes flitting between the two of them. "Did I interrupt something?" His fear was subtly masked behind his enthusiasm. Both she and Janssen waved away his concerns. "Lee Taylor is a piece of work, I can tell you."

"How so?" she asked him. Janssen handed back the photographs and she took them before pulling out a chair and sitting down.

"He doesn't seem particularly bothered about us having potentially found his missing girlfriend," Eric announced, breathing hard. He must have been practically running to the ops room to be so short of breath. "To be fair to him, it does seem as if he's convinced himself she did a bunk years ago to get away from him, rather than coming to an untimely end. He's definitely moved on. I checked on the way back, he's married with a child. No repeat of the domestic incident reported during his relationship with Tracy. Although, he received a caution for possession of a class B substance and was disqualified from driving for six months a couple of years back, so he's not squeaky clean."

"What's your instinct telling you?" she asked, keen to see the development of his intuition.

"He was evasive, noncommittal and remarkably

unconcerned about the possibility she was murdered. Me asking questions seemed only to irritate him rather than make him nervous. I didn't get the impression he was on the back foot at all. His line manager gave him the heads up I was coming though, so he could have prepared himself. But then there's his version of events. What he told me this morning blows all manner of holes in the initial statement given when he reported Tracy missing."

"That is intriguing," Janssen said.

"He tried to backtrack and pass it off as forgetting details because he was tired having just finished work but I'm not buying it," Eric said with confidence. "When I challenged him on whether he was with his mates or working when she disappeared, he lied to me."

"How can you be sure?" she asked.

"He thought about his response. When he did, he looked up and to the left."

"So?"

"Basic brain chemistry," Eric countered. "The left hemispheric part of the brain deals with creativity, the right with memory. He had to concoct an answer, not draw on it from memory. It's a neurological reaction from his eyes, he wouldn't be aware of it."

"Where on earth did you learn that?"

"Discovery channel," Eric replied with a smile. "Besides, moments like that, loved ones disappearing, they can stay with people their entire lives. Some peoples' lives are defined by them. They're not the type of events easily forgotten whether you move on with your life or not."

"Sounds like you didn't like him," Tamara said.

"That's neither here nor there," Eric countered, sounding defensive. "I'm careful not to let my feelings cloud my objectivity." She was impressed, although it did sound like he was quoting a textbook. "Although, you're right. I didn't care for him."

"Good man," she said, trying not to sound patronising. She was genuinely pleased with how the young detective was settling into his role, seemingly unfazed by the magnitude of the events he was investigating. "I want you to do two things for me. First, follow up on Clare Hardy, see if she has reappeared somewhere else and the system hasn't picked it up and then start trying to assemble the DNA profiles of the missing girls to help with identification. Hardy has form. I read she was picked up for solicitation a couple of years prior to her disappearance. We started taking mandatory DNA swabs from people arrested back in 2004, so we should be able to find hers on file. Likewise, see what we can get on the others. We'll need to advise Sophie Maddox's mother of our investigation, so perhaps she'll consent to giving us a sample for consideration."

"We might have a job finding her. I looked yesterday and she's left the area. If she's registered on an electoral roll somewhere, it'll be easier," Eric replied, furiously scribbling notes in his pad.

"If not, try the local drug and alcohol outreach programs. Perhaps we can track her through the NHS."

Janssen followed up on her thinking. "Lesley Abbott was estranged from her family. We'll need to reach out to them anyway out of courtesy and they may be willing to help us. Tracy Bartlett will be a different matter. I recall she had no living family."

"We'll have to make do with whatever we can get," Tamara replied. "Anything that can narrow this list down will be a help. The pathologist has promised to have the autopsy report finalised for us by tomorrow morning."

"Working a Sunday. You must know people," Janssen said, standing up. She laughed. "We also have another lead to follow from the business card pulled from the victim's bag." She looked at him quizzically. With the surprise at her arrival and the team splitting to follow up on the potential victims, he must have forgotten to tell her. "I'll fill you in on the way."

CHAPTER THIRTEEN

DRIVING through the gated entrance to the Malloy residence, Tom Janssen immediately saw the figure of Beatrice on the far side of the courtyard. She was underneath a fixed canopy, crouching before a cylindrical object, raised off the ground on a frame and sitting at waist height. She glanced in their direction but continued on with what she was doing. Her hair was swept back from her forehead and tied at the base of the neck. A set of goggles sat atop her head and she was wearing a thick leather apron and matching guards on her forearms. As he got out of the car, she opened a door at the front with a gloved hand and he realised she was standing before a small furnace. The interior glowed a deep orange. Closing the door, she cast the glove aside and stepped out from under the canopy to await their arrival. Her face was covered in a sheen of sweat and she looked tired, as if she hadn't slept. Janssen remembered her that way the other night. Perhaps she always looked fatigued.

"Back so soon, Inspector," Beatrice said through a sideways smile. "You must really like my jewellery."

"You are more than a metalsmith, I see," Tamara said. Beatrice followed her gaze beyond her, back to the furnace.

"Glass blowing is quite a skill. You also work larger pieces, I see." She pointed to a forge a few metres away.

"I see you know your way around a smithy," Beatrice replied with a smile, wiping sweat from her brow with the back of her hand. "I dabbled in sculptures for a while, working lengths of discarded metal. I figured I'd develop a theme around post-industrial rebirth. That was a while back though, they never took off. Decided to stick with what I knew. Have you worked metal yourself then?"

"It's been a while and nothing on this scale. Sometimes it seems like a different life," Tamara replied, offering up her warrant card. "DCI Greave. We were hoping to speak with your daughter, River. Is she about?" The warm welcome rapidly dissipated at mention of her daughter. Beatrice's expression narrowed and she cast a glance towards the main house.

"Yes. She's here. If you're in luck, she might even be out of bed."

Beatrice beckoned them to follow and she led them over to the house, pushing open the front door. "River!" she shouted at the foot of the stairs but there was no reply. "She might be out the back." Continuing further into the house, an old farm cottage, they entered a small kitchen to the rear. On the far side of the room, the top half of a stable door to the outside was open with a small walled garden visible beyond. Climbing plants shrouded the doorway, rising up the exterior brickwork and threatening to encroach on the interior. Beatrice opened the nearest window overlooking the rear, barking at her daughter once again. "River! Police are here to see you." The breeze carried the sweet and unmistakable aroma of cannabis to them and the officers exchanged knowing looks.

The sound of a metal chair scraping on tile could be heard and the shadow of a figure approached the rear door. "What people?" River asked, appearing at the door. Her face dropped at sight of them and she discarded what was in her hand, exhaling smoke away from the house.

"I said *police*," Beatrice replied, lowering her voice and emphasising the intonation. River ducked back out of sight. "I'm sorry. She's… been like this for a while. I can't get her motivated."

"Smoking weed will help with that," Janssen replied, stepping past her and heading for the door. Tamara followed. He didn't care about River's personal habit. They were dealing with far greater issues.

They found River sitting on a cast iron chair, set around a circular table, with her feet resting on a second. A packet of hand rolling tobacco, lighter and cigarette papers were alongside an ash tray on the table. There was no sign of her drugs, no doubt concealed in the pocket of her fleece or more likely stashed in the nearby flowerbed to await retrieval after they left. "Hi River. We're not bothered about your recreational habit. We won't be sending you back to prison for a possession infringement. I've got better things to do with my time." He felt the need to point that out, needing her onside and if she feared him, that would be less likely.

"Maybe you wouldn't but your mates would," she retorted. "Do what you like. Green's easier to get hold of on the inside anyway." He got the impression it was bravado, a need to maintain control in front of the police. Unsurprising seeing as she only recently gained any form of influence back in her life after being granted parole.

"I don't doubt it," Janssen replied, gesturing to the chair River had her feet on. She relented, lifting them off and he pulled it away and sat down. "This is DCI Tamara Greave." River looked up at her with an impassive expression. Tamara smiled but River looked away without a response.

"We've been made aware you were once friendly with Sophie Maddox," Tamara said. "The girl who was being fostered by the Grables—"

"Yeah. I knew Sophie," River replied, "so what?"

"Were you good friends?" Janssen asked. River met his eye.

She nodded. "Did she talk about her background very much, her family for example?"

"Nope, sorry." Her reply was curt. He raised his eyebrows to convey his irritation at her attitude. Her expression softened a little. "Look, she didn't ever want to speak about her past. I guess it was too painful for her.

"What about a boyfriend?"

River threw her head back with a laugh. "Nah, not likely."

"You seem quite sure," he said, drawing her gaze back to him. The laughter switched into a broad grin. Her eyes sparkled. It was a knowing expression. River seemed to be revelling in her new found power. "What is it you're not telling us? Because I know there's something."

She exhaled deeply, the smile fading. "Sophie wasn't into anything permanent, you know. She wasn't looking to stick around. A boyfriend wouldn't fit with her plans."

"What plans?" Tamara asked, standing off to her right.

River rolled her eyes skyward. "Plans. Life plans. The future. All of that." The answer was too vague and Janssen encouraged her to continue. "Sophie was on her own, had been most of her life. That's the way she wanted it too. No one looked out for her so she would look out for herself. That way, no one would ever get the chance to let her down."

"Such as her parents?"

"I guess so," River replied with a shrug. "Like I said, she didn't talk about it."

"And Sophie said all this to you?"

"As good as, yeah." River looked between the two of them. "Why do you ask? Sophie's not been around here for ages as far as I know. I've not seen her since she took off." Janssen chose to ignore the comment for the time being.

"When did you last see her?"

River thought hard. "Not sure. Around the time your lot fitted us up." She must have been referring to her conviction. Every criminal he'd ever arrested and who was found guilty accused him of corruption. It was quite normal. The nation's prisons were filled with the innocent, if you listened to the inmates.

"Was she associated with you and your... *group*?" Janssen couldn't find the right word.

"If you're asking me if she cared about animal welfare and the soul of the human species... then yes, she was part of *my group*. It's a pity more of you aren't. Something might get done about it."

"The company you targeted, what was it called again?" he asked, intentionally keeping his tone neutral. She glared at him, eyes narrowing.

"You've obviously read all about me. They deserved everything they got and more besides."

"And yet, you were fitted up?"

"I didn't have anything to do with that break-in. None of us did." He looked away, annoyed that he'd allowed the conversation to become side tracked.

"Was Sophie one of the activists? It might help with our investigation."

"Investigation into what?"

"Whether it is Sophie we found buried in the dunes out by Wells."

River's mouth fell open and within moments her eyes glazed over. A period of silence followed before River, blinking furiously, shook her head.

"No, can't be Sophie, just can't be. She left."

"She told you she was going?"

"No, not exactly." The attitude was absent. It was as if she'd transformed into an entirely different person. "She said she would one day, had plans to but never actually said when. She'd talk about things she wanted to do, where she wanted to go... new places and stuff... and she wouldn't tell anyone beforehand. She knew people would try and stop her if she did, her foster parents and the socials. I figured it was all talk. You say stuff when you're a kid but you don't do it, do you?"

Janssen inclined his head towards Tamara, who nodded. Stepping forward, she passed River a copy of the photos found among Sophie's possessions. River took the pictures, holding them up before her. Passing them from one hand to the other, she skipped over the pictures of the parents quickly before lingering on the shot taken at the party. "Can you tell us who this is?" Janssen asked softly as she came to the strip from the booth. Staring at them intensely, he thought for a moment there was a flicker of recognition but the longer the wait for her reaction, the less confident he became. Putting the pictures down on the table, she met his eye.

"No. Sorry." Something about her tone resonated with him, raising a doubt in his mind as to whether she was being truthful. Only moments ago she was adamant her friend was unlikely to be seeing someone and now, faced with evidence to the contrary, she appeared distinctly unmoved by the revelation. He maintained the eye contact but she held firm.

"Okay, what about the name Darren? Does that mean anything to you, particularly in relation to Sophie?" The barricades surrounding River were back. It was as if learning of her friend's potential death pulled them down but the respite was brief. She shook her head.

"No. I don't remember anyone called Darren."

"Think hard. Perhaps it was someone here on holiday, a friend of a friend. Maybe someone mentioned in passing."

River took on a hard edge as she spoke, calm and controlled. "No. I can't help you. I wish I could but I don't know him. And to answer your earlier question, no."

"No?" Janssen queried.

"Sophie wasn't one of the hardcore activists. She'd come with me on protests, hand out leaflets and that but no. She didn't want to get involved."

"Involved in what?" Tamara asked. River appeared to reel,

perhaps fearing she'd spoken too freely already. Shaking her head, she crossed her arms in front of her.

Sensing the futility of further conversation, Janssen thanked her for her time. River didn't reply but her eyes tracked him as he stood. The impression of reticence was strong. Was she withholding to protect her friend or herself? Perhaps it was her animosity towards the police. Either way, there was more to River Malloy than they knew already. He would have to keep digging.

Entering the kitchen to find Beatrice leaning against the worktop, close to the open window, he was aware she must have been listening to the entire conversation. Not wishing to be overheard herself, she gestured for them to follow her into the hall and out of earshot.

"Please don't judge River too harshly," Beatrice asked in a hushed voice, nervously glancing past them back into the kitchen. "She's found adapting very difficult since… since she came home. I hear her sometimes at night… crying. She likes to make out how tough she is but that's all it is, an act."

"We are investigating a potential murder, Mrs Malloy," he was firm but at the same time could see the anguish in a mother's face. All she wanted was to protect her daughter. "After this length of time, we need to press every lead we have."

"I understand, Inspector. I really do. River was such a sensitive child. I wasn't around much… it was just me and her, you see. I worked three jobs to make ends meet and River needed me far more than she needed the extra money. I see that now." She stared towards where her daughter was sitting, as if she could see through the solid wall.

"What can you tell us about her friends?" Tamara asked. "Sophie Maddox in particular, if you knew her." Beatrice reacted to the name. It was fleeting but noticeable all the same.

"I knew the girl." If the words hadn't been tinged with venom, the expression accompanying them would have conveyed her feelings. She looked at each of them in turn.

"Looking back, I can't say I approved of the friendship. Sophie was flighty... jumped from one thing to the next... never could settle into anything for any length of time." Beatrice took on a faraway look, her expression softening as she absently fingered her necklace. "I guess it shouldn't come as a surprise bearing in mind where she came from."

"What do you know about her past?" Janssen asked.

"Oh, nothing much. Only whatever River shared at the time. I just meant her living with the Grables. They were always willing to take on any waifs and strays who needed somewhere to bed down. I guess the girl was always looking for somewhere to belong. Much like my River." The last was said with clear regret.

"Like River?" he asked, seeking clarification.

"Yes. I was never around and she needed support... love, a place to belong. She found people to fill those gaps in her life."

"You're talking about the animal rights activists, are you?" She nodded, looking down at the floor. "They gave her the consistency you couldn't."

"As well as a purpose," Beatrice added. "That's where my River and Sophie departed from one another. River wanted somewhere to belong whereas Sophie was only looking to take what she needed."

"That's quite a disparaging view you have of her, Mrs Malloy," Janssen said, ensuring he didn't come across as judgemental.

"Well, if you're going to drag that girl back into our lives then you ought to know what you are dealing with. It's very easy to paint the unfortunates in our society purely as victims. There was far more to that girl than many realised, even River. *Particularly* River."

"Are you speaking from personal experience?" Tamara asked. Beatrice shook her head slightly.

"I just saw the shenanigans she got up to with my daughter, toying with her emotions... getting her to jump through hoops for her. When you've been around the track like I have over the years, you develop a nose for these people."

"Did Sophie buy any jewellery from you?" Janssen thought she would have mentioned it already if she had but it was worth asking.

"That girl never paid for anything, mark my words. Sophie Maddox would bleed someone dry and move on to the next. If it's her you've pulled out of the ground, you should bear that in mind."

"Could you look at these for me," Janssen asked, holding out his hand towards Tamara. She produced the photos found among Sophie's belongings and he passed them to Beatrice. She examined them with a frown. Shaking her head at the strip from the photo booth, she handed them back.

"I'm sorry, Inspector."

"No matter, worth a look," he replied, noticing how her gaze lingered on the others. They appeared to have captured her attention. She noticed him watching her.

"Are these family shots… of Sophie's relatives?"

He nodded. "We believe so. Would you know them?"

"No, how would I?" she said, smiling. "No matter what type of girl she was, if it is her you found out there then it's a terrible waste of a young life."

"Very true. If River opens up do you think you could encourage her to give us a call? We want to get this cleared up as soon as possible."

"I'll do what I can, I promise," she replied.

CHAPTER FOURTEEN

LESS THAN A DOZEN people were present in *The Black Dog* pub. It was early evening and Janssen expected a larger turnout even on a Sunday. Waiting patiently at the bar to be served, he kept half an ear on what the locals were saying. The pub had been closed for the previous two nights, a precautionary decision against the threat of the storm surge. As it happened, the building came through unscathed. A couple of the older patrons were discussing how it wasn't as bad as several they'd experienced in their youth and they were grateful for that. Although the weather was still a popular subject, much of the chatter was around the discovery of the body on the beach. Unsurprisingly, gossip was rampant with suggestions as to who the victim may be and what happened to her. Janssen listened in.

The smart money seemed to be on a suicide or an accidental fall from one of the passing North Sea ferries. The former seemed the most popular amongst those joining in on the discussion. A dissenting voice argued as to why no mention was made of someone missing on board a ship only to be shouted down with talk of currents and riptides. As far as they knew, she could have fallen from a vessel off the Scandinavian coast and carried to Norfolk over a period of weeks. No one particularly wanted to countenance the possibility that a murderer once moved among them, let alone one who could still be present.

After what felt like a needlessly long wait, the barman approached him and he ordered himself a glass of orange juice and spring water for Tamara. Accepting the change from a ten-pound note, he returned to their table by the bay window, alongside the entrance door. Tamara smiled her thanks, accepting the drink. For a moment he considered apologising for his reaction to her presence that morning. Embarrassed by his petulance, he thought he'd leave it unless she raised the subject.

"What was all that earlier, at the Malloy place?" She looked at him quizzically. "Have you done a bit of glass blowing yourself?"

Tamara laughed. It was a gentle sound, softening her angular face which had seemed altogether too serious during the day. "Not really, no," she explained. "It was considered important for us to experience all manner of things when we were young."

"You mean at home, family?"

"Yes. Our parents wanted us to see what was on offer in the world." She smiled, taking on a faraway look. He figured she was remembering those occasions. "That meant a lot of family days to cultural events. Folk music festivals, museums and art galleries. Our mother, in particular, always managed to tune into these pop-up craft classes at local fairs or those organised as part of living history exhibitions."

"Sounds like you have great parents." The smile faded as she bobbed her head and he wondered if he'd said something amiss. Not sure how that was possible, he picked up his drink and scanned the lounge allowing conversation to drop.

"Quiet tonight, don't you think?" she asked him. He assessed those clustered around the bar. He guessed they were locals by the way conversation flowed easily. He felt comfortable spotting the tourists. Despite approaching the end of the season, usually they were still present in large numbers. No doubt kept away by the weather warnings, as were many of those with second homes in the area, the knock-on effect to the town was obvious. They would return soon enough.

"Let's hope the group haven't cancelled their plans," he replied. At that moment, the door opened and half a dozen people entered. The man in the lead greeted the barman and he indicated towards the rear. With a smile and a thumbs up gesture, the small group passed through the lounge and into another room that Janssen hadn't realised was there. Casually watching them as they filed past, he couldn't help but think they looked very plain and ordinary. The youngest was probably in their fifties with the age range spanning upwards another couple of decades. They struck him as an odd bunch for a teenager or twenty-something to be associating with and even less likely to be practising the occult. None of them bore even a passing resemblance to the unknown male Lesley Abbott brought home with her. Although, factoring in possible ageing as well as a change in appearance it would be difficult to be sure. The door was left ajar and angling his head, he could see into the room beyond. They were removing coats and chatting with one another.

A couple came out of the room heading for the bar, catching his eye. He'd been rumbled. Tamara rose from her seat, he followed her lead, and they approached them just as they were ordering drinks for the group. Subtly displaying their warrant cards, they identified themselves. Far from being in any way alarmed, they were curious as to why the police were taking an interest in their meeting.

"I'm a little bemused by what you think the purpose of a *moot* is," the leader of the little group, a man by the name of Charles said, a half-smile developing as he spoke. "We're Pagans not practitioners of the occult." Janssen glanced to Tamara who took the comment in her stride.

"You'll have to forgive our ignorance," she replied. Charles led them back into the meeting room. "Is there not something of a crossover?" The question was met with derision and for a moment Charles appeared to take offence. The moment passed and he gestured for them to take a seat while introducing them to the group. The response was mixed but on the whole it was positive.

"I suppose to the uninitiated, and I mean that in a very general sense, our views could be misconstrued," Charles said, inclining his head to one side and acknowledging the consensus of those assembled. Another picked up the thread, the woman they'd met alongside Charles at the bar, Eva.

"We are a diverse group, drawing from many traditions. As Pagans we look to learn from our ancient ancestors and explore the spiritual path. We meet regularly, listen to teachings from the elders and seek guidance on our path."

"It sounds very much like a religion, in that sense," Tamara replied.

"We are no different to any other religion in that regard," Charles replied. "We follow a poly or pantheistic nature-worshipping religion, the one true humanity-wide religion. Pagans see the cycle of the natural year, and its emphasis on the different seasons, as a model of spiritual growth and renewal, the passage of which is marked by different festivals celebrating divinities who have an affinity with those points in the year."

"So, you have multiple gods?" Tamara asked.

"Our divinities are not necessarily humanoid," Charles continued. The man was eloquent and articulate, clearly highly educated. "There are many who are elemental or collective. There are those who see our contemporary beliefs as somehow neo-pagan rather than true representations of our ancestral heritage, however, we tend not to get bogged down in such discussions. People are free to believe or worship as they see fit. Tolerance is key within Paganism. We seek to put humankind back in harmony with the world around us and as such embrace modern science and the values of people in general. We are not so dissimilar to any of you who possibly view us as out of touch with the modern world. The reality is quite the opposite."

"How does the occult fit in to this?" Knowing where the dividing line might be and therefore differentiating between the two might prove necessary.

"Occultism? Are you referring to the practice of witchcraft?" Eva asked. "Forgive me if I'm interpreting your tone wrong but you sound as if you speak only about negative energy."

"I'm on new ground, I must say," he replied, mustering a warm smile that was returned.

"We are more of a *folk religion*," Eva told him. "What you are referring to are more *Neopagan* or *Druidic* practices. This is modern paganism, where the practice of magic is widely regarded as paramount within the religion. All are welcome here and we have had solitary devotees of *Wicca*, as well as some of the *Gardenarians*, attend with us from time to time, so we are not ignorant of the belief structures. The practice of magic or witchcraft can be assigned to black and white, the former is concerned with the more malicious acts of revenge, torment or coercion whereas white magic can be used to foster love, protection or safety, to name but a few." Her explanation garnered murmurings of agreement from among the group. "Sadly, the practitioners cannot be so easily defined."

"Why not?" he asked, genuinely finding himself curious at this different take on the world.

"Well, for instance," Charles began, "Wiccans see magic and spell craft as essential to their religion, although you don't need to be a Wiccan to practise magic, as you are free to practise any spells you see fit. There are no set rules to follow, no dogma or indoctrination. You will find solitary practitioners just as you will find covens who have their own particular focus. The difference lies within the person casting the spells… what they perceive as their gifts and what they set out to achieve."

"Will there be those who are... I don't know how to put this without risking offence... not as ethical, or wholesome, as you describe?" he asked, looking around at the assembled faces. No one appeared overtly offended by the question. A few expressions hardened but there was no sign of dissent. Charles answered, apparently choosing his words carefully.

"There will always be those who lean towards a darker version of reality, it is true. There are not many, and few that I have come across in my time and I've been a practising Pagan for thirty years. However, with a vast number of avenues to consider, one should always choose carefully when associating with a new group. We have connections to a national federation and there is also the Pagan Council who will guide new entrants to the religion as best they can, although, there are no official vetting procedures I am aware of."

"You said you've come across a few. Any of them local to us here, in Norfolk?" Janssen asked. Charles glanced sideways towards Eva who looked down, failing to meet his eye. The movement was obvious. "Charles?"

"We had one, some time ago now." His tone and body language conveyed his reluctance to speak of it. "He joined us for a while, not for long I hasten to add. He held views that were... inconsistent with our ways."

"What happened with him?" Tamara asked, intrigued.

"We asked him to leave of course." Charles looked up, glancing between the two of them.

"We should have known from the outset," Eva chimed in. "He was odd from the very moment he arrived." Charles placed a gentle yet restraining hand on her forearm. She stopped talking, pursing her lips and shaking her head.

"He was a charismatic young man, remarkably knowledgeable about our customs and enthusiastic," Charles said, his brow furrowing. "His company was naturally infectious, as some people tend to be, and we saw it as an opportunity to bring new blood to the group and indeed, our religion."

"New blood?"

"Oh… drawing in some younger people is what I meant. We really want to make a difference to the world we live in. This is an earth-focussed religion after all. We felt to bring in younger members might allow us to broaden our reach. Conn seemed like just the type of chap we were looking for. For a while, he seemed to do just that but then it all changed."

"What was the problem?"

"Perhaps we misjudged him… or his intentions. I say *we* and to be honest, it was me. Eva and some of the others were uneasy with him from a much earlier point but I was stubborn."

"You still are," Eva muttered. Charles acknowledged the comment with a flick of one eyebrow.

"Conn began pushing us to celebrate both the seasonal festivals as well as the *Esbats* – lunar rituals combining both religion and magic elements. Wiccans believe in the power of the moon with differing energy levels depending on which phase the moon currently sits in. The respective energies have particular uses, according to those who believe at any rate. There are twelve, sometimes thirteen, new moons each year. Conn sought to direct us towards this… well, in any event, it wasn't for all of us."

"But it was for some?" Janssen seized upon the particular choice of words. Charles sat forward, shifting his weight in his seat.

"Yes, there were some who were of similar beliefs. For a time, we continued as before believing in our collective spirit before there was an inevitable parting of the ways. As I said, we are tolerant and everyone is welcome. After all, Paganism is a widespread religion with beliefs in many deities and practices. However, there is one stipulation – your actions must not seek to harm others."

"And he did?" Janssen sought to clarify. Charles met his eye, as did Eva, although she struck him as nervous and on edge. "Did he seek to harm others?"

Charles nodded, breaking the eye contact.

"When was this?"

"Oh… years ago. Four, maybe five." Charles looked to Eva beside him for assistance, Janssen figured they were a couple.

"Closer to six, I would say," she corrected him. "It was the year after that terrible Yule… the worst winter period in decades. You remember?" Charles nodded that he did.

"Yes, I would say six is probably accurate."

"And this *Conn*, do you have a last name for him?"

"Conn was what he called himself, it meant something else, *disciple* or *leader…* something like that. Whether he officially adopted the name or not, I couldn't say."

"Was he a local?" Janssen asked, making a note. Charles shook his head. "Can you describe him to me?"

"He knew the area well enough. I'd place his accent as East Anglian but whether he was from these parts, I really don't know." Janssen noticed Tamara looking around the group, she was contemplating something. He could tell.

"Are there usually more of you than this?" She aimed her question at Charles.

"We used to number more, it is true."

"That parting of the ways you mentioned?" Charles nodded solemnly. "So, would it be fair to say more of your group were quite taken with the notion of the magical elements Conn evoked?"

"Particularly the more… impressionable ones, yes."

"The younger ones," Eva added.

"Young women?" Tamara pressed.

"Both."

Janssen exchanged glances with Tamara and he saw her draw a deep breath. "I want to run a few names past you, if I may? Let me know if they sound familiar, maybe as visitors to the group or mentioned in passing. Stop me if you do," he asked, checking each member of the group were comfortable. Everyone seemed willing. "Darren or Clare?" Collectively they shook their heads, seeking confirmation from one another. "What about two young women by the name of Lesley or Sophie?"

"There was certainly someone called Les, I remember one of the others calling her by name," Eva replied, pleased with herself for recollecting it. "I'm sure because *Les* struck me as such an odd nickname for such a pretty girl." Janssen glanced to Tamara but she only had eyes for Eva.

"How about River?" she asked. Eva turned to her, tilting her head to one side but it was Charles who responded.

"River, yes, definitely." Eva agreed and a couple of the others supported them. "A tough one to forget, River. Very focussed, driven. She knocked around with another girl and that Lesley you are speaking about."

"Could this other girl be Sophie? She would have been in her mid-teens, blonde…" Janssen allowed the description to tail off as they openly discussed their mixed recollections between themselves. He felt a tingle of excitement or trepidation in his stomach, he was unsure which. The debate subsided with everyone turning to him, unable to confirm or dismiss the possibility.

"Perhaps if we had a photograph," Charles said, sounding apologetic. Janssen remembered he'd snapped a copy of the images with his mobile. Irritated he hadn't thought of it earlier, he quickly brought up the gallery of Sophie in the photobooth. Enlarging it with thumb and forefinger, he passed the handset across. Both Charles and Eva leaned. The response was immediate and emphatic. "That's her. She was here. The three of them."

"But not the male? That's not Conn," Janssen clarified, pointing towards the image. Charles shook his head, offering the handset around to the others with Janssen's approval. None of them could put a name to the face either.

"Sorry, never saw him. But that's certainly her. After the

falling out with Conn, the three of them made up a part of those who never returned to the group." Charles sat back with a broad smile, blowing out his cheeks and marvelling at his contribution. Turning to Tamara, this time he found her looking directly at him, her eyes sparkling. They came here in search of a lead and would be leaving with several.

CHAPTER FIFTEEN

"THAT WOULD CERTAINLY EXPLAIN the reason why both Sophie and Lesley were likely to be wearing similar jewellery," Tamara said as they crossed the road, leaving the pub behind them. "What was it you said earlier about the pendant? Something about it depicting the three phases of the cycle of the moon and the worship of the goddess."

"Yeah, that's it," Janssen confirmed. "If they were in awe of this Conn, then it follows they might be wearing it for more than just fashion trends."

Tamara's phone rang and she answered it, surprised to hear Eric's voice on the line. "Are you still at the station at this hour?"

"Yes. You said to follow up on Clare Hardy. I got a hit on the database but I wanted to get a concrete answer before I called. They've only just come back to me. I was thinking they'd forgotten and headed off to the pub."

"Eric," she said, adopting a stern tone, "I want you to take a deep breath… and then tell me what on earth you're going on about please."

"Clare Hardy, the missing sex worker," he said tentatively. She felt bad for ribbing him then, clearly, he wasn't yet sure when she should be taken seriously. "She's not missing." Tamara stopped. Janssen continued on for a few steps before realising and then he too, stopped to wait.

"You found her?"

"After a fashion," Eric replied. "She's dead. A drug overdose, three years ago down in London. There were no suspicious circumstances and the coroner ruled it a case of accidental death. I guess no one cross-referenced the name she was living under with her maiden name. Or her maiden name was the one we knew her by—"

"Eric… go home and get some sleep. I'll need you fully alert tomorrow morning."

"Will do."

"And Eric?"

"Yes, Ma'am?"

"Good work young man." She could almost feel the pride emanating from him transferring down the line.

"Thank you, I'll see you tomorrow."

"One more thing before you go," she paused, ensuring she had his attention, "please don't call me ma'am again."

"Erm… okay…"

"Goodnight, Eric." Hanging up on the call, she turned back to Janssen. "And then there were three!" she said with a smile. "Come on, you can give me a lift back to my hotel." He seemed preoccupied, mulling over whatever it was in his mind. "What is it, Tom?" He looked back towards the pub, sucking air through his teeth.

"Something Manafort said to me the other night, at the grave site. The victim had a contact card for a local company whose focus was heavily associated with vivisection. There was quite a furore surrounding them a few years back. It's the firm River Malloy and her activist friends were convicted of breaking into. He thought it odd that an employee of the company would be associated with someone who used ethical cosmetics. I have to agree."

"So, what are you thinking? Could he have been an inside

man – someone who helped them gain access?"

"That's what I'm thinking. Whatever the connection is, you'd imagine if these girls were so tight presumably, they would know of it, and River said she'd never heard of a *Darren*. She's done her time. We wouldn't be able to put her on trial again."

"If the involvement of an insider didn't come out during the trial, perhaps she's worried about implicating him now? She may have completed her sentence but he hasn't."

Janssen inclined his head to one side. "Yeah, you're probably right. It's Monday tomorrow. I'll pay the company a visit and see if we can track him down. Whether he was involved in the attacks on the business or not is one thing, but I'll be more interested to know if he knew our victim."

"If you were a betting man, who would you have your money on at this stage?" she asked, resuming her course back to the car.

"I have been known for a flutter in the past but I learned one thing years ago."

"Which is?"

"Never to bet on a sure thing."

He fell into step alongside her. She didn't ask him to put a name to his *sure thing*. In her mind, they were still some way off a positive identification. "Besides tracking down the elusive Conn, we'll also need to speak to some of River's associates. Right now, she's the only person who we can tie to any of these women, aside from Lee Taylor, and something tells me he will be less than forthcoming." Approaching the car, parked in a small car park along the quayside Tamara cast an eye out to the sea. "The body was discovered not far from here, wasn't it?"

Janssen pointed to Beach Road running directly away from them up to the holiday park with the beach beyond. "Yeah, just around from the point there."

"Show me." He agreed and they got into the car.

Parking where the road met a locked gate, alongside the entrance to the beach café, as close as they could get to the dunes, they got out. From their slightly elevated vantage point at the top of the incline, Tamara looked across the collection of static homes noting how the majority were in darkness. There was no indication the holiday makers were returning just yet. Janssen pointed the way and set off with her a step behind. Their route through the dunes took them past a number of colourful beach huts clearly visible under the bright light of the new moon, many of them painted in varying shades of yellows, pink and blues. Footings jutted out of the ground where others recently stood, violently ripped from their standings no doubt by the recent surge. Only now did she realise the true scope of the damage. Safely inland when the storm made landfall, she'd obviously seen the reports and heard the warnings but to her it was still a distant event that never threatened her directly.

Coming to the edge of what was the crime scene, Janssen indicated where the remains were found, describing the positioning of the burial. There was no sign of what had been hidden for years by the sands, only revealed now by a freak of nature. The police cordon had been removed along with all the evidence, the dunes left to be reclaimed by the wind and the sea. Without a once in a generation storm event, who knew how much longer the victim would have lain there undiscovered.

"He had some nerve," she almost whispered. Janssen glanced towards her.

"Say that again."

"The killer. He had some nerve to bury the body out here," she replied, looking up and down the beach before turning and gauging the distance to both the woods and the campsite behind them. "It's perilously close to the holiday homes."

"There's always the possibility the killer was staying in one of them. It would make sense. He'd have pretty much direct access to the dunes. Makes the concealment easier."

She thought on that point. It was a logical conclusion. "That might help to explain why no one saw anything odd at the time. Usually somebody sees something they consider innocuous in the moment but tie it to a crime later. With our three women, no one saw anything."

"At the risk of jumping the gun, do you think we could be looking for more than one body?"

The breeze was light, carrying cool air off the sea and onto her face and she took a lungful. "I'd be lying if I said the thought hadn't occurred to me. But let's keep focussed on what we have. There still isn't a link between Tracy Bartlett and the other two, let alone River. If something materialises, then we won't be able to pass it off as a coincidence. First thing tomorrow I'll have Eric run down the past records of the holiday camp, try and see who was around at the time."

"That will be one heck of an undertaking. Thousands of people pass through here every season. Many of them are privately owned, often rented out to friends, family or acquaintances."

"Eric will manage." She was confident in his abilities. If the killer turned out to be transient, passing through either on holiday or masquerading as such, unless he had a previous record they would be hard pressed to identify him. If not, then he was a local. "Quite a risk bringing the body here, even in the dead of night. If you come by car there's only the one access road leaving you visible to the town for the length of it. A car would stand out at an odd hour. Likewise, we parked as close as we could. To do so earlier in an evening would draw less attention, but to empty a body from the vehicle, even one wrapped in a sheet without anyone seeing would be impossible."

"Not to mention the number of locals who walk this route every night. Dog walkers, tourists. Couldn't be done. Not unobserved," Janssen replied. "There's always access from the woods." She turned her gaze on the nearby pine trees, their interior shrouded in darkness. It was possible.

"Can we estimate how awkward that would have been?" She hadn't been able to discuss the physicality of the victim yet, although the missing girls they were focussing on were all slight in stature.

"It's hard to tell from the bone structure alone but the medical examiner and the CSI agreed the victim was roughly five foot six in height. That puts our three names in the frame and if so, then it's a manageable weight to move over a short distance."

"The woods are clear from brush?" she asked, straining to see detail beyond the tree line.

"Absolutely, yes. If you knew your way around, you could easily manage to slip through unnoticed."

"Still taking a risk. That's unusual for..." she let the thought tail off. Murders committed in the heat of the moment, an unexpected surge of fury instantly regretted seconds later, but too late for the victim, often resulted in the killer immediately fleeing the scene. The body would be discovered shortly after. Even in those cases where the body was removed, hidden somewhere or taken to a new location to detract from the culpability of the murderer, usually a friend or acquaintance, the rushed and poorly thought through nature of their actions would lead to early discovery. Murders where the body lay undiscovered for years, or never found at all, were mostly committed by those with premeditated tendencies. They already knew where they would conceal the body, how to go about it and given great thought to putting as much distance between themselves and their victim as possible.

This victim fitted neither scenario particularly well which left her with another possibility. The killer wanted to keep the victim close by. Perhaps so they could revisit the scene on occasion, enjoying the sensation of power that came with knowing what no one else did – who was buried in the nearby dunes. A chill passed through her at the thought. If it were the case, then the person they were hunting was a cold, calculating individual. Someone to be feared.

"Okay, I'm done. Shall we head off?" she asked, Janssen

nodded. "We'll follow up on the activist angle. They were prepared to break into the vivisection clinic, trash it and set it alight, so there's a tendency to violence there."

"I can't imagine River's past associates will be pleased to see us knocking at their door," Janssen said. "I don't know how cooperative they'll be."

"Let's rattle their cages anyway, no pun intended," she added, catching sight of his smile in the corner of her eye. "You can run down this Darren character, see how he fits in. Do you need to head home or do you fancy a drink?"

Janssen looked at his watch. It was shortly before ten o'clock. "A drink sounds good."

RAISING her glass and finishing the contents, Tamara signalled the barman requesting another glass of prosecco. Putting the empty glass back on the bar she caught Janssen's expression in the corner of her eye. When she looked at him inquisitively, he averted his eyes. "I know," she said drawing her palm across her cheek, aware of how quickly she'd finished her second drink. They'd barely been back at the hotel for half an hour. "Do you need anything?" she asked, eyeing his half full glass of mineral water. He was driving, so refused to drink at all which she thought admirable. He shook his head slightly.

"Are you okay?" he asked. His tone was soft, his manner gentle.

"Rough few days. Weeks, if I'm honest," she told him, gratefully receiving a fresh glass and charging it to her room.

"Anything you want to talk about?" She assessed his intent. Tom Janssen wasn't one to pry nor gossip as far as she knew. He seemed genuinely concerned for her. She laughed, curling her fingers around the stem and gently turning the glass on the bar, but it was without humour.

"No, but thanks," she replied, feeling the smile fade. She was drinking too fast, feeling light headed. "Have you heard anything about the proposed boundary changes?" She could tell by his lack of reaction that he had, although the redrawing of the area boundaries was supposed to be a closely guarded plan at this stage.

"I've heard a few things said, yes."

"It could shake things up a bit."

He inclined his head. "I reckon that's why they still haven't given me a DS. They're waiting to see what happens with the changes."

"You think there will be a reduction in cover?" she asked him, seeking to pick his brains for the lay of the local land.

"I would expect so. There will be a cost saving element in play, isn't there always? Why do you ask?"

She considered brushing aside the question. It would be the best course of action. Maybe it was the wine, or the company, she didn't know but she answered directly. "There could be an opening for a DCI... here, with your team." Again, she was surprised at his reaction. He was not only clearly aware of the possibility but a flick of his eyes and a subtle shift in his seat told her he was bothered by the comment. "Did I say something?" He shrugged, glancing past her and across the bar. There were barely a handful of people present, mainly residents of the hotel this close to eleven o'clock. "I was thinking I might go for it... if it happens." She paid close attention but this time, he didn't flinch.

"How would... Richard, isn't it?" he asked, eyes narrowing. She nodded, picking up her glass and sipping from it, looking at her own reflection in the giant mirror set behind the drinks' shelves of the bar. "How would he feel about that? I recall he works in London." There was something about his tone that was different, an edge maybe. She couldn't be sure.

"He spends most of the week in the city now. I don't think it would make that much difference." The words sounded bitter to her ear, judgemental. She caught Janssen looking at her via the mirror. *Those dark eyes, the finely chiselled features.*

"I can imagine," he said, breaking the eye contact and raising his own glass. "Sometimes it's hard enough when you live in the same town, let alone get separated by work as well as distance."

"Oh..." she said, chuckling. "Do I detect a similar level of relationship apathy?" He smiled, looking down at the bar.

"Something like that, yes," he confirmed, draining his glass and replacing it gently on the bar. "Things don't seem to be going the way I expected. In this job," he shook his head slowly, staring ahead at nothing in particular, "maybe *that is* to be expected." A few seconds passed with neither of them speaking. Tamara sipped at her wine. Janssen's demeanour shifted from threatening melancholy to mild amusement. "Tell you what, though, I was thinking of putting in for that position. Quite fancied being a DCI." His tone wasn't angry nor assertive, she didn't feel he was trying to stake a claim. Glancing at her sideways, he smiled ruefully. "I didn't think I would be up against stiff competition."

"I'll try not to make you look bad," she replied, drawing a laugh out of him. "Hell, it'll probably never happen anyway. You know how often these plans come to nothing. I'm just sick of being in limbo."

"Are you referring to being an acting DCI or about you and Richard?"

Taking another mouthful of prosecco, she felt the bubbles run up her nose. The sensation stung and made her eyes water. She ignored his question. "I think I need to call it a day." Rising from her stool she wavered, forcing her to reach out for the bar in order to steady herself. Janssen leaned over and placed a hand on her arm for support. She'd had more than enough to drink bearing in mind she hadn't eaten properly since breakfast and that was roughly sixteen hours ago. "I'm okay," she whispered, glancing to him. "Really. I just need to get my head down."

"I'll walk you."

They left the hotel bar. It was a small place, a dozen rooms for paying guests over the first and second floor. She was on the first, with a suite overlooking the marshes and the entrance to the harbour. The short walk was good for her. Although still unsteady on her feet, climbing the stairs forced her to concentrate and Tom's presence was helpful. Not to help her walk, mind you, but she was terrified of embarrassing herself. Reaching her room without incident, she fumbled in her pocket for the key card before struggling to slide it into the slot. The card slipped from her fingers and fell to the carpeted floor. She cursed. Before she could react, Janssen knelt and retrieved it. He made to put it in the slot for her just as she reached for it and their hands touched. She felt something. A spark, a flutter in her stomach. Their eyes met and he smiled warmly. She could smell his aftershave, feel his breath on her skin. Suddenly self-conscious she stammered her thanks. The green light lit up and the sound of the door unlocking came to ear, breaking the spell of the moment. She cracked the door open and turned her head towards him. "Sorry… about earlier."

"No need to apologise," he replied. That was nice of him to say but she wasn't quite sure what she was apologising for. She needed to get into the room. The door was heavy, the self-closing mechanism rigid. Pushing it open, she crossed the threshold. Turning to him, she bid him goodnight. It was an awkward moment as he lingered. *What is he waiting for? He had to go.* She didn't want him to which was exactly why he should.

"Goodnight," Janssen said softly, his eyes flitting further along the corridor and back again. Still he lingered, only turning to leave when she released her hold on the door. It closed and she turned the latch, locking the door. Leaning against the wall, she clamped her eyes tightly shut and drew a deep breath. Picturing Tom standing in the corridor on the other side of the door, she considered opening it to see if he was still there, unsure of what she would do if he was. A wave of dizziness passed over her and she dismissed the idea, instead, walking across the suite towards the bed.

I really need to lie down.

CHAPTER SIXTEEN

PARKING SPACE APPEARED to be at a premium as Tamara Greave pulled onto the forecourt. There was a queue for the pumps, Monday morning commuters filling up on their way into work. Squeezing through the only available space she drove around to the rear where the signage indicated the workshop would be found. Here, the allocated bays were already filled with cars booked in for work. She parked behind two cars set aside to await an MOT inspection. Getting out, she crossed to the reception. A buzzer sounded as she entered, two customers sitting inside the waiting area glanced up at her but said nothing. One was scrolling through a social media feed and the other sipped at a cup of coffee from the vending machine located in the corner. The smell of oil and rubber hung in the air.

Approaching the counter, she caught the attention of a figure in the workshop beyond and he came through, smiling warmly. She offered him her ID. He was surprised, the smile flipping from welcoming to nervous.

"I wanted to have a word with Niall Bradshaw. I was told he'd be working today."

"Niall? Yeah, sure. He's out back. Come through." The man stepped to one side and lifted a hatch, beckoning her forward.

She followed him through into the workshop where the day's bookings were already underway. The sound of a pneumatic wheel gun greeted their approach as she was directed to where Niall Bradshaw was carrying out a tyre change on an estate car. He had his back to her and the noise masked her approach. Startled by her presence, he jumped when he turned to face her. She showed him her warrant card and he rolled his eyes.

"Well, that didn't take you long, did it?" he said, placing the gun on the floor and defiantly crossing his arms.

"How do you mean?"

"I've not even been out six months and you're already on at me." He was agitated, glancing across the workshop at his colleagues. Tamara could tell they were curious, looking over at them but trying to do so surreptitiously and failing miserably. "They told me this is how it'd be."

"I don't understand. Who told you?"

"The guys on the inside. It doesn't matter what I do, the moment anything happens you'll be sniffing around and trying to attach me to it. That's how it works, right? Once you have a record, that's you marked for life. My probation officer helped me to get this job. I don't need you lot screwing it up for me. Jobs are hard enough to come by around here as it is!"

"Yes, your probation officer told me where I could find you. He's been quite impressed with your attitude since your release. I don't hear that very often."

"Yeah, great," he replied, glancing sideways towards the reception and the man who'd showed her through.

"Your boss?" she asked. Niall confirmed it with a brief nod. "I'm not here to cause trouble for you, Niall."

"Then why are you here?" he asked, picking up a rag and wiping his hands.

"To ask you about River Malloy and some of your other associates."

"Seriously? Haven't I been through it enough times already?"

His annoyance was clear to see. "I don't think I'll have much more to say than I have already."

"I've been through the case file as well as the defence your barrister put up at trial. You didn't have all that much to say then either."

"That's because there are only so many different ways you can say *I wasn't there.*"

"The jury didn't believe you though, did they?" she countered. Niall cast his head backwards, staring at the roof and letting out a deep sigh. "Besides, I'm not here to go over that. I'm looking into another matter."

"Something else you're looking to pin on me and the others?" She ignored the comment.

"Do you remember a couple of girls by the name of Sophie Maddox or Lesley Abbott? They were associating with River around the time she was active in your campaign targeting *Norfolk Reactive —*"

"*Targeting...* we weren't targeting anything. We were peacefully protesting outside their premises against their barbaric immorality. It was hardly a campaign. You make it sound like we were at war or something."

Tamara revisited her notes. "You were not only permanently encamped outside the company's perimeter fence but you also protested outside employee's homes, leaflet dropped their neighbours as well as actively naming people in social media feeds... that's not merely a peaceful protest. You were actively damaging these people's lives."

"Yeah, well... what goes around and all of that."

"Sophie and Lesley, ring any bells?"

"What's it about?"

"If you could just answer the question." Something about the expression, his stare, made her think he wasn't likely to cooperate unless she gave a little ground. "I'm investigating a potential murder and trying to get to the bottom of what happened to her. At this time, we are trying to narrow down who it might be." Niall's eyes narrowed and then his stance softened. "Now, Sophie and Lesley."

"Yeah, I knew them. Not well," he added with a shrug, "but they were around."

"Were they active campaigners?"

"I don't really remember. They were River's friends, not mine and there were a lot of us back then."

"Joining your protest?"

"Yeah, what I would call twenty or thirty hardcore… those who lived with us at the encampment. Numbers fluctuated. People drifted off to do work and that. We all had to make ends meet somehow but we managed to maintain a presence. We wanted to shut them down. We knew we'd have to keep the pressure up and it'd be the long game."

"They did shut down, or at least completely changed their business model and it was nothing to do with the protest in the end."

"Ah… right, is that what they say?"

"You disagree?"

"They always spun the line that we were not having an effect on their business but I saw the owner's face every day when he drove past. He was feeling it. I could see it in his eyes."

"Then why set the fire? If you were wearing him down." She was intrigued. The subject still brought Niall's passion to the surface despite his desire not to rake over the past.

"That was exactly my point at the time… why would we ruin all our hard work by torching the place? They were on the verge of folding… I knew it." Niall lifted himself upright, a smile creeping from the corners of his mouth.

"You seem pretty sure."

"They were in trouble, I saw the…" he fell silent, averting his eyes from her gaze as the smile dropped away. *Was he about to let something slip and caught himself in time?* "Ah… what the hell… like you said, the jury didn't believe me, so why should you?"

"Can you remember anything about the girls, River's friends?"

"Sophie was alright. Proved herself to be useful whenever she came along with River. She was about a fair bit for a while. The two of them were pretty much inseparable for a bit. River had it bad for her, it was so obvious. Not sure if it was reciprocal though." Tamara was thrown. She hadn't realised.

"They were an item?"

"Oh, yeah," Niall replied, rubbing at the two-day stubble growth of his chin. He was dark-haired and despite only being in his early thirties his beard growth was already heavily flecked with grey. He kept the hair on his head cut short, probably a result of a prematurely receding hairline. "But like I say, I don't think Sophie considered it an exclusive arrangement."

"What makes you say that?"

Niall shrugged. "Just didn't strike me as the type. I wasn't surprised when she took off."

"You remember that?"

"It's what River told me... or words to that effect. Sophie stopped coming to the protests. I guessed they'd split and River wasn't handling it too well. She had her own demons, you know. Looking back on it all, I wonder if she was only part of it as a way to vent the frustrations of her own life."

"That's profound," she said, trying not to come across as condescending.

"I did a lot of thinking when I was inside," Niall explained, ignoring her scepticism. "I met a lot of people... and I listened, learned."

"It sounds like you found God."

"I stand by the fact I should never have been in there in the first place, but I never want to go back. Whatever I've done in my life that I didn't get pulled up for, I've paid my dues many times over. I'm sure I can spend the rest of my days arguing the injustice and screaming about it but you... everyone else, ain't gonna listen to me, so I'm wasting my breath. I've put it behind me and I could really do with you lot leaving me alone to get on with my life."

"What about Lesley? Where does she come into it?"

"Barely knew her." He was dismissive. "She was one of those middle class new-age types, wanting to break out from behind her privilege whilst living off the family money as far as I could tell." He met her eye, she read him as genuine. "Don't get me wrong, she picked up the tab a few times and I wasn't gonna object but... hey, we've all got to eat, right? She liked River, though. They really seemed to hit it off."

"If they weren't heavily involved with the protests together, how come they found one another in the first place?"

"That'll be the weirdo they were hanging out with." She encouraged him to continue. "This guy thought he was some spiritual guru or something, called himself *Coll* or something. Odd name. Odd bloke. I asked River about him and she said it wasn't his real name but it suited his image."

"Any idea what his real name was?"

"At the time, no but I've seen him since."

"Where?"

"Here," Niall said, indicating the garage with a flick of his head. "Brought his car in a couple of times. He was in last week for a service, drives an old VW Golf. Pretty impressive it's still on the road. He's changed a bit but definitely him. He's got something about him, a look, I don't know. Gives off a weird vibe. You don't forget him."

"Name?"

"Yeah," he laughed then, "I had to find out what it was – Collyer, Mike Collyer."

"Thanks for your time," she said, scribbling the name in her notebook.

"Please don't rush back," Niall called after her as she walked away.

Bypassing the reception area, she headed outside. The

manager who'd initially greeted her appeared from the main entrance and hurried to catch her up.

"There isn't a problem is there?" he asked, looking over his shoulder, back into the work bays where the mechanics were getting on with their jobs.

"No, nothing I am aware of. Why do you ask?"

"I don't know really," the man said, his eyes furtively moving around. "Just, police interviewing Niall... I thought it might be because someone made a complaint after what happened the other day."

"What *did* happen the other day?"

"Niall was involved in an altercation with a client... I don't know what it was about or who was the aggressor. You do get some trying people through here and... although I didn't see the incident – I wasn't working on Saturday – but the duty manager said Niall was not at fault. Bearing that in mind, I gave him the benefit of the doubt."

"Who was the client?"

"One of our regulars, Mr Collyer. He's been coming here for years. He is a loyal customer... if a little odd," the manager said. Tamara looked past him, seeing Niall returning to work but apparently with half an eye on them. "Is your visit anything to do with that? We have a company policy to help the wider community, a social responsibility if you will, offering jobs to those who might not be able to get one with their past... I'd hate for one of our staff to jeopardise that policy. I'm sure you understand."

Tamara turned back to him and smiled. "No, there's been no complaint made. It's unrelated." Reassured, the manager backed away, smiling apologetically for holding her up. It would seem her radar was a little off. Niall Bradshaw wasn't as open as she'd first thought. "You wouldn't happen to have an address for Mr Collyer?"

"Erm... yes, but I thought you said it was unrelated."

"That's true, it's not. Could I have it anyway, please?" The man nodded, looking confused. She could understand but felt no need to explain. She waited patiently while he disappeared back into the building, returning a few minutes later with a handwritten address scribbled on a piece of paper. He passed it to her nervously. "Thank you very much." Without another word, she turned to leave, noting how Niall was nowhere to be seen.

CHAPTER SEVENTEEN

NIALL BRADSHAW CROUCHED DOWN and retrieved the wheel gun. From the corner of his eye, he could see the detective speaking to Marcus, the branch manager. *The man was so transparent.* He either cosies up to someone like the sycophant that he is or he's spitting venom in a pitiful gesture of dominance. Pretending not to notice the two of them glance in his direction, he made a show of getting on with his work. Marcus returned to the reception but the policewoman didn't leave. Instead she lingered, occasionally looking in his direction. He'd expected someone to show up sooner or later. After Saturday, it was almost inevitable. Although it surprised him that Conn hadn't given him much of a chance to think about his reaction. *Maybe that was the point.* His expectation was that Conn would make a second play, much as he'd done last time. This time it would be different. He'd misread the situation before, believing it all to be a bluff. Only it wasn't and it'd cost him. The heavy price of naivety – five years of his life.

Slipping out of the workshop unnoticed, he passed through the staff room and out of the fire door. Here, he lit a smoke. Leaning against the outer wall of the building he tilted his head back, eyeing the passing clouds. The police were already asking questions but that's all it was so far, more questions. They were fishing. She didn't have any facts, nothing concrete, at any rate. That meant Conn hadn't gone through with the threat. Not yet, at least. Maybe this was just a warning of greater things to come. They were not idle threats either. There was no doubt in his mind Conn had the ability, as well as the prerequisite lack of conscience to carry out the threat. Last time, it was his belief in the system that gave him the confidence to ignore it. Now, with a criminal record behind him, the odds were even less in his favour.

Anger flared within him and he wanted to scream out in frustration but instead, he drew another lungful and shook his head. A face peeked out from inside, expectantly looking around. It was Marcus. The moment his eyes fell upon him, he stepped out. Hands firmly on his hips, he sneered at him. Niall cut him off before he had a chance to speak.

"Give it a rest, Marcus, would you. I'm taking my fifteen minutes." He looked away, exhaling smoke along with the words.

"Don't you think you've had your break already… with the police. That better not become a habit!"

He looked across at the chubby, diminutive control freak. The temptation to slap him was almost irresistible. "Don't worry. It won't, Marcus."

"Well, it better not. We have standards around here. I can't be dealing with trouble brought in by…" It was almost as if he didn't know how to finish the statement. Instead, he let out a sound which could have meant anything and disappeared back inside. His voice carried from some distance across the staff room, "I want you back in five!"

Sighing deeply, Niall took a final draw on his cigarette before tossing the remainder to the floor and grinding it into the tarmac with the ball of his foot. "Yes, Boss," he whispered to himself.

What he needed to figure out was a plan of action to ensure he put himself on the front foot. Adopting a passive stance failed him last time. He needed to be certain how far he was prepared to go in order to stay out of prison. Rubbing fiercely at his face with the palms of his hands, he set off back to work.

CHAPTER EIGHTEEN

THE LOBBY FELT MORE like the interior of a car dealership than a medical research firm. The floor was laid with black porcelain tiles, the walls painted a brilliant white. Strategically located foliage in planters broke up the otherwise sterile, if contemporary, presentation. The receptionist glanced up from behind her desk returning his smile just as the phone rang. She looked away, picking up the handset. Normally a patient man, Tom Janssen was becoming irritated by the wait. To ensure his visit caused as little disruption as possible, he'd called ahead but still found himself standing in the lobby three quarters of an hour later.

The opening of a door nearby echoed in the surroundings and he turned to be greeted by the approach of a middle-aged man, probably in his late fifties. Despite his age, he was well built, almost the same size as Janssen himself. He was well tanned with a round face and flushed cheeks. Both of which stood out in stark contrast to the thinning, almost white hair and equally pristine teeth. His face split a broad grin as he offered his hand.

"Inspector Janssen?" He took the offered hand, returning the smile. "Shaun Robinson. Forgive me for keeping you waiting.

Monday mornings… what else can I say?" He raised his hands in an open gesture of supplication to signify a lack of control over the events. His tone conveyed contrition and he led them back towards the door with a gentle touch to Janssen's elbow. "I understand you have some questions about one of our colleagues going back a number of years?"

"That's correct," he replied, waiting while a code was punched into the door before they were able to pass through it and into the corridor beyond. This part of the building's appearance was far more like any other office he'd ever frequented. Dark blue carpets, hard wearing, along with pastel painted walls. The décor lacked the grandiose impression of the statement reception lobby. His escort appeared to notice.

"Usually visitors don't come back this way. They are shown directly to the conference room. This business is not unlike any other, perception is of equal if not greater importance than the actual performance." They continued on until they reached the last door in the corridor which his guide opened, allowing Janssen to walk through first. Offering him a seat in front of a large glass desk, highly polished and contemporary black, Shaun waited for Tom to sit down before taking his own seat opposite. "Now, what is it I can do for you?" Shaun asked, leaning forward at his desk and cupping one hand in the other.

"I'm trying to trace a man who would have been working for you roughly five or six years ago."

Shaun blew out his cheeks. "A lot's happened since then. Do you have a name for me?"

"Only the first name, I'm afraid. The remainder of the business card was damaged and we've been unable to reconstruct it," he explained, reaching into his pocket and taking out the copy he brought with him. "A man by the name of Darren."

"Unfortunately, quite a common name. No one springs to mind," Shaun said, reaching out and taking the copy. Peering at it intently, his brow furrowed. "Yes, it certainly looks like one of our cards from that period." He looked up, raising his eyebrows. "In what manner have you come by it?"

"It was found in the possession of a deceased female. We've yet to identify her and we are hoping your employee might be able to help us with that."

"I see," Shaun said, putting the paper down on the desk and sitting back. Spinning his chair to the right, he woke up his computer, tapping in a password and activating the screen. "I'll see what I can find for you. I hope you haven't had a wasted trip, though."

"I'm presuming the mobile number is one registered to your company. That will help, won't it?"

Shaun shook his head keeping his eyes on the monitor in front of him. "Not necessarily. We used to employ a number of contractors around then. Although we printed them business cards, they were not issued with full company benefits. They were, however, allowed to apply their own mobile numbers to the cards if they chose to." He continued his search of the database. Moments later, he turned back to Janssen. "As I thought. We have no one with that first name currently on our books. He must have moved on. Unsurprising really. There has been a great deal of change in the past few years. Our business is radically different to what it was around that time, requiring personnel with vastly different skill sets."

"So, I gather," Janssen replied. "How many employees do you have now?"

"Fewer than a hundred. However, that's staff on permanent contracts. We still hire in agency personnel and contractors as and when we need to. That policy hasn't changed."

"I understand you moved away from vivisection."

"I prefer the term *scientific research*, if you don't mind." The tone indicated the statement was offensive which wasn't his intention. "But yes, a few years ago I took the company in a different way."

"You no longer test on live animals."

"No, no. We are purely a medical research-based business now." He held his palms up as he spoke. "We run trials on behalf of drug manufacturers prior to them receiving full approval and going into mass production."

"So, you do your testing on humans now? That's a significant change. What part did the protests play in that decision, if you don't mind my asking?"

"Ah... you remember that?"

He shook his head. "Before my time here but I'm still interested."

"That was a very difficult time... for all of us," Shaun sank back in his chair, angling his head so he could look out of the window. Janssen followed his gaze but there was little of interest. "I was getting it from all angles at that time, the protestors, journalists, clients, as well as the employees believe it or not. It was a bizarre period of my life, I must say."

"The employees?"

"Oh, yes. Some of them were being followed home. Excrement pushed through their letterboxes, smeared on their windscreens. Somehow, they expected me to ensure their safety. *Me!* As if I hadn't enough to do already. That was your job!" He waved a hand in his direction, before dismissing his own gesture. "Not you, obviously. I meant the police in general. We had to upgrade our security due to the vandalism and break-ins, try and redevelop the main gate so as we could get in and out without being swamped by the great unwashed sitting at the gate."

"You mean the protestors?"

"Of course! They were living on my perimeter. I've no idea who funded them but it was a glorious day when your lot finally arrested them and they were put away."

"One of them died I understand." To celebrate such a tragedy, even if it worked in your favour, seemed to him to be a little crass.

"Oh, don't get me wrong. That was awful, awful... shocking

but put yourself in my position for a moment. Two years they were at my gate baying for blood, how is that for a delicious sense of irony, and then overnight it was all over. Commandeering the moral high ground, they'd done their level best to ruin my reputation, my livelihood and disrupted our business no end with their stunts but ultimately, we prevailed!" He grinned, bobbing his head with satisfaction.

"Why did you change the nature of the business... seeing as the battle was won, so to speak."

"The fire played a large part in that to be fair." Shaun shook his head, the triumphalism dissipating. "The damage was so extensive that it wiped out most of our laboratories, all of the testing equipment as well as our stock."

"The animals?"

"Yes, everything. The core of the business was gutted. Our active testing cycles were destroyed. It would be months before we could get back up and running. Clients were furious and contrary to popular belief, there are many companies who carry out the research. It's a competitive business. Others were snapping at my heels before the fire. It was an opportunity for them to finish me off. As it turned out, the fire was something of a blessing. With the money I was able to reinstate the labs but take the business a different way. Not that it was without pain, mind you. I had no choice but to release most of the staff. The back-up team working in administration had transferable skills but many of the others had to go."

"A rebranding and a different approach," Janssen said, a comment heartily welcomed.

"Exactly. I'd had enough of all the drama. Besides, I had made many contacts within the sector over the years and I was able to secure new contracts quite soon after we rebuilt. The last few years have been quiet and that's how I like it, profitable... and quiet."

"You must still keep records on your former employees, though."

"Yes, of course, but do bear in mind the fire tore through the complex. Much of the detail was lost with only the financial data and regulatory requirements downloaded to our data servers."

"I don't understand, do you have it or not?"

Shaun Robinson looked him in the eye. "I'll have someone trawl through the backups to be sure but, from what I see here," he indicated to his monitor, "we have nothing for you. I'm sorry. Give me a couple of days and I should be able to confirm it for you. Here, look for yourself." Angling the screen in Janssen's direction, he stood up and leaned forward. A list of names generated from the company files was there, displayed in alphabetical order. There was no one by the name of Darren. He felt deflated. His attention was drawn to a double photo frame sitting beside the monitor. They were pictures taken on graduation days, degree ceremonies by the look of them. Shaun was in both, the first alongside a blonde female and the second a dark-haired young man. The latter had the build of his father, although probably carrying much more weight in face and frame.

"Your children?" he asked, sitting back down.

Shaun looked at the frames, nodding with a smile on his face. "Yes. They've both completed their doctorates in the last couple of years. A great deal of work went into them. Proud days. Do you have children of your own, Inspector?"

He shook his head, although his mind drifted to Saffy, Alice's daughter. He hadn't seen either of them for days and he felt a pang of regret at that. "No, I don't."

"Well, when you do, mark my words it will be the greatest experience of your life when they achieve something of note. You'll be living your dreams through them."

Janssen smiled politely, quietly considering it an odd stance to hold. In his experience, parents who lived their dreams through their children often had rather unhappy children. "If you could make that search a priority I would appreciate it," he said standing up.

"Of course, I'll get someone onto it immediately. Tell me, is this related to that poor soul found out by Wells at the weekend?"

"I wouldn't like to say at this stage, Mr Robinson. There's no guarantee this employee even knew the person in question."

"Too right. I don't need another blast of negative press. People have largely forgotten about us over here and I'd like it to stay that way."

"Our inquiries will be discreet. I can assure you."

———

STARTING THE CAR, he checked the time. If he was quick, he was confident he could make it. The car journey took less time than he thought and he even managed to make a short stop en route. Arriving at Alice's house, she was on the driveway in the process of clipping Saffy into her car seat. Upon seeing his arrival, the little girl squealed in her mother's ear, much to her irritation. Alice withdrew from the car, turning to see the approaching Janssen. He handed her the flowers he'd picked up along the way. They weren't particularly special, far less than he would have liked. She cracked a smile but it wasn't the ringing endorsement he'd hoped for but more than he probably deserved.

"Hey," he said. As a greeting, it was lame and he knew it.

"Hi, Tom," Alice replied, accepting the offering graciously. "That's very thoughtful of you."

"I'm sorry about the weekend, things ran away from me a bit."

"I read about it in the paper… and it's the talk of the surgery," Alice said, glancing into the car and checking her daughter hadn't performed another miraculous escape. He noticed she was in her uniform, heading for her shift as expected. "Listen, I'm already running late. Can we talk later?"

"Yes, of course," he said, trying to mask his disappointment and failing miserably. Alice put the flowers on the passenger seat, closed the door and leant in to kiss him, turning her cheek towards him as he responded.

"Thank you for the flowers," she said, turning and heading around to the other side of the car. Janssen crouched and waved to Saffy who blew him kisses with her left hand. The car reversed past him, backing out into the street. Alice gave him a half-smile and he offered her a salutary wave as she drove away, waiting until the car rounded the bend and disappeared from view.

"I think you're in trouble, Tom," he muttered under his breath, turning and making for his own car.

CHAPTER NINETEEN

WATCHING the departing form of the detective as he crossed the car park and got into his vehicle, Shaun Robinson waited until he saw the car reverse before turning and walking back towards his office.

"Mr Robinson," Camille, the receptionist called after him.

"Not now," he replied gruffly.

"But I have your wife on hold—"

"I said *not now!*" he barked without looking over to her. Instead, he marched out of the lobby without another word, leaving the beleaguered woman to field some kind of excuse.

Once he was back behind his desk, he loosened his tie and undid the top button of his collar, freeing the neckline. Picking up his mobile phone, he scrolled through his contacts. Locating the number, he dialled it and waited, drumming his fingers on the desk in front of him. His desk phone beeped. Camille was calling through but he ignored it. Eventually, his persistence was rewarded and the call was answered.

"So," he began, speaking softly, "I've just had an interesting visit from one of Norfolk's finest, asking all kinds of questions."

"About what?"

"About what went on six years ago." He allowed the

comment to hang in the silence that followed, listening to the sound of breathing coming down the line. It was more ragged than normal. His health must have deteriorated since the last time they saw one another. "Now *you assured* me that this wasn't going to come back on us," he said, sitting forward in his chair and looking around, as if fearful he would be overheard. No one else was present but he was on edge. They were never supposed to be speaking about these events. He expected it to be consigned to the past but here they were, going over what he thought was long buried.

"Nothing's changed. I can't see as you have anything to worry about—"

"He was asking about Darren," Shaun said, cutting him off. "Tell me, how is that possible? And make no mistake, this isn't only *my problem* if all of this comes to light. I wasn't keen on—"

"Don't be so soft, Shaun! You knew exactly what you were doing. I seem to recall you had very little choice in the matter and far fewer options when it came down to it. Have you removed any reference to him from the company records?"

"Darren? Yes, of course, I have! That's what we agreed."

"Then you have nothing to worry about. As far as you are concerned, the fire wiped out much of the hard copy records, and digital files are so easily corrupted over time. Honestly, I don't see why you're so easily rattled. We always knew there was the potential for a rocky period where we might need to brace ourselves. I had you down as a man with much stronger mettle than this."

Shaun drew himself upright, inhaling a deep breath. "That *period* was five years ago and none of this was even mentioned back then, so why now? I don't understand." There was a pause in conversation. Checking the handset, he feared the line had dropped but the connection was still active. "*Why now?*" he repeated. Moments passed before he got a response. When it did arrive, it was unsatisfactory.

"I don't know… Tell me, who was it who came to see you?"

"Erm… an Inspector Janssen. Tom Janssen, I think. I don't know him, never come across him before."

"Hmm… no, nor have I."

"He's going to come back… he wants all the information we have on Darren and I said I'd look into it."

"Well, that was foolish."

"No, you don't understand. He has a business card in Darren's name, or a part of it. I passed it off as probably belonging to a contractor but it's only a matter of time until they find some other link. I get the impression he isn't going away. He struck me as… determined."

"What else does he know?"

"Apart from the business card? Nothing, really, as far as I can tell." Shaun called seeking reassurance but the conversation wasn't going as he hoped. "But he's going to keep asking, I know it." He recognised the desperation in his own voice. Hearing it only seemed to compound his fears.

"Take a deep breath and for goodness' sake, man, hold on to your nerve. How did he come about this card?"

"Some dead girl washed up on the beach over the weekend."

"Yes, I heard about that."

"Apparently, she had it amongst her possessions. I don't see how but there it is. They're hoping Darren could help to identify her."

"That is unfortunate. And could he? Help them, I mean?"

"How should I know? The last thing we need is Darren talking to the police *about anything*."

"Agreed. In which case, it might prove advantageous to have him drop out of sight for a while. Do you still have that place in Spain?"

"No, we sold it last year."

"Shame. It would have been the perfect place for him until all of this blows over."

Shaun thought hard. "I'll think of something."

"Do so and make it soon. If this chap is as efficient as you seem to think, he won't let the grass grow under his feet. In the meantime, I'll make a few discreet inquiries of my own, see if I can put your mind at ease."

"Thank you. I would appreciate that." Finally, his concerns were being addressed.

"Probably wise if you don't call me for a while as well, under the circumstances. Plausible deniability and all of that. I'll catch up with you at the club over a round later in the week."

"Yes, sounds good."

"One more thing, though, Shaun."

"Yes?"

"Don't ever try to threaten me again. It's not a good look on you, is unwise... and is not good for your health. You understand, I'm sure?"

He swallowed hard. "Yes, of course. I... don't know what I was thinking."

"You're rattled. It's easily done but now is the time for you to remain focussed. You got to do things over, and it has all worked out well for you. For both of us. Let's not be doing anything rash that might undo all our hard work."

"Absolutely. I'll speak to you—" The line went dead. He sank back in his chair, tossing the phone on to the desk in front of him. His stomach churned and a wave of nausea passed over him. His desk phone beeped again and this time he answered it. "Yes, Camille. What is it?"

"I have your wife for you, Mr Robinson."

"Okay, put her through." He glanced to his right, eyeing the photos of his twin children taken at their respective graduation ceremonies. After the passage of this much time, he once again felt as if he was on the brink of losing everything. That couldn't be allowed then, nor could it now. The call came through. "Hi darling, sorry about before. I was caught up on another line."

CHAPTER TWENTY

TOM JANSSEN WALKED into the ops room to find Eric with his feet up on a desk, munching his way through a packet of crisps. At sight of his arrival, the constable threw his legs aside only to overbalance. The castors of his chair pushed off and he landed in a heap on the floor. Scrambling upright, he flushed red with embarrassment.

"Are we not keeping you busy enough?" he asked, hanging up his coat. "I'm sure I can find more for you to do."

"That *was* my breakfast, I've been at it all day," Eric protested. Janssen waved away the need for an apology.

"Are you working through the residents at the holiday park?" Eric replied with a look that morphed into a grimace. "That bad, is it." Eric rubbed at his cheeks before stretching out his arms and interlocking his fingers in front of him.

"I managed to get a probable date range from pathology to help narrow down our time frame. The management of the holiday camp were nice enough to email across a list of all those recorded on site from the earliest date. I say *nice of them*, but it's basically a data dump of names as long as your arm. It's going to take ages to wade through."

"Best make a start then."

"I already have. What do you think I've been doing all morning?" Eric countered, grinning. "I've been feeding the names into the police national computer and it spits out anyone with a record, violent or otherwise." Janssen was interested, looking across at Eric's screen he tried to imagine what might be churned out. "Have you any idea the number of petty criminals who drop into our patch for a week away? It's frightening, it really is. I'm amazed we don't see our own mini crime wave every season."

"Criminals need down time too, you know," Janssen replied, grinning. "Anyone we need to take a look at?"

Eric shook his head. "Not so far. Mind you, part of the issue I'm coming up against is that the person making the booking is the recorded guest. As I understand it some families book in one name with a party of four and then three sets descend at the time, kipping on air beds and what not. It makes it damn hard to know who was there."

"Those guests are unlikely to be our killer though, are they? You're looking for a single person or a couple. If they show a history of violence or arrests for sexual offences pin them up. Other than that, move on. You're going to need to get through that lot before next year. Is Tamara not back yet?" he asked looking around and spotting her coat hanging up.

"Yeah, she's been back for a while. She's in briefing the chief super, I think. At least that's something you won't miss." Janssen shot him a dark look. Eric looked away, his neck flushing red just as it did every time he was either embarrassed or thought he'd dropped a clanger. His attitude hadn't changed once Greave arrived to head up the case. He didn't think so at any rate, although now he doubted himself. Eric was as honest a character as he'd ever worked with and despite a tendency to occasionally read far too much into something, in reality, he wasn't usually far off the mark with his assessments. Janssen considered pressing the young man on how he reached his conclusion but

Tamara's arrival spared him the scrutiny, which was probably for the best.

"I've managed to get a name for the mysterious Conn," she said, dispensing with a greeting, formal or otherwise. Janssen couldn't hide his surprise.

"Where did that come from?"

"Niall Bradshaw handed him to us. And that's not all. Apparently, the two of them had a bit of a spat at some point during Saturday."

"Over what?" Eric asked. Tamara shook her head.

"No one knows. He certainly didn't mention it to me. He also places Sophie Maddox, Lesley Abbott and River Malloy together as a unit of sorts. Both were present among the animal rights protest group, alongside River, although Lesley was involved to a far lesser degree. What's more, he alleges River and Sophie were a couple. River taking it badly when, in his view, Sophie broke it off."

"Well, I'll be…" Janssen said, tucking his hands behind his head and interlocking the fingers. "I wonder why River didn't mention that when we interviewed her. What's she hiding?"

Eric's eyes lit up. "Hey, you don't think… you know…"

"What?" he asked.

"That River might be the killer. The result of a lover's tiff. It happens all the time, doesn't it."

The notion wasn't as daft as it sounded leaping from Eric's consciousness.

"We'll add that to the theories for now," Tamara said with a smile.

Eric frowned. "Sorry, I got a bit carried away."

"Until we've established an evidential case, we can't rule anything out, Eric," Tamara reassured him. "She didn't feel comfortable telling us about it or doesn't want us to know. Maybe she's concerned about becoming a suspect. There could be any number of reasons."

"Maybe it's not us she was worried about," Janssen said,

thinking of Beatrice. "Her mother's a... formidable woman. Maybe she didn't want to be outed to her mother as part of a murder inquiry, and who could blame her?"

"Niall Bradshaw. He's an interesting character. I'm not sure what to make of him just yet," Tamara said, her expression turning pensive. "I got the impression he's really trying to turn his life around. Albeit, he still doesn't accept he should have served time."

"I've not met an offender who thinks they should have," he joked.

"No, this was different. If you'd seen the look in his eyes, the passionate way he spoke about the injustice of it all, I reckon you'd question it too."

"And yet he was coy when it came to the altercation involving Conn," Janssen countered.

"True. I never said we should qualify him as a stand up pillar of the community, though. Do we know who was assigned to investigate the original case, the attacks on the vivisection clinic as well as the arson? It would be good to garner their insights."

"That would be my predecessor, I should imagine, DI Samuels. He's retired now, isn't he Eric?" he looked to the DC for confirmation. Eric was still the longest serving officer in Norfolk Constabulary present and their *go to man* for local knowledge.

"Medically pensioned off. As far as I know, he's still in the area. I'm friendly with his niece. I'll give her a call and find out." Janssen was impressed.

"Is there anyone in this county you don't know?" he asked. Eric took the question seriously, thinking hard on his response. Janssen waved it aside and Eric realised the joke. "Find out where he is and we'll pay him a visit."

"I wouldn't expect a warm welcome though," Eric said shaking his head. Upon finding both senior officers eyeing him and waiting for him to elaborate, he continued, "I remember him when I was first on the job. He was old school, intimidating. I'm not sure they teach his methods in training anymore. Anyway, I dare say he'll not take kindly to anyone questioning his diligence."

"I'll look forward to that," Tamara said. Something about the way she said it made him think she wasn't passing Eric's comment off and would genuinely relish challenging someone with a reputation like Samuels. Tamara Greave was far from a pushover. "While you're looking things up, can you pull anything there is regarding Mike Collyer from the system? He's the one better known as Conn. Cross reference him with Niall Bradshaw and see if there's a link. Review the case file of the investigation into the activists and their attacks on the vivisection clinic. Maybe Conn was called as a witness or interviewed, I don't know. I suspect they have a history of sorts. Anyone else find it coincidental that the day we turn up a body on the beach, Conn and Niall have a coming together? Maybe it's nothing but these people are all navigating the same waters and keep coming back to one another." Looking to Janssen, she inclined her head. "I already have an address for Collyer. Come on, you and me can go and see what the mysterious Conn has to say for himself. Eric, if there's anything you think that's immediately relevant you can call us on the way."

"Will do," Eric replied, turning back to his screen, evidently pleased to have a break from the tortuous monotony of researching historical holiday makers.

Picking up his coat, Janssen quickened his pace in order to catch up with Tamara as she left ops. "I like the maritime analogy," he said smiling.

"Well, seeing as I'm on the coast now, I thought I'd try and fit in more."

"How was the meeting with the super? Is he pleased with progress?"

"It's still early days, he knows that."

He was surprised by the lack of depth in her response. It was still early in the investigation, that was true but, in his experience, there was always a keen interest from above in charting the development of a murder case. The super always wanted to be made aware at every stage of major investigations. He didn't press the issue, sensing Tamara wouldn't be forthcoming. What he couldn't fathom was why.

CHAPTER TWENTY-ONE

THEY FOUND the address in a small lane, sited to the south-east of the village of Docking. A traditional flintstone semi-detached cottage, two up, two down, it mirrored the other property perfectly. A narrow driveway ran down the side of the building, dominated by heavily overgrown foliage and tree growth. The car barely managed to fit onto the drive and allow them both room to get out comfortably. A hatchback was parked at the end of the drive, in front of an old concrete prefabricated garage located to the rear. Even from this distance, the garage appeared somewhat dilapidated. Tamara Greave eyed the front door but the vegetation spreading from the front garden formed an impenetrable barrier and they were unable to reach it. A mixture of wildflowers and spreading ferns, at some stage it must have been a well-tended garden but that was evidently some time ago. The door itself looked like it hadn't moved in quite some time. The pale blue paint was peeling from the bottom half of the door and coming away further up, blistering in places. At the foot of the door, the lack of protection revealed blackened wood beneath, a sign of wet rot.

The net curtains in the front room of the adjacent property moved, drawing her attention. The windows were closed so it wasn't symptomatic of the breeze. She tried to see who was behind them but they shrouded the occupant well. Glancing to Janssen, she indicated they should head to the rear. The driveway itself was gravel lined but even this was in the process of being reclaimed by nature.

Rounding the corner to reach the back of the house they found a small kitchen, coal shed and an outside toilet attached to the main building. Judging by the length it probably housed the bathroom towards the back of the kitchen. The garden stretched back but as to how far was difficult to tell for here, too, Mother Nature made her presence felt. In the absence of a bell, Tamara knocked on the edge of the door to the left of the obscured glass. The curtains were drawn and she saw no movement from within. Janssen placed his palm flat on the bonnet of the car, feeling for heat. "It's cold," he said. Conn hadn't been out recently. Checking the time, it was well after midday. She hammered her fist on the door this time, following up by rapping her knuckles on the glass.

Within moments a shadow appeared on the other side, a key turning in the lock. The door cracked open and curious eyes peered out through the gap. Tamara brandished her warrant card. "Mr Collyer?" she asked, he nodded. "Detectives Greave and Janssen, Norfolk Police. May we have a word?" The man nodded once more, opening the door wider. He wasn't quite what she was expecting, assessing him to be in his mid-forties but the full beard and wild hair made him appear far older than his years. The facial hair extended several inches away from his chin, wispy at the ends and streaked with grey. His hair was equally unkempt, in no discernible style, and appearing to defy gravity by standing on end. All of which combined to give him something akin to the look of a mad professor, aided by his narrow-set eyes. They were strikingly dark and piercing. She had the impression he was weighing them up just as much as they were him.

Standing back from the door, he beckoned them to enter. He

was a slightly built man, easily over six feet tall and somewhat rangy with arms that looked out of proportion in their length. He wore jogging bottoms over a collarless shirt, the buttons of which were undone to the mid-chest. A leather necklace was visible beneath sporting a metal pendant, the design of which she couldn't make out the detail of. He didn't wear a watch or rings on his finger but in his left ear lobe was a gold hoop.

"What can I do for you?" he asked with a smile. His lips parted to reveal teeth heavily stained yellow with receding gums, adding to the prematurely aged appearance. The kitchen had a strange smell to it, not merely of cooked food and a bin well past needing to be emptied, but more of stale air mixed with damp and general poor cleanliness. Flies buzzed around the single-glazed window above the sink, itself stacked with crockery evidently sitting in water for some time. There were many more dead flies lying on the sill.

"Do you also go by the name of *Conn*?" she asked him.

"I do, it is something of a nickname."

"It is unusual."

"Perhaps it is here, certainly, but not in the Celtic nations. There it is more prevalent."

"What's the etymology of it?" she asked. He angled his head slightly.

"Some would say it means *wisdom* and to others it denotes a *leader* or *chief*."

"I see why you chose it."

"Is this why you came to see me, to discuss the derivation of bygone names? Surely not?"

"No, forgive the passing interest. I'm sure you will have heard about the remains of a woman found over at Wells over the weekend."

He nodded. "Yes, a sad business, I don't doubt."

"We thought you might be able to help us to identify her."

Conn's eyes widened and he looked to her and then Janssen, standing behind and to her left.

"Really? You had best come through." He turned and guided them from the kitchen into the next room. It was separated from the room at the front of the house by a dividing wall. The stairs to the first floor were open and led up from one corner of the room. Conn pulled open the thick curtains allowing light to stream in but the window was small and the improvement slight. Tamara looked around. A two-seater sofa was positioned beneath the only window within the room and two high-backed chairs were set to either other side of the open fireplace. Against the wall beside the access to the stairs stood a fifties vintage sideboard, the top protected by a lace runner. The walls were lined with a floral print paper that clashed with the colours of the print on the sofa. Various family photographs graced the walls but Conn wasn't visible in them as far as she could tell, although with a haircut and a change of clothing it might be harder to recognise him. The sound of the wind rattled down the chimney, carrying the smell of soot and ash into the room.

Conn offered them a seat, preferring to stand himself. Janssen declined, standing in the doorway to the kitchen. Yet to speak, he was intent on observing. Tamara saw a light switch next to him and made him aware. Janssen flicked the switch but nothing happened. Conn remained in the centre of the room for a moment, folding his arms across his chest and waiting patiently with an expectant look on his face. Looking over his shoulder at Janssen, he then crossed the room and sat down in one of the chairs next to her. Even then, he perched himself on the edge resting his elbows on his knees.

"I have no need of artificial light," he said. Conn struck her as confident, doing his best to convey an image of himself as warm and open. The ticking of a carriage clock dominated the silence while she took out her notebook.

"We are working on the theory that the person discovered on the beach was known in the area. We have narrowed the list of potential names down and several witnesses have placed these women in your company. We are also of the strong belief that this woman was the victim of a homicide. She was murdered."

"Right."

She waited but he offered nothing more, just remained focussed on her with those dark eyes. "You don't have anything to say about that?" She was curious about his reaction. There was no outward display of shock or disgust. No indication of denial or outrage despite her linking him with a dead body, a murder victim no less. Conn didn't flinch in the slightest. "It doesn't bother you?"

"No! Why should it?" he said with a shrug, holding himself upright and flicking his eyebrows in a matter-of-fact gesture. "I've known lots of women over the years. If she is local, as you say, then I suppose it is quite possible that I knew her. What makes you think I would?"

"These women were known to have a strong interest in the occult. As, we are told, do you."

"Ah… now I see. Is this an issue for you?" he asked meeting her eye before glancing over his shoulder towards Janssen.

"A person's spiritual or religious beliefs are their own. I have no issue."

"But others do…" he smiled but it was mocking and insincere. "People fear what they don't understand."

"They don't understand you? Is that what you're saying?" she pressed.

"People are conditioned by their surroundings and their upbringing. Mostly, people live in fear of their own lives… the insignificance of their time on earth, their lack of impact. Modern humanity leans towards materialism, desiring what we see around us and no matter how much we gather to us it is never enough to satisfy the thirst. We are slaves to our ego whereas, in reality, we are surrounded by the elements. Embracing this fact and celebrating the natural world and our place on the wheel is the only way we will ever find our true purpose."

"As you say, it is a matter of personal belief," she held his eye contact before breaking off and glancing around the room, Conn following her gaze. "Do you remember your time with the local Pagan group, around six years ago?"

"It was short-lived but yes, I remember. Not fondly, I must say. Why do you ask?"

"That was around the time we believe our victim was killed."

"Ah… and… you think one of my followers could be your… victim?"

"*Followers*… that makes it sound like they were part of some kind of a cult… and that would make them your what, disciples?" Conn grinned. For a moment she saw the flash of charisma, an easy charm that could appeal to an impressionable mind, perhaps those who were disenfranchised, vulnerable or seeking relevance in a world that apparently bordered on perceived chaos.

"Living the life of a Wiccan is a very personal spiritualism. Those of you who believe only in a monotheistic religion find our ways too complex or confusing to comprehend." There was the easy smile again, knowing, reassuring. Conn sought to both guide and control the conversation. "It is true, the various pantheons are not easy to understand. To trace their connections to one another, let alone how they exist in elemental form takes a great deal of study. Perhaps only one god will reveal themselves to you, sometimes none. To come together and join as one we can invite them into our rituals, demonstrate our worthiness and reflect their qualities." He sat forward, leaning in her direction. She saw Janssen take a step further into the room, sensing some kind of mood change. Conn stared into her eyes, the smile fading. "You need to look for the signs that your god walks beside you. Then you will be able to walk your path of life with confidence."

"And what if no god reveals themselves to you? What do you do then?"

"Your relationship is a long-term commitment, requiring

belief, worship and attentive behaviour. If your god rejects you, then you must seek another."

"Where are your followers now?"

"We are all free spirits and must walk our own path." He sat back once more, spreading his hands wide.

"Amongst those people who followed you, when did you last see... Sophie Maddox, Lesley Abbott or Tracy Bartlett... when did you last see or speak with them?"

Conn blew out his cheeks, scanning the ceiling as if he would find an answer searching there. "The passage of time means little to me. I couldn't say for sure."

"Would you care to hazard a guess?"

"Years, certainly."

"And how did your little group split? Was there a falling out between anyone? Even spiritual people suffer from relationship issues."

"Not that I recall," Conn stated, dismissively shaking his head. "I worship *Mother Nature* herself and Her consort, the *Wild Man*, seeking to ground myself in the earth's elemental energies. In doing so I harness Her power. The others chose their own spiritual path and moved on, as we are called to do so."

"Do you miss it, the group? Being together?"

"We all exist on the wheel and ultimately, will meet again. It is the nature of things."

"Were you involved in any form of relationship with any of these women, I'm thinking more in the traditional sense than the spiritual?"

"No. To do so would cloud the mind."

"Do you have any idea as to how one of your followers could have ended up buried in the sand?"

"How would I?" he replied, straight faced.

"What is it that you do, Mr Collyer?" Janssen asked. Conn turned to him with an inquiring look. "For a living."

"My worship of the elemental realm brings me everything that I need."

"So, you don't have a job."

Conn fixed Janssen with a stare, slowly shaking his head. "I am fortunate in that I do not require one in order to live in the physical realm." The two men held eye contact for a moment, only breaking when Tamara stood. She'd gathered more than enough to satisfy what she came for.

"Thank you for your time, Mr Collyer. If we need to speak with you again, we will be in touch."

Janssen backed out of the room, stepping through into the kitchen and opening the door to the outside. The air smelt sweet and refreshing. Tamara took a deep breath as she rounded the corner to the side of the house, hearing the key moving in the lock behind them. Neither of them spoke until they got into the car. Janssen glanced across to her. "Do you think he's quite as bonkers as he wants us to think? I reckon he's playing us. He didn't flinch when you brought up the women, more or less confirmed Tracy Bartlett was one of his *followers*."

"Yes. I thought I would chance it. Until now we didn't have a connection. A lack of a denial isn't proof though. The three of them going missing around the same time makes me ask the question as to why."

"I know he's playing us," Janssen said. "Even so, he's not all there but a killer? I'm not so sure."

"I think he's a very calculating individual. He rates his intelligence as on a higher level than ours," she said, staring back at the house. Janssen put the car into reverse and backed out into the lane. "All of that was just an opportunity for him to showcase himself in front of us. Playing childish games for his own amusement. We weren't going to get anything useful out of him."

"Agreed," Janssen said, putting the car into first and pulling away. "Not knowingly anyway."

"Stop a second!" Janssen braked hard, as if fearing something unseen was in front of them. Tamara unclipped her seatbelt and got out of the car. A man stood outside the house next door, seemingly pleased he had caught her attention. She approached him, smiling. He looked around nervously, leaning on a solitary crutch for support.

"Are you estate agents?" he asked.

Tamara frowned. "No, police," she replied, showing him her ID.

"Pity. I hoped he was selling the place."

"Your neighbour?" she clarified. He nodded. "Do you know him well?"

He scoffed at the notion. "I wouldn't let *The Angel of Death* anywhere near us."

She was intrigued. "Why do you call him that?"

"Because it's fitting. Maureen used to live next door... with her husband before he passed away. She used to keep the house and garden lovely. Now look at it." He waved his crutch towards the front garden of Conn's house. "It's such a shame. Maureen struggled... living on her own, like you do when you reach our time of life and your health is failing. You can only do so much with what you have. I helped as much as I could, mind you, but it was never enough. She needed help. Proper help."

"Is Conn her relative?"

"No! Her family weren't much use at all. Her children live far away from here, one is in Scotland I think, the other somewhere in the midlands. They would come back from time to time but they were just too far away. I don't know how this one," he indicated next door, "came to be on the scene or where he's from. Maureen started to get some funny ideas after Terry passed away, continuing to speak with him and whatnot... anyway, that man turns up... doing her shopping, taking her out for trips to the coast, odd jobs and that."

"Conn?" she asked, glancing next door.

"Yes. At first, we thought he must be from one of these charities who help out vulnerable folks... but, no... he was nothing like that. Maureen left him the house. That didn't go down well with her children, I don't mind telling you."

"I'll bet it didn't," she agreed.

"They took it through the courts – what with Maureen's dementia and all but I guess they lost."

"What do you make of him, your neighbour?"

"Strange. Keeps odd hours, up at all times of the night doing who knows what. Very strange goings on, gives the wife palpitations when he so much as looks at her."

"I see. I don't suppose you've ever seen any visitors to the house, people he mixes with?"

"No, never. He's always on his own, curtains drawn all day and night. For a moment I thought we might be getting shot of him. What do the police want with him anyway? Should I be worried for me and the wife?"

"He was just assisting us with our inquiries. Nothing for you to be concerned about… but, if you're ever in doubt please feel free to give us a call and someone will stop by. Thank you for your time." She made to leave. Almost as an afterthought, she turned back and took out one of her contact cards, passing it over to him. He squinted at the print, presumably he was in need of reading glasses.

"Norwich? You're some way from home, aren't you?"

"The telephone number still works, just in case you need to talk," she replied, smiling. He tipped the card to his forehead in thanks, slowly turning to head back inside.

Tamara walked back to the car. Janssen looked across as she got in. "What was that about?"

"I think I have an answer for you as to why he doesn't need to work for a living. The old lady who owned the house passed away," she said fastening her seatbelt. "Being the good Samaritan sometimes pays dividends."

"You have to love nosey neighbours. By the look of it the money is running out if he's not paying his utility bills."

CHAPTER TWENTY-TWO

ERIC COLLET WAS SO ENGROSSED in what he was reading he failed to note their return. The constable jumped when Tamara Greave rested a hand on the back of his chair, leaning in to see over his shoulder. "Anything for us?" she asked. Eric looked like he'd been beavering away while they were out, amassing a pile of paperwork around his desk. He gathered himself quickly.

"I've been going over the case history regarding the activists' targeting of *Norfolk Reactive Sciences*, from the initial protests right through to the arson and the subsequent trial of Niall, River and their co-conspirators. Both River and Niall were considered the driving forces behind the arson, Niall being the focal point for all the protests up to that point."

"Why was River given a higher profile when it came to the arson?" she asked, curious as to why her status was elevated.

"After the fire, the protestors were top of the list of suspects and a number of search warrants were executed on them. Most of them were living at the semi-permanent encampment on the perimeter of the site, coming to the area specifically to become part of the protests whereas a few were local residents. River was among them. The group were rounded up and search warrants initiated. Beatrice Malloy's home was searched and trace evidence was recovered linking River to the arson."

"And the strength of that trace evidence?" She turned her attention to a whiteboard Eric had been populating while they were out. There were several pictures taken following the arrests, she recognised River alongside Niall. The three other faces, who were also sent to prison, were unknown to her. Eric stood up and crossed to the board, pointing out a couple of crime scene photographs presumably taken during the searches.

"Clothing of hers was found with the same accelerant on it as was used in the fire. Granted, it was petrol but she had no plausible reason as to why her jumper and a pair of jeans were so heavily soiled. Nor could she sufficiently explain the third-degree burns suffered on her right forearm and right cheek. In fact, she offered no explanation at all. There were empty petrol cans found on the property as well, but River didn't drive and the property uses a diesel generator as back-up to the mains supply."

"That was still pretty circumstantial," Tamara said.

"Two beer cans and an empty bottle of gin were also found within the premises themselves, at the break-in point." He pointed to an image of a smashed window set aside a floor plan. "They entered the building here at a weak spot in the building's security and then travelled through to the laboratory testing wing. That was where the seat of the fire was. It started with petrol but the chemicals stored and used in the processes increased the intensity of the flames, allowing it to spread throughout before the fire brigade were able to arrive on site and tackle the blaze. Forensics were able to retrieve a number of fingerprints from both the window's glass and frame, along with others found on the cans and bottle."

"Which was able to place all five at the scene?" Janssen asked. Eric confirmed it. "But one of the arsonists died in the flames… and that person was never identified."

"Correct," Eric said, pointing to another section of the board.

"The case files suggest the investigating officers strongly believed these five weren't the only ones to have been present but they couldn't place anyone else at the scene. Four of the five flat out refused to admit their role in the break-in or the arson."

"And the fifth?" Tamara asked.

"River Malloy," Eric stated. "She didn't have anything to say for herself at all. Never once asked for legal counsel and failed to utter a single word in any police interview. Besides that, when called to give evidence in her trial she was found in contempt of court for refusing to answer questions. I read the transcript and it is the most bizarre case I've ever come across."

"How long was she given?"

"Five years for the involuntary manslaughter and three for the arson."

"I'm surprised the court let her off so lightly if she was so uncooperative at trial," Janssen said.

Eric consulted his notes. "Her defence team argued her paranoid schizophrenia played a pivotal role in both her taking a part in the protests, the arson and her reactions to the court proceedings. Several doctors were called to confirm her condition. Although not considered unmanageable, it does look like it helped."

"So, her team didn't continue to protest her innocence at sentencing," Tamara said. She found it highly unusual to plead not guilty and then use their client's mental state to justify her role in a crime she professed not to commit.

"Due to her lack of testimony at any point, her counsel was given autonomy to proceed as best they could. At least, that's how I understand it."

She thought it through. "If you include time served on remand, prior to trial... she must have been out in around five years. Is that right?"

"Model prisoner by all accounts," Eric stated, checking his notes to confirm dates. "Served just shy of sixty percent of her sentence."

"What about the others? What defence did they offer?" she questioned. Looking across the information gathered to date, somewhere in there was a link that tied all of these people together. If they could find it, she was certain they'd be able to not only put a name to their murder victim but understand how she came to be buried in the dunes.

"The four of them denied involvement from day one. Three of them were each other's alibi, claiming to have been with each other at the encampment but denied breaching the perimeter. Niall was the remaining defendant who claimed he was with another person at the time of the attack and nowhere near the premises. The investigation team and the CPS didn't buy it. Nor did the jury."

"Who was Niall's alibi?" Tamara asked, seeking clarification.

"That's just it, he refused to name her when interviewed. And even when it went to court, he still refused. Effectively, he could just as well have been arguing he was partying with Elvis at the time for all the good it did him. The forensics alongside the weak alibis did for all of them. They were convicted by way of joint enterprise on a unanimous decision and given sentences ranging from five to eight years in total. We already know Niall and River were given the stiffest. Her because of the strength of the forensics and perceived belligerence towards the investigation, and Niall because he was long held as the leader of the group. In the judge's summing up, he highlighted the group's failure to identify the person who died as immoral and a *reprehensible dereliction of friendship*."

"To what lengths did the investigators go to in trying to identify the person who died?" she asked. "It's quite plausible this victim is one of the three missing women we are investigating. Were any of the names mentioned at the time?"

"No, Ma'am… sorry, Guv," Eric stammered.

"Tamara will be fine going forward, Eric," she said. "Good work, Eric. Have you had a chance to track down Tom's predecessor yet?"

"I have," Eric trotted across to his desk, returning with a slip of paper and passing it to her. She read it, an address in Sheringham. Eric turned to Janssen.

"You had a phone call while you were out, from pathology. I think they've emailed you the findings from the autopsy."

Janssen turned to his computer screen and checked his emails. There was indeed a file waiting for him. He double clicked the attachment to open it. Tamara crossed the ops room to join him and watched as he scrolled through the report to the end, stopping when he reached the conclusion. He read out the salient points.

"*In the absence of evidence regarding any further injuries... the cranial fracture most likely would have caused massive internal haemorrhaging to the brain... leading to a high likelihood of death without immediate medical intervention...* So, there we have it, confirmation should it be needed, we have a clear case of homicide," he stated softly. "*The victim is estimated to be between the age of seventeen and twenty-five... chemical analysis of the DNA suggests she originated from and also lived in East Anglia for all of her life... to date no matching dental records or DNA are held on file... search ongoing.*" He stopped reading, looking up at her. "Where do you want to go from here?"

"Eric, I want you to keep going over this case. Pull everything we have on it and go through looking for references to any of the characters we have on our radar now. Come at it from any angle you can. Maybe something was missed at the time."

"What are you thinking?" Janssen asked, his eyes narrowing. "This is all linked somehow?"

"Two unnamed bodies die around the same time as this activism campaign is in full swing, both circling River Malloy, Niall Bradshaw and Conn... and no one is giving us straight answers then or now. Something was missed."

"I agree but where?" Janssen replied.

"We'll have to sound out DI Samuels before we know that. Too many people weren't talking back then…"

"Or the right questions weren't being asked," Janssen added.

Sitting back in her chair, she thought hard. "When I was talking to Niall, he intimated he knew their protest, activism… whatever you want to call it, was having an effect on the business. He stopped short of explaining how but I got the distinct impression he thought they were about to win the battle. What I'm wondering is how could he be so sure? The only way they could claim victory is if the business either announced it was changing direction or shutting down completely. From his point of view, committing the arson was counter productive."

Janssen twirled a pen absently with his right hand, his eyes drifting across the information boards. "If he was right, there would be no need to take such a risk as to burn the place down. They would be certain to be the prime suspects. That doesn't make a lot of sense, it's true."

"Highly committed people are often guilty of not seeing reality, though," Eric chimed in. "Zealots will throw all logic and rational thought under the bus if they are only focussed on the end goal."

"Good point," she replied, taking in what both of them were saying. "There is the possibility Niall and the others realised they were mistaken about the business' troubles and that resulted in a spontaneous over reaction – the fire."

"But… you don't think so, do you?" Janssen said pointedly.

She shook her head.

"Niall was certain… but he stopped short of telling me why, which brings me back to what he knew and how?"

"And why he couldn't say, even now," Janssen added. "Of course, if you're right then that leads us to another issue."

"Which is?" she asked.

"The forensics had them nailed on as being in the building. Don't forget, Niall and the others had the duration of a trial to discredit it and failed. All we currently have is your instinct."

"Fortunately, I also have a massive ego and a level of arrogance second to none."

Janssen grinned. "Presumably you'll not be throwing all of this at DI Samuels this afternoon," Janssen said with a half-smile.

"No, don't worry," she replied. "Certainly not *all* of it anyway."

CHAPTER TWENTY-THREE

TOM JANSSEN FELT a familiar sense of belonging as he guided them into Sheringham, navigating his way to the other side of town and the address where the former incumbent of his role retired to. The sun was out today, the sky clear. This was a far better representation of life on the east coast than Tamara had seen in the past few days. They could just have easily skirted the town on the main roads, coming back on themselves and avoiding the likely traffic queues, but he wanted her to see where he grew up. He wanted to see where he grew up.

The thought occurred why he rarely came back these days. True enough, the need wasn't there anymore. His father passed away when he was in his teens and his mother never sought to leave, aside from when she finally gave in to her infirmity. Even then, he managed to place her in a residential home close to the town. He was lucky. Their family were well known, respected. It certainly helped. Taking the next left, he drove them along the esplanade. The sea was a picture of calm in stark contrast to a few days before.

"You say you grew up here?" Tamara asked, looking along the coast across the golf course positioned at the edge of the town. "It's beautiful."

"I know," he replied, genuinely pleased she saw it as he did. "I never used to think so. We couldn't wait to get away."

"We?"

"Me, my friends…" he said, his tone edged with regret. "There are only so many campfires you can build on the beach and cans of beer you can drink before it all gets—"

"Boring?" she finished for him. He smiled.

"Exactly."

"I think most of us feel that way about where we grow up. As teenagers you can't wait to get out of there and form your own life." He turned again, heading away from the coast and cutting across the nearby centre. "So, where did you run to Tom Janssen?" she asked playfully, rolling her head in his direction. He couldn't see her eyes through her sunglasses but he felt her gaze upon him.

"London. Isn't that where we all want to be, where we think everything is at?"

"Not for me," she countered. "Birmingham. The principle's the same, mind you. Drawn to the big city, bright lights and twenty-four-hour takeaways."

"We set our sights too high." Thinking of himself, he hadn't appreciated his home town anywhere near enough. The drama greeting him in the capital was intoxicating for a while. Now, the sleepier feel of his home town was more of a draw these days.

"Do you regret it?" she asked, breaking him free of his momentary reminiscing.

"What? The move to London? Nah," he shook his head. It was true. Everything experienced in his ten years in the Met made him what he was today, albeit seeing the world in a harsher light. Or maybe that was a result of the job. "You?" he asked, glancing at her.

"Sometimes… I go home and visit my mother a couple of times a year… then, not so much."

He laughed. That was the first time he could recollect her sharing anything personal with him. Tamara Greave was something of an enigma. She didn't seek to draw attention, styling herself in a very understated manner and yet her interactions with those around her saw her stand out as very much a people person. He felt at ease in her company, everyone did. She was natural. Open, approachable and at the same time reticent and guarded. He found the confliction in her personality intriguing.

They came to the turning he was looking for, an unadopted road angling back towards the coast. The properties were all detached, most were three storeys high as they were set into the hillside. The house they sought was set back slightly from the others. A stone walled driveway opened up from the entrance gate, massive retaining walls holding back the hillside leading up to the house itself. The first and second floor had large balconies running almost the full width of the house, set beneath the overhang of the pitched roof and no doubt granting impressive views over the cliffs and the sea beyond. A figure was seated outside on the second floor, he rose as they parked their car. Leaning casually on the rail, he looked down on them as they made their way up to the house.

Janssen glanced up, shielding his eyes from the glare of the sun with the palm of his hand. Presumably, that was Peter Samuels, former DI of Norfolk Constabulary but they'd never actually met. Samuels sat back down in his chair, disappearing from view as they reached the front door. Tamara rang the bell and it was answered shortly by an affable lady. At first, they thought she must be Samuel's wife but she quickly identified herself as a carer, ushering them inside. The layout was interesting. The kitchen and what he imagined was a study were located on the ground floor, a confined space bearing in mind the footprint of the house. Leading them up the nearby staircase, Janssen noted the house opened out into a far larger open plan living and dining area. The building must be sculpted to fit the hillside rather than cut into it. The stairs continued up to the next floor but a figure was making their way down to meet them.

Waiting patiently in the living room, a white-haired man appeared, gingerly taking the last few steps very carefully as he reached the landing. His eyes flicked between the two of them, brows arched inquisitively. He was slim but far from frail despite moving with the aid of a walking stick in his left hand. He appeared to assign his weight disproportionately to his right side. He was tanned and greeted them with a broad smile, revealing white teeth.

"I so rarely get visitors," he said grinning. "To what do I owe the pleasure, detectives?"

Janssen was surprised. "How do you know—"

"Forty-two years in the job, young man. That's how. Besides, you have it written all over your faces." Gesturing for them to head out through the patio doors and out onto the balcony, he looked to the woman accompanying them. "Perhaps a cup of tea would be in order, Beverley," he said.

She smiled.

"Of course, I'll be right back."

She set off back down towards the kitchen while Samuels followed them out onto the balcony. Janssen looked over his shoulder. The man didn't appear to be struggling to walk. Four chairs were set around a circular table and they each took one as Tamara introduced them both.

"Both a DI and his chief inspector. This must be interesting," Samuels announced once introductions were complete. He rubbed at his left knee with his right hand, grimacing slightly.

"Is that the cause of your early retirement?" Janssen asked. "I understand it was a medical decision."

"No, nothing to do with it! This is arthritis… a cursed result of aging. No, no. My retirement came about after a micro stroke."

"I'm sorry to hear that," he replied.

"Oh, don't be. It was well past my time at any rate. I was starting to stink the place out. The job had moved on but I wasn't one for change. Do you know what I mean?" He grinned once more, seemingly comfortable with his decision.

"I guess so," Janssen replied.

"Is it just you here?" Tamara asked, glancing around before settling back on their host. She removed her glasses at that point.

"Afraid so," Samuels replied, arching his back and stretching slightly. "The kids have moved on, as has the wife." He must have read their expressions and chose to elaborate, Janssen for one wasn't sure what he meant. "She lives over in Lynn now. *With* her new husband." Janssen flicked his eyebrows, unsure of the correct response. "Don't worry, lad. It comes with life and… often with this job. Are you married?" he asked him, then looked to Tamara. They both shook their heads. "Probably for the best. I have Beverley to help me out. To be honest, I don't need round-the-clock help but it certainly beats doing all the donkey work yourself." He aimed the last comment at Tamara. "You must find that as a DCI, having a few lesser mortals such as us," he pointed to Janssen, flicking his forefinger between the two of them, "to do the grind on your behalf?"

"Well, I'm an acting DCI… so, I know what you mean."

"Acting, hey? Well, well, young man," he leaned forward tapping Janssen on the knee, "and she's got your promotion as well as the rank. Best pull your finger out, eh? You'll be pensioned off before you know it, and pensions aren't what they used to be, are they?" Janssen smiled politely. Eric's assessment of DI Samuels was proving accurate. He was old school on many levels. Tamara didn't seem deterred in the least, segueing into the reason for their visit.

"We've had an old case of yours come up in one of our current investigations. We were hoping to have a discussion with you about it."

"By all means. It's been a while since I've had to put the uniform on. Go ahead. Which case?"

"The arson at *Norfolk Reactive Sciences*. I expect you recall it well."

"I certainly do," he said, looking to Janssen. "That was a big case. High profile what with the ongoing protests, the permanent camp outside. It was like Greenham Common, back in the 80s. You remember?"

Janssen shook his head. "I read about it. That was a missile protest, though. Nuclear disarmament, wasn't it?"

"Absolutely. Very similar though. A group of idealists trying to change the world to fit their beliefs. Wasting everybody's time. This lot were no different."

"I thought we aren't supposed to take sides," Tamara countered.

Samuels looked to her and then back at him. "We don't, do we... at least, not officially," he grinned at him, tapping the side of his nose. Janssen felt self-conscious at being the focal point of his responses. Tamara took it in her stride.

"Mr Samuels," she said, before pausing to choose her words carefully, "was there ever any doubt in your investigation as to who started the fire?"

He stared at her, his eyes narrowing. "No, I can't say I doubted our conclusions in the least. It was obvious who had the means and the motive. They were practically living on site, so they certainly had the opportunity. Not to mention the forensics. It was probably the easiest conviction of my career. Why on earth do you ask?"

"Because of their protestations of innocence," she countered. He burst out laughing. The reaction was part humour, part incredulity.

"Don't they all! Honestly, I never encountered such an open and shut case in my entire career. What on earth makes you want to take the word of a bunch of hippies and travellers like that lot for?"

"Why do you think you couldn't identify the person who died?"

"That lot wouldn't tell us, that's why!"

Beverley returned at that moment bearing a tray of cups and

a pot of tea. She read the expression on Samuels' face, glancing at the others. Tentatively, she spoke, "I brought some biscuits for you as well." She then excused herself, apparently conscious of walking in on something.

"I'll tell you this," Samuels stated, sitting forward and waving a finger pointedly in Tamara's direction, "if that lot had one iota of conscience, they would have admitted who was there and allowed us to notify the poor girl's family. But they didn't, none of them!"

"Girl?" Janssen asked, Samuels met his eye. "I thought the body was too damaged to identify."

"It was… but, I chose not to refer to her as an *it*. The size of the body, and anyway, most of the protestors were women… somehow enthralled by that Bradshaw boy. Heaven knows why."

"But you did try to identify the victim?" Tamara pressed.

"Of course, we did. The intensity of the fire hampered identification. The flames burned so hot that the body was destroyed beyond recognition. The materials they keep in those labs were such that all the connective tissue fused the skeleton together, we couldn't even draw a match from dental records nor extract a usable DNA profile." He drew himself upright, looking back to Janssen. "Sadly, unless that bunch chose to tell us who she was, we had no way of finding out."

"What about reviewing those protestors who were in the area or the local MisPers as they came in down the line?" Tamara asked, seemingly intent on applying some pressure.

"Oh… for it only to be so easy. Do you think I'm daft, woman? As soon as that building went up and we began rounding them up for interview, they scattered to the four winds. There must have been upwards of forty different people present at any one time. They don't exactly have a registration system either. I'll bet most of them didn't know who was missing by that point. Moving on to the next protest, no doubt."

"And the missing persons reports?"

"I don't know what it's like these days, young lady, but back then we weren't flush with officers on the front line. I had a full caseload of criminals I was trying to put away. I didn't have time to keep returning to the death of an arsonist, however unfortunate it may have been. We're always hearing about budget cuts, are you sure you're managing your resources properly?" Tamara smiled. Janssen knew the difference between genuine and forced. "Besides, I figured one of them would give up the name post-conviction in any event, perhaps to curry favour with the judge prior to sentencing."

"But they didn't," Janssen concluded.

"Quite right. Shameless!" Samuels said.

"To do so would have confirmed they were present," Tamara said.

"Too right, they were bloody there, girl!" Samuels rolled his eyes in Janssen's direction. "I've no idea what they teach you these days, I really don't. Haven't you got enough to contend with in the job without raking over past convictions?"

"Provided they were *sound*," she said.

"It's as sound a conviction *as any* I had in a very long and productive career. River Malloy set that fire and under the law of *Joint Enterprise*, they were all just as responsible. I sleep well at night knowing I put the right people away." He glared at her. She held the eye contact, unmoving. "Maybe once you've been in the job a little longer, you'll understand how things work." Samuels was patronising her. To Janssen it was obvious. Tamara cleared her throat.

"May I use your bathroom?" she asked, Samuels grunted, leaning forward to pour tea from the pot into the nearest cup. Tamara stood.

"Be sure to leave the seat up when you're finished," he muttered under his breath without looking up.

"I also have a few calls I need to make," she said, looking to

Janssen. "Why don't you finish up here and I'll meet you at the car." She walked away without any final words for Peter Samuels, not that he seemed bothered by the slight.

CHAPTER TWENTY-FOUR

TOM JANSSEN WATCHED Tamara return into the house and descend the stairs to the ground floor. Her confrontational approach had not gone down well with the retired detective but he didn't think she would be too disturbed.

"Sugar?" Samuels asked, heaping two spoonfuls into his own cup.

"Please," Janssen replied. To his horror, his cup received the same amount before he could protest.

"Milk and two sugars... NATO standard we used to call it." Janssen was puzzled and it must have shown in his expression. Samuels smiled. "Common standard for tea drinking by NATO personnel – milk and two sugars. Have you never served?"

He shook his head. "No, my father and grandfather both did but I took a different path."

"Yours is just as worthy, young man. As long as you didn't come in via the graduate programme as one of those plastic policemen?" He looked at him, staring across the rim of his cup, blowing the steam from the brew. Samuels was searching, trying to assess him. It was like viewing his own routine in a mirror.

"I graduated with a degree but came up through the ranks," he replied. "No accelerated promotion for me."

"Good man. The best way if you ask me." Glancing back into the house, Tamara was nowhere to be seen. "I'll bet your boss has found a way to get ahead, eh?" A sideways grin crossed his face for a fleeting moment. "I notice she's not wearing a wedding ring. A woman of her age, single… you can tell she hasn't had children as well. Has she?" he asked seeking confirmation of his assertion. Janssen shook his head.

"Not that I'm aware of."

"I wouldn't be surprised if she's not into men at all. You can tell by the clothing. Dead giveaway. That's another way for women to get up the chain of command these days. It used to be slipping between the sheets… now, you just have to be of the right *persuasion* to benefit from positive discrimination. Must be a pain to work with, eh?"

"To be fair, this is only the second case we've worked together… and I wasn't expecting to have her along for the ride on this one either."

"Decision from above?" Samuels asked. He nodded. "Right you are. They do that, interfere. If they just let you crack on nicking villains, this country wouldn't be in the state it is now! As for her… my advice, don't pay too much attention to whatever she pushes you towards. Don't drag your feet. Get the case tied off and move onto the next. That's how you build a career." Samuels retired at Janssen's current rank and he was half the man's age. He let the matter pass. "What's your take on all of this then?"

Drawing a deep breath, Janssen scooped up one of the biscuits provided to them by Beverley. Talking through a mouthful, he shrugged. "Seems like a bit of a waste of time, if you ask me. Forensics placed the scrotes at the scene. River Malloy did nothing to advance either her cause or any of the others at trial. Like you said, they were guilty." Samuels was watching him intently as he spoke. Picking up his own cup of tea, he sipped at the incredibly sweet liquid. "But… we have to dot the *is* and cross the *ts* so to speak."

"So, why are you trawling through the arson? What's all this about?"

"We turned up a body on the beach last weekend. You'll have heard, I'm sure," he said, Samuels nodded. "Anyway, it looks like it is one of those who had strong links to the protestors and... keep this to yourself... she had a business card in her possession belonging to an employee of *Reactive Sciences*."

"Ah... I see. Hence why you're looking at the old case, trying to put a name to it."

"Exactly."

"And the nature of this *body* you've found is?"

"The more I look at it, it has to be a murder. At this stage we're running down potential leads."

"So, your acting DCI is running around interviewing as many of the old players as possible, trawling far and wide trying to build this into a bigger case?"

"Yeah," Janssen admitted. "Trying to make it larger than it needs to be, probably looking at cementing the promotion. You know how it is."

"I do, lad, yes. Climbing the pole as fast as she can. Officers like her... they'll do whatever it takes, mark my words. Even if that means trampling on the good name of those who have gone before or those around them." He leaned forward, tapping his knuckles against Janssen's knee. "They don't realise you don't *shit* on people on the way up, because you have to pass the same people on the way back down! Watch your back, lad. Keep your eye on the detail and remember everything. Keeps you right, trust me."

"Wise words. Thanks, I will," Janssen replied. "Tell me, when you were investigating all of this back in the day, did the name Darren ever come up?"

Samuels looked at him, his eyes drifting up and to the left. He shook his head. "Sorry. I can't say as it does. Why? Who is he?"

"No matter," Janssen said, "probably nothing anyway. There

were a number of girls who went missing around the same time as, or shortly following, the arson case. Did you look into any of those?"

"Erm... not sure I did. Rings a bell, so I guess I must have."

"Keeping your eye on the details?"

Samuels chuckled. "True enough. Now that I come to think of it, there were one or two."

"Three," he corrected.

"Yes... three. Let me think..." Samuels sat forward, rubbing at his chin. "There was one who was probably fleeing domestic abuse... some rich kid who was a bit of a drifter... I'm afraid you'll have to remind me about the other. Since the stroke, my memory isn't quite what it was."

"A teenager, presumed to be a runaway from her foster home."

"That's right, yes," Samuels exclaimed, wagging a finger in the air. "Took off from Gerald Grable's place. Yes, I remember. They were mortified, Gerald and Ann. They'd never lost one before... not permanently anyway. They always came back. I don't remember a Darren being involved with any of them at the time, though."

"Did you find anything untoward in those investigations?" Janssen asked, helping himself to another biscuit.

"Untoward? Such as?"

"Strange associations... behaviours... any indication at all that it wasn't a simple runaway situation?"

"No, not that I can recall. People go missing all the time. Let's be honest, without a blood trail or a smoking gun there isn't a lot to go on with an adult unless we have a strong indication of foul play. There wasn't in any of these cases. I remember the boyfriend of one was a bit quick with his fists but... crimes of passion, you know. Heat of the moment. Women can drive you a bit mad sometimes, can't they."

Janssen nodded, replacing his cup back on the table. "You

never came across Mike Collyer, or possibly under his nickname, Conn?"

Samuels met his eye, responding immediately, "No. Never heard of him. Why do you ask?"

"He's come up alongside Niall Bradshaw, the lead agitator—"

"Yes, Niall. A piece of work that boy. Trust him about as far as you can throw him."

"They were having words. It could be unconnected but just covering the bases for the DCI. You know how it is."

"I certainly do, don't worry. Was there anything else?"

"Oh, yes. There was one more thing I was curious about."

"Ask away, old chap," Samuels replied, smiling warmly.

"Regarding the arson… I know it's a waste of time… but one thing got me thinking. The entry point, where they broke in… how did they know to do it there?" Samuels met his eye. Janssen narrowed his gaze, unblinking.

"I'm not sure I follow."

"Well, the protestors were on site for a number of years. The business owner, Shaun Robinson, as well as the employees were coming under a great deal of pressure. He told me they had to review and upgrade procedures, consider extra security, revamping of entrances to the complex and so on. It was very disruptive."

"Yes, I don't doubt it. So?"

"The entry point was a weak spot in the building's security. They slipped in avoiding the CCTV and managed to get inside, cross the complex and start a fire significant enough to wipe out much of the complex. All before security were able to raise the alarm. By the time the appliances arrived to tackle the fire it was already burning out of control." Janssen sat forward, resting his elbows on his knees and cupping his chin with one hand, striking a thoughtful pose. "How did they know where the weak point was, let alone manage to pass through the security doors of the complex to reach the labs and start the fire? I was there yesterday, speaking with Shaun Robinson, and we needed a swipe card to access the offices… and they are of far lesser importance when compared to the labs themselves. We aren't talking about a specialist black ops team after all. This was largely a bunch of youngsters looking to change the world."

"Yes… yes, I see your point." The smile faded from the retired detective's face, as he nodded along, clearly contemplating the question. "Quite a conundrum. I… have no answer for that but I didn't need one. Once we had the forensic evidence, the rest was purely gravy."

"I guess so," Janssen said, smiling. "It's still quite a question. I'm pleased not to have to come up with the answers either."

"Quite so!" Samuels laughed. "Listen, don't mention it to her downstairs. Not unless you want to be digging over my old case for the next ten years." He grinned. Janssen returned it. Checking his watch, he arched his brow.

"Well, I'd best be off. The DCI will be busting my balls if I don't head out," he said, tilting his head slightly in the direction of Tamara. He could see her down below, leaning against the car and casually watching them.

"Keep her sweet, by all means. Just don't let her stop you doing your job."

Janssen grinned before finishing his tea and standing. "Absolutely right. Pity you're not still in the job, Peter."

"I don't miss it in the slightest. Did my time, earned my rest! There's one more thing you need to be aware of, lad."

"Oh? What's that?"

"Pension. Get yourself set. Retirement comes up on you quickly, believe me." He shook his head before breaking into a broad grin. "Always make sure you have a plan."

"I'll think on it. Thank you very much for your time as well as your memories. It's good to hear how things used to be. Makes you wonder how far we've actually come. No need to come down, I'll see myself out," Janssen said, offering Samuels his hand. They shook and he left the retired detective alone on the balcony.

Beverley was busy in the kitchen and she offered him a polite wave as he passed the entrance, heading for the front door. Once outside, he walked down the driveway taking care not to appear too keen under the watchful eyes above.

"About time!" Tamara snapped as he unlocked the car. Shrugging, he opened the door. She got into the passenger side while he leaned on his door, looking up at Samuels. Shaking his head slightly, he was sure he saw the older man grin. Then he got in and shut the door. Starting the car, he reversed out of the drive. Once clear of the house, Tamara looked across at him. He smiled in return. "Productive?"

Janssen sighed. "He's a pleasant man! You made quite an impression on the bigoted old sod." He grinned. "Are you naturally gifted at winding up men like him or do you have to work at it?"

"I've spent years perfecting my style."

"Surprising. You are so natural with it." She laughed. "He has you down as sleeping your way to a promotion and at the same time being a lesbian. That's good for your career, too, positive discrimination."

"Is it? I'll have to bear that in mind," she said, shaking her head. "Cantankerous old... *lesbian*, did you say?" She fixed him with a puzzled expression.

He nodded. "Yeah. Apparently, it's the way you dress. Gives it away. Who would have known?"

"Hey! I like the way I dress. It's professional and... functional."

"Don't blame me, they're not my opinions," Janssen said, stifling a laugh. "Mind you..."

"What?" she asked, waiting for him to finish the sentence.

"Nothing..." he glanced over to her, she was still smiling expectantly.

"Seriously, what?"

"I was just wondering if you have to go to a specialist *lesbian shop* or something… I mean, to get the required look?" She swiped a closed fist in his direction, striking him on the upper arm. He feigned shock and indignation, breaking into laughter.

"Go on, what did he have to say?" she pressed. "Besides tips on my fashion sense and sexual orientation."

"More than I reckon he would if we had the conversation again. I'd put money on it the arson investigation was pretty half-arse at best. Once they had the forensics to place Niall, River and the others at the scene they did little else to figure out what went on. A decent barrister should have torn the case to pieces."

"Forensics, though… with that we all know a jury are likely to convict. Hell, most of us struggle with the science. Throw in fingerprints along with DNA and we pretty much have a slam dunk. I'll bet the defence was all about mitigation rather than proving innocence."

"True," he agreed.

"What about the girls?"

"Barely investigated I should imagine. He pretty much indicated Tracy Bartlett's boyfriend was a known abuser but he wrote it off as actions resulting from a *crime of passion*. Women annoying their partners and so on."

"Strewth." She shook her head, irritated. "I know the force was littered with dinosaurs like him in the past but he was serving until pretty recently."

"His attitude to a teen runaway wasn't much better," he continued, pulling the car out onto the main road to head back inland. "Interesting though, I mentioned Darren and he dismissed it but… and you'll love this… he mentioned not having heard about a Darren seeing any of the missing girls. Now, it could be he misinterpreted my asking and then linked the two questions but…"

"No one seems to know Darren… except he may have been in a relationship with one of the girls."

"My thoughts exactly," he agreed.

"Why would he lie?" she asked, turning her attention to the passing landscape. "Or, maybe not lie as such but not mention it?"

"I'm still thinking Darren was the inside man at *Reactive Sciences*. That's why his business card was in the possessions at the beach and, if I'm right, why the company have no recollection of him."

"Or so they say."

"Yeah, Shaun Robinson knows about him I'm almost certain. Call it a hunch. He tried to throw me off yesterday, but the man's a poor liar. I'd play a hand of poker with him any day."

"So, what's your thinking? Shaun denies any knowledge of this Darren because… he wanted to cover up an employee's involvement in the activist's campaign."

"Possibly, yes. Maybe he was an activist himself, smuggled in under false pretences for the very reason of undermining the company. He could have helped them bypass security. Shaun and his company wouldn't want that to become common knowledge."

Tamara fell silent, seemingly mulling over the theory. "That doesn't explain why DI Samuels would go along with it."

"No, it doesn't," he agreed. She had a strong point. Where the retired detective came into it, he was less certain. "Professional reputation? If Samuels missed it… he might not want to blot his own copybook." The motivation sounded weak in his head as soon as he uttered the words.

"And yet, he seemed able to link Darren to at least one of the missing girls," Tamara reminded him.

"That's only my supposition, though. I could be way off the mark."

"No!" Tamara replied immediately. "That man is holding a lot back. All of that sexist crap he was spinning… I don't doubt he believes a lot of it but that was mostly for my benefit."

"Because you're a woman?"

"No, not at all." She shook her head. "Because he was trying to throw us off, both of us. Me in particular. By putting my back up, he not only draws us away from the difficult questions we were there to ask but, at the same time, puts the seed of doubt in my mind as the lead investigator."

"How so?"

"Think about it, how much of our job is instinct? You get a feel for the person you're talking to and from that you form your opinions and choose a course of action. By being such a pig, he has me remembering how much I dislike him. If I have an instinctive response to him, I could be just as likely to brush it off as act on it seeing my dislike of the man as clouding my judgement. He knows something and he's not telling us. Something that isn't in the files or the court transcripts."

He looked across, reading the determined expression on her face as she stared at the road ahead. "You were right. I wasn't sure but you were bang on," he told her. She glanced over. "That was *exactly* the right way to play him."

"And I'll tell you something else, we're going to keep digging until we find out what DI Samuels doesn't want us to know."

CHAPTER TWENTY-FIVE

ERIC COLLET PRESSED thumb and forefinger into both eyes, closing them tight. They watered. Hours spent trawling through pages of raw data on the screen was taking its toll. Reading through the transcripts of the arson trial was both time consuming and monotonous. Much of the testimony covered similar ground. Employees describing a systematic campaign of intimidation. Witnesses identifying each defendant as present at the encampment and recounting exchanges on their way into work as well as near their own residences. The experiences would have played well to alienate the jury from the defendants. However, by the time he read to the conclusion there was precious little which he considered to be of use in their current enquiry. The process felt like a personal failure. After mulling it over for a while, he hit on the idea to come at it from another angle.

Greave and Janssen arrived in ops, handing him a paper bag. They'd brought him lunch on the way back from their trip to interview the former DI. He struggled to contain his enthusiasm. Leaving early for the station, skipping breakfast and his mother's new found desire for him to become self-sufficient resulted in a vending machine meal consisting of a packet of crisps and a chocolate bar. There would have been more if he hadn't used the last of his change.

"I've noticed you're not being catered for these days," Tamara said to him, holding a sandwich in one hand and taking a seat. He fished out his own, coronation chicken. That would do. Tamara was eating something stuffed with green leaves as usual. He was pretty sure she was a vegan or close to it. How anyone could live like that he didn't understand.

"Yes, well… Mum has changed her stance recently," he said, taking a bite. Janssen was sitting off to his left, a knowing smile threatening to grow at the corners of his mouth. "She thinks I should be finding my own way more." He spoke with a mouthful, trying hard not to spit food as he talked.

"Does that mean she's got you doing your own laundry as well?" He looked at her, trying to see if she was teasing him as she often did or genuinely curious. The warm smile suggested the latter.

"Mum's got a new man," he offered, wiping his mouth with the back of his hand. "Nice bloke. Doesn't think she should be chasing around after me… at my age and that."

"Got a point," she agreed.

"I suppose."

"And tell her the rest," Janssen said. The smile was now a broad grin. Eric looked down. He could feel his cheeks flushing.

"Since I took up with… Becca… Mum thinks that… you know." Tamara arched her brow, eyes wide, encouraging him to continue. "That Becca should… maybe… take on some of it."

"Ah… your mum sees the new woman in your life and thinks she should be taking care of her little man?" The last was said affectionately as opposed to mocking him.

"Yes. That's it exactly."

"And what does Becca think about this?"

He blew out his cheeks, shaking his head vigorously. "Are you mad? I wouldn't mention it to her. She would go… well, not be very happy about it I'm sure."

"Have they met, your mum and the prospective daughter-in-law?" Now she was mocking, he could tell.

"Yes."

"How did that go?"

"I don't want to talk about it," he countered. Janssen burst out laughing at his discomfort. Instead of being angry, he found himself laughing too. "What do you do when you have two women as strong willed as one another anyway? *It's impossible.*"

"Keep your head down, Eric," Janssen advised, wiping a tear from the corner of his eye. "They only have to meet one more time on the wedding day... perhaps more if you also have children."

"Don't joke about it, please," he replied, running a hand through his hair.

"You'll figure it out and if you need a bit of help, I'm sure Tamara and I can keep you right. Wouldn't you say?" Janssen looked to Tamara. Eric turned with a smile on his face. It faded when his gaze fell on her. She looked lost. Staring into space at nothing in particular. For a moment he feared she was annoyed by their lack of professionalism but she'd been all in on the banter a few moments ago. Something had changed. He decided to change the conversation, wanting to move away from the trials of his personal life. Janssen met his eye and Eric could tell he thought the same.

"I went over the transcripts as you asked. Believe me, there isn't a lot there. Then I got to thinking. Families and what not watch from the gallery and I remember this was quite a contested trial. There was a lot of antagonism, threats surrounding the case from other activist groups acting to support those in the dock. So, I checked up on the security arrangements."

"What did you find?" Tamara asked. Her tone was neutral, a little flat in comparison to when they first got back in Eric's mind.

"They increased security at the crown court. Anyone wanting

access to the building had to present ID as well as pass through the usual security checks, bag searches and metal detectors. Then, if you wanted access to this particular courtroom everyone had to sign in again. The judge was fearful of acts of disruption halting proceedings… or worse. It was one step short of a closed courtroom but they didn't go that far."

"Probably afraid of a backlash if they did," Janssen suggested.

"My thoughts too. Anyway, it took some digging but I tracked down the list of everyone recorded as present each day over the fourteen-day trial."

"I sense you've found a person of interest?"

"There were a number of journalists, local and national, who covered the trial who I've been able to verify through their credentials. Some were from abroad, that's how big this story was. Beyond that there were family members who are easy to chalk off. This brought me down to around a dozen, presumably associates of those involved in the case, curious members of the public and so on. However, there is this one guy who attended every single moment of the trial up until the final day, a *D Robinson*."

Janssen rose from his seat, crossing the ops room enthusiastically. Eric turned the relevant document in his direction, handing it over. "Do we know what the *D* stands for?"

"Not recorded in the paperwork we have I'm afraid."

"*Robinson*," Tamara said aloud, "any relation?"

"My thoughts exactly." Eric spun his chair back so he was facing his computer screen. Tilting the screen so the others could see he brought up a social media page. "I give you *Darren Robinson* and according to his *About page* is a recently qualified doctor in molecular biology. He graduated from Cambridge six years ago, continuing to work on his research project for his PhD. Sadly, the only links within the social media are to his sister, Yvonne. However, it didn't take me long to confirm who their father is. You'll not be surprised to know—"

"Shaun Robinson, Managing Director of *Norfolk Labtech*," Tamara finished for him.

"Formerly *Norfolk Reactive Sciences*. The very same," he confirmed, gesturing theatrically with an open hand, sweeping from left to right.

"Outstanding work, Eric," Janssen said, tapping the constable's shoulder. "Have we got anything to tie him to the company?"

Eric shook his head, the enthusiasm waning. "No. There isn't any mention in his digital bio. I've brought up numerous papers he has published over the last few years. He's been researching the effects of experimental drugs on the human condition in conjunction with other members of the medical scientific community. Nothing in his research ties back to his father's company though."

"Thinking back to the time," Janssen said, eager to find a link, "he would have been an undergrad, possibly working for his father as an intern or assistant during the holidays. That might be why it's so easy to remove him from the company record."

"Your suspicions could well be right," Tamara said. Janssen leaned in to see a close up of the profile picture on the web page. Eric clicked on it, making it full size. Janssen's eyes narrowed.

"How old is he here, do you think?"

"He's twenty-seven now," Eric stated. "Although, I don't know when this picture in particular was taken. Why?"

"If we could roll the clock back on him, I wonder what he would look like having hit his twenties," Janssen wondered.

"I can help with that," he said, opening up another tab on the screen. Eric typed in a google search bringing up a facial recognition app. Opening that, he downloaded Darren's profile picture and uploaded it into the app. "Not very scientific but it will give us an idea." Eric clicked a feature and Darren's face morphed slightly.

"Can you give him different hair with that?"

"Yes, I can try. What type?"

"Longer, darker and wavy. Slim him down a little as well, in the face. Whatever you can do." Eric clicked away. Tamara came to join them. Once Eric was done, he clicked the process button and the image changed again.

"Well, I'll be…" Tamara said quietly.

"That's close," Janssen agreed. They were looking at a face remarkably similar to the one seen in the photobooth pictures taken with Sophie Maddox. "Close enough to justify a search warrant, I'll bet."

"Eric," Tamara placed a gentle hand on his shoulder, "get us everything you can on Darren Robinson. Where he lives, any priors, associates, PAYE records… even his school report if you could access it. Anything at all that we can use as leverage."

"Yeah, I'll get right on it. Why do you think he would skip the last day of the trial? It seems odd bearing in mind he was present at every moment of proceedings prior to the conclusion."

"We can add that to the list of questions, without a doubt," she replied, turning to Janssen. "I wonder if there was anything else Shaun Robinson was hiding when you met him?"

"I reckon it would be a good idea to take a look at Shaun's business prior to the change of direction. You said Niall Bradshaw was adamant the protests were having their desired effect. Perhaps we could see what information they hold at Companies House. It could give us a steer."

"I'm very keen to hear what Darren has to say for himself as well."

"Shaun had photos of his kids on the desk when I was talking to him. Darren was right in front of me the whole time."

"It looks like Shaun is a better poker player than you gave him credit for."

CHAPTER TWENTY-SIX

TITCHWELL WAS one of the many small villages dotted along the main coastal route passing through north Norfolk. Barely a stone's throw from the nature reserve separating the village from the sea, Janssen slowed the car. The address they sought was set back from the main road and he didn't want to miss it.

"There," Tamara said, indicating to him as they approached a turn off.

It was a narrow lane and as he took the turn, they could see the residence up ahead. Coming to a solid wooden gate, they found it open and drove through into the gravelled courtyard in front of the main house. Once this would have been a working farm managing the surrounding farmland. These days the land was largely combined under the umbrella of larger organisations with many of the buildings surplus to requirements. Over the years these were converted into residential accommodation with many taking on a new lease of life in the modern economy, such as tourism. Not so in this case.

The flintstone complex of buildings were set out in a U shape, the main farmhouse with ancillary buildings attached at either end wrapping around them up to the boundary. From the upper windows of the main house, Janssen was sure of a clear view overlooking the marshland making up the wildlife reserve with the sea beyond. A Mercedes estate was parked in front, the door to the boot raised. Pulling the car alongside, they noticed suitcases were set on the ground waiting to be loaded into the interior and the front door to the house was wide open. They got out of the car, a voice calling to someone from the inside carried to them.

"We'd best get a move on. The flight is scheduled to leave Norwich at six."

"I'm almost ready," another voice replied, softer and sounding deferential. A figure appeared at the threshold of the door, stopping immediately upon seeing them. He was clutching a holdall in his right hand and as Tamara reached for her warrant card, he flinched, taking a step back and half turning. Janssen thought he was about to bolt judging from the open-mouthed expression on his face. The thought must have been fleeting because he turned back to face them, apprehensive. Tamara showed him her ID, identifying them both.

"Darren Robinson?" she asked. He faced her, eyes wide, looking furtively between the two of them before glancing back over his shoulder into the house.

"It's a simple enough question, Darren," Janssen said, coming alongside Tamara. The young man nodded.

"Yes," he replied.

Janssen eyed the suitcases as well as the holdall and indicated to the former. "Going somewhere?"

"Erm..." he replied, tracking his gaze down to the bags.

"Anywhere nice?" Janssen pressed. Footsteps sounded on a tiled interior, the frequency of the steps growing quicker as they approached. Shaun Robinson stepped out into the afternoon sunshine moments later, seeking to take the situation in hand.

"Detectives... I do wish you had called ahead. I'm afraid you've picked a terrible moment. We're taking a short family break, seeking to extend the warmth of summer that little bit longer," he said, aiming his comments to Janssen before nervously glancing at Tamara Greave.

"Funny you didn't mention that yesterday, Mr Robinson," he replied. "I'm still waiting to hear back from you about your employee search. Although," he pointed to Darren, "I think we've found our answer."

Shaun Robinson scoffed. "Surely, you don't mean my son? Darren was only with us for the work experience. He was hardly an employee—"

"You can argue semantics all you like, Mr Robinson. In the meantime, we would like to have a chat with your son about a few things."

Shaun glared at him. "I'll call my lawyer." He reached into his pocket, producing his mobile.

"Do as you wish," Tamara told him. "While you're making that call, we'll have a dozen uniformed officers pull your house apart." Shaun stopped searching his contacts, his finger hovering over the screen as he looked at her.

"What? Why… would you do that?"

Janssen stepped forward, unfolding the search warrant they'd brought with them and handing it to him. "This authorises us to take your house apart one brick at a time in search of evidence."

"What… on earth do you expect to find?" Shaun protested.

Tamara produced a copy of the photos retrieved from the possessions of Sophie Maddox. Holding it up in front of Darren, she pointed to the pictures. "Maybe you would like to have a chat with us about your relationship with Sophie, Darren. This is you, isn't it?" Darren stared at the images and then looked to his father, either for guidance or permission, he couldn't tell which. To Janssen, he appeared ready to cry. Turning to Shaun, she continued, "Obviously, it is up to you. We can play it however you choose. Depends on what you have to hide."

Shaun lowered the mobile to his side. "We have nothing to hide, do we, Darren?" It was rhetorical. His son shook his head. He was scared. It was written across his face.

"You might want to cancel that flight," Tamara said to him. "I think you'll be otherwise engaged for the time being."

"We should go inside," Shaun replied, stepping forward and dropping the boot of the Mercedes. Placing a hand on Darren's shoulder, he guided him back indoors. Darren placed the holdall on a chair in the hallway. Janssen fell into step alongside Tamara, the two of them sharing a silent communication with one another as Shaun led them through into a large open-plan kitchen and diner.

"Will your wife and daughter be joining us?" Janssen asked. Shaun looked past him, out of the window and into the manicured garden beyond.

"No… she's out for the evening and our daughter no longer lives with us."

"Just the two of you on this family getaway then?" Shaun didn't reply, offering them a seat at an expansive dining table positioned alongside a wall of glass overlooking the garden. "I suppose there's no point me asking to see *your* passport?"

"Ask your questions," Shaun stated through gritted teeth. "And then you can leave."

"I think we'll be the judge of that, Mr Robinson," Tamara advised him. Evidently, Shaun was a man not used to people speaking to him in a condescending manner. He bristled but offered no further objection. Sliding the strip of photographs across the table in front of Darren, she tapped alongside them. "How long were you and Sophie an item?" Darren stared hard at the photos, his expression a mixture of concentration and controlled emotion. Janssen noted his breathing was rapid and uncontrolled. Turning away from the photos, he glanced to his father who nodded. It was a gesture conveying encouragement.

"Not long. Six… maybe seven months." The tone of his voice was soft, quiet and barely audible.

"Were you together when she went missing?" she asked.

Darren met her eye, the corner of his mouth twitching in an involuntary moment.

"I… I wasn't aware she was missing," he replied, looking between the two detectives with the expression of a frightened ten-year-old. "I mean… I know she hasn't been around—"

"For *six years*, Darren," Janssen stated firmly. "Where do you think she went?"

"Now look here! I don't know what you're imply—" Shaun interjected. An outburst immediately put down by Tamara.

"It's your choice, Mr Robinson. We can discuss this here or take your son back to the station. If you interrupt again, I will arrest him and we can do this on tape." Shaun visibly tensed but looked away. Tamara took it as a signal of acquiescence and turned back to Darren. "Where do you think she went?"

He shook his head, looking at the table's surface. "I don't know." His response was barely above a whisper.

"Come on, lad," Janssen protested. "You're going to have to do a lot better than that."

"It's true! I don't, really I don't," he protested. "If you knew Sophie, knew what she was like then you'd understand." Finally, Janssen could see some animation within him.

"Then tell us," Tamara countered, adopting a softer more encouraging line.

"She wasn't like anyone else I'd ever met… before or since!" Darren said, looking directly at Tamara. Janssen could see tears welling in his eyes. "So energetic, full of life. Nothing was going to stop her."

"Stop her from doing what?"

"Anything she chose to. That was it with her. The world was there to be explored, experienced. She wasn't bothered about exams… or careers… or all this other stuff." He waved a hand to one side in a dismissive gesture. "Sophie was all about lived experience. I guess… I was drawn to her because she was the opposite of everything I was told…" He glanced briefly at his father. "Everything I believed in. She was wonderful."

"Little slapper." All eyes turned to Shaun, sitting with his arms tightly crossed in front of him, a sneering expression on his face.

"I assume you disapproved of the relationship?" Janssen asked.

"I would have," Shaun replied hotly, "had I known about it. You can do better than the likes of her, boy."

"And what would you know, Dad?" Darren countered. Shaun visibly baulked at the assertion. Janssen silently wondered how often, if ever, his son addressed him in that tone. He assumed never. Darren continued unabated. "We saw a lot of each other over that autumn and winter period. It was special." He looked at his father, the corner of his lip curling as he spoke. "She was special."

"You knew her?" Tamara directed her question to Shaun. He shrugged.

"Only as one of those silly protestors at the gate."

"You must have known more than that," she countered. She was right. He must have known of her name as well as her background to make such a disparaging remark.

"Part of that extra security I mentioned yesterday," he indicated to Janssen. "I had to take measures of my own when they started targeting employee's homes."

"Private investigators?" he asked.

"Yes. We hired a couple to do some digging, find out what we were up against."

"And what were you up against?" Tamara pressed.

"Middle class eco-warriors, in the main. Along with a few strays looking to cause trouble."

"Did you consider Sophie to be one of those?" Janssen asked. Shaun shrugged again, looking away. Tamara turned her attention back to Darren.

"What happened between you? Did the relationship come to an end?"

"I never found out," Darren said, sounding despondent. "I thought maybe she... got bored with me and moved on or..."

"Or?" Tamara asked, lowering her head and forcing him to make eye contact with her.

"I wasn't any more use to her, I guess," he said, arching his brow. Now, they were getting somewhere.

"Were you providing information to her and her associates involved in the protests?" Tamara asked. Darren looked to his father, who stared at him with an impassive look on his face. "Forget what your father might say, Darren." He looked back at her, chewing on his lower lip. "We know someone was on the inside providing them with information on company practices, financial information and possibly security details as well. Until now, we'd found no connection between those outside of the gate and the company. Now we have you, so please don't waste our time. It's been six years!"

"All right! Yes, I told Sophie... *things*. Nothing about people, where they lived or stuff like that, I swear."

"But you fed them information on the stability of your father's company, how it was getting on under the scrutiny?" Janssen asked. Darren's gaze fell upon the table once more, his head bobbed briefly in acknowledgement. Janssen looked to Shaun whose expression remained unchanged. This wasn't news to him.

"When was the last time you saw or had contact with Sophie?" Tamara asked.

Darren's brow furrowed as he thought hard. "A few weeks before the fire... maybe but it might have been more. Like I said, she wasn't looking to spend much time with me. It all kinda fizzled out over the previous Christmas and new year period. I saw her a few times in the January and February but it was sporadic. I had to hassle her for the time and she didn't like that a lot."

"Were you aware of her relationship with River Malloy?" she asked. A snort of derision came from Shaun who immediately held up his hand in apology, even if he didn't appear to mean it. Darren nodded, pursing his lips. "Did that bother you?"

"I'd be lying if I said it didn't. Like I said, Sophie wanted to experience all things life had to offer. I hoped… like an idiot… that maybe I would be different, that I would mean as much to her."

"That you would remain in her life?" she suggested. He agreed. "Tell us, why did you attend the arson trial. You were there every day, weren't you?" He looked at her, his eyes narrowing. Janssen thought he might be considering a denial. As it turned out he merely smiled weakly. "Why were you there?"

"I thought I might get to see her… if she came… or find out what happened to her, where she went."

"But you didn't attend on the final day of the trial. Why not?"

"Sophie wasn't mentioned… she hadn't shown up. I didn't see why that would change on the last day."

"What do you think happened to her?"

"*I don't know.* I wish I did. I wondered if… she might be the one… you know, in the fire." The final words were uttered quietly, as if he couldn't bring himself to say them.

"Do you think it could have been her, the one who died in the flames?" Tamara asked. He shrugged. "It is at least plausible, so why didn't you come to us, to the police? She disappeared and you let it go. Why?" Darren shot a look across to his father who was watching him intensely. Something unsaid passed between them that no one but father and son would understand.

"I don't know. I think I was afraid my father would find out about us, me and Sophie. At the same time no one else seemed bothered about her going away. I don't think they cared about her. I approached River and some of the others in the camp but… they didn't want anything to do with me. Most of them knew I was the son of the owner and didn't trust me… and didn't know I'd been helping them all that time."

"How did it make you feel," she turned to Shaun, "to find out what your son had been doing? You did know. That's one reason why you've been giving us the run around."

"I was… unhappy, to put it mildly," Shaun stated. If he was angry about it, the feeling must have passed for he was calmly discussing it now. "But he was young, idealistic… and thinking with his… well, we all do things we regret in the name of love, don't we. I moved past it. If anything, Darren's actions helped me to review what was important in my life. He helped me to see what needed to be changed. If anything, I owe him for what he did at that time even if it was unwitting. After the fire I decided to take the business another way, build something my family could be proud of rather than trying to hide it."

"And yet you chose to hide your son's involvement?" Janssen stated.

"What would you have done, Inspector? You know how the press work in this country. Any link between my son and these protestors would have been print dynamite. His reputation ruined and our family name dragged through the mud, and why, because of a childish infatuation with some little tart."

Darren stood up, his chair screeching as it scraped across the tiles. Glaring at his father, he stormed from the room. Janssen made to follow but Tamara indicated with her eyes to let him go. Instead, she looked at Shaun. "I expect you to cancel this little trip you had lined up for your son." Shaun met her eye and nodded. "You know, I'm sure Darren's involvement should have been made known to the case officers and properly investigated at the time. He may well have been complicit in an event that led to manslaughter. That was why you chose to keep it quiet, wasn't it?"

CHAPTER TWENTY-SEVEN

"How dare you!" Shaun protested, rising from his chair. "Do not try to second-guess my motivation because you have no idea."

"Either way, this will need to be looked at irrespective of how much time has passed since the trial, along with your attempts to block it coming to light. I dare say you could face charges of obstruction of justice as well yourself."

"Now you are being ridiculous," Shaun stated. "By all means, do what you must. My solicitors will have a field day with you, I'm sure."

Tamara fixed him with a stare. "If I were you, I'd make that call now. I guarantee they'll be pleased to take your money in exchange for their much-needed services." With a flick of the head, she encouraged Janssen to join her and they made to leave.

"We'll see ourselves out," Janssen told him with an accompanying smile. Shaun sat back down at the table shaking his head slowly from side to side, his hands clasped before him. He didn't look up nor utter another word.

Darren was leaning against their car outside when they came out of the house. His hands were thrust into his trouser pockets and he looked at them sideways as they approached.

"Honestly, he makes me so angry when he talks about people like that." The explosive outburst appeared to have subsided. "You mean Sophie?" Janssen asked.

"And others. Anyone he doesn't rate, doesn't see as worthy of him or the wider world. I mean, *he didn't even know her!*"

"Sophie and your father were worlds apart, it is true," Janssen said, "in background as much as world view. Both are arguably the result of their life experiences to date."

Darren laughed. It was a bitter sound. "Yeah, aren't we all?"

Tamara reached into her bag and withdrew something. Drawing Darren's attention, she took out the other photos found among Sophie's possessions. "Sophie kept hold of these alongside the ones of the two of you. She didn't keep much. I suspect they meant a lot to her. What do you think?" She offered them to him and he took them begrudgingly. Janssen wondered if being so close to anything meaningful to her was at the opposite end of the scale to comforting. He quickly passed over those depicting her parents before hovering on the one taken at the party. "Have you seen these before?" she asked. He didn't answer, maintaining his focus on the image in front of him. "Darren?"

"Sorry... what was that you said?" he mumbled, looking to her, open-mouthed.

"Do you recognise these pictures?"

"No... no, I don't... sorry." He shook his head and thrust the pictures back into her hands, stepping away from the car.

"What about these?" she said, passing him pictures of the jewellery found in the dunes. "We found them in the possession of a murder victim discovered buried—"

"I know where you found them. My father told me how all this has come about," Darren cut her off. "Besides, you'd have to have been living under a rock not to have heard about it." The reaction to the images was immediate, intense. Neither of them needed verbal confirmation. Darren's index finger slowly traced the line of the necklace, pausing when he reached the pendant. Tears welled and Janssen thought he was set to break down. The moment passed and he lifted his head to face Tamara.

"They were hers, weren't they?" she asked.

Darren's lip trembled as he spoke, passing the pictures back as he did so, "That was Sophie's... the necklace... definitely."

"You are certain?" she asked again.

"It was a gift... for Christmas, I think. At least, that's when she started to wear it, never went anywhere without it. I'm sure." The young man was crestfallen, his shoulders sagging and he suddenly looked fatigued beyond measure. Even without hearing the words, it was obvious to him the significance of the confirmation.

"We will need to speak with you again," Tamara said. He acknowledged that fact with a bob of the head. Janssen pressed the key fob and the car unlocked. He opened the driver's door. Darren caught his eye and he looked across the roof as Tamara got in her side.

"I loved her you know... Sophie. I still miss her, even now."

"I can tell," he replied, getting into the car. Closing the door, he smiled to Tamara.

She flicked up her eyebrows, a gesture conveying intrigue. "Do you think he loved her enough to kill her?"

Janssen blew out his cheeks as he started the engine, glancing over his shoulder at Darren who was still standing there, watching them leave. "What was it, Shaun said back there? *We all do things we regret in the name of love.*"

"It's true," Tamara agreed with a rueful smile as they pulled away, "but I never came close to killing anyone."

"It only takes a second... and everything changes," Janssen replied, watching the departing form of Darren Robinson re-entering the house in the rear-view mirror.

Tamara's mobile rang and she answered, noting it was Eric Collet. She put the call on speaker so Janssen could hear as well. "Go ahead, Eric."

"I've just come off an interesting call with Robert Beaufort, you remember him?"

"No, I don't," she replied, looking to Janssen. He shrugged. "Should I?"

"He says he spoke with you yesterday, shortly after you paid Conn a visit."

"Oh… the neighbour? Yes, of course. I don't think I ever took his name. What was he doing calling the station?"

"That's just it," Eric explained. "He tried to call you directly but he said he couldn't get through."

"I had my phone switched to silent. We were speaking with Shaun Robinson and the mysterious Darren."

"Right."

"Eric, what did he want?" She sounded mildly irritated to Janssen, not that he would ever voice it aloud. Eric could have that affect.

"Oh, yeah. He said you'd told him to call if he was ever alarmed."

"It was a spontaneous decision. I never thought he actually would need to call, though. That didn't take him long to make use of the courtesy."

"He said there were some weird noises coming from next door late last night. His words, not mine," Eric clarified.

"We got the impression Conn was something of a night owl," Janssen said.

"Beaufort mentioned that. He said it was *very* different to what they usually hear. He said he was minded to call last night but it was past midnight."

"I'm pleased he didn't. That'll teach me to be so quick in handing out the contact cards," Tamara said, shaking her head. Janssen stifled a laugh. "What does he expect us to do, Eric?"

"Well, I told him you'd look into it."

"Fair enough. Can you arrange for a unit to drop by?" she said, turning her gaze to the outside of the car.

"Oh… well…" Eric stammered. There was something he was

unwilling to say. It was obvious to the two of them in the car. They exchanged glances.

"Eric. What did you say?"

"He asked for you specifically."

"Eric?"

"He said you told him you would go back if needs be."

"I meant... *us*... the police. Not me personally."

"Oh... I see."

"You took his telephone number?"

"Erm..."

Tamara exhaled a frustrated sigh, "Leave it with us, Eric." She looked to Janssen. "We'll stop by... and if it's a waste of time I'll leave him with a flea in his ear. In the meantime, it looks very likely Sophie Maddox is our murder victim. Focus on building her specific timeline."

"That won't take long," Eric countered. He was right. They knew very little about the missing teenager's movements with her case treated as a runaway.

"She was in a relationship with River Malloy and also Darren Robinson. That gives us reference points to jump off from. Start cross-referencing everything we can between the three of them. You never know, things might start to make more sense now. Darren has also confirmed himself as the insider feeding company financials to the activists using Sophie as a conduit. We should take Niall Bradshaw's comments about the company being in dire straits as credible."

"I'll get onto Companies House and see where it takes us."

"Good. We'll be back once we've been out to Docking," Tamara told him. "And Eric?"

"Yes, Ma'am... Tamara."

"Today, you get to call me Ma'am, Eric. When we get back, I had better be impressed." She hung up the call before he could speak. Janssen slowed the car, pulling across the oncoming traffic, turning around and accelerating away back the direction they'd just come from.

"Docking isn't too far out of our way," he said, accompanied by a smile. "He's young. He'll learn."

"He will learn fast now that I'm here."

There was something in her tone, something unsaid. He thought about asking her about it but quickly chose not to. If there was something for him to know she would say when it was right. She wasn't the type to hold back from him unless she had good cause. Tamara must have felt his eyes upon her. She turned, seeming to assess his expression.

"What is it?"

"Nothing," he said, hoping she would drop it. Thankfully, she did just that. "I wonder what Conn has been up to that's spooked the neighbours?"

"It had better be worthwhile. I don't want us drawn into some continual spat between residents."

WITHIN FIFTEEN MINUTES they approached the village of Docking. Veering away to the south when they reached the outskirts, they turned onto the little lane running down to the isolated semi-detached properties and pulled up outside. Nothing had changed since their previous visit, much as Janssen expected. This was Tamara's situation to deal with and he allowed her to take the lead, setting off to see Conn's neighbour. Barely had she put a foot on his driveway than the man appeared at the front door. He struck quite an agitated figure. The man hovered in the doorway, reluctant to step out of the house, one hand bracing on the frame and the other held his walking stick. His arm was trembling. The overall state of his appearance was somewhat dishevelled. Janssen turned off the engine and got out, sensing something was genuinely amiss.

"Mr Beaufort?" Tamara asked, her tone edged with concern. "Is everything okay?"

"It's next door... I don't know what's been going on," the

elderly man said in a quivering voice. He was rattled. "Something very queer happened last night."

"Can you describe it to me?"

"It started around eleven… not unusual… with his chanting. It happens, very odd. Then everything went quiet and I said to the wife how great it was that he'd stopped early for a change… we were in bed, you see." Beaufort looked to his right, as if he could see through the party wall and into the interior next door. "Then there were voices, not just his. He had someone else there. It sounded to me like they were arguing. Not that we were listening in. Not intentionally, at any rate."

"Arguing about what, do you know?"

He shook his head. "It went on for some time and then the shouting seemed to stop before other noises… thumps and thuds, then quiet. I heard a door bang, like it was closed too fast and bounced off the frame. I was at the front window by then, trying to see what was going on. Just curious, you understand?"

"What did you see?"

"Nothing really," he shrugged. "It was very dark. I heard footsteps on the drive… whoever it was, was moving quickly. I thought I saw someone running off down the lane. In that direction," he said, pointing to the way they'd approached.

"Could you describe them?"

"No, I shouldn't have thought so. As I said, it was dark… it was more a shape than anything else and my eyes aren't what they used to be. I think they were wearing a dark hoodie or a coat. Either way, I couldn't make out any features."

"How about a vehicle, headlights moving off shortly after?"

"No, sorry," he confirmed. "It was so strange, the sounds that followed. It was eerily quiet… I can't explain it better than that. It's not like that here. You can always hear something, if not the man next door, it's the wind or gulls. Always something. Not last night, though. It was the damndest thing."

"Did you venture out?"

He shook his head emphatically. "Maureen told me not to.

Not that I would have. I glanced over the fence this morning but that's as far as I was prepared to go. That's your job, not mine."

"Okay," Tamara said, glancing back to Janssen. "We'll take a look. Have you seen any movement today?" Again, he shook his head. "All right. Leave it with us." Beaufort closed the door before she'd even rejoined Janssen on the road. Together, they headed next door.

CHAPTER TWENTY-EIGHT

JANSSEN FELL into step alongside her as Tamara strode down the driveway to Conn's house. His battered old Volkswagen Golf was still parked in front of the garage where it had been on their last visit. The grass growing behind the wheels stood several inches from the ground. It hadn't moved for a few days. As they found before, the curtains were all drawn in the house. The door to the rear was ajar, slowly rocking on its hinges with the pressure from the breeze. Raising her hand to knock, she stopped, her attention drawn to the frame. Pointing it out to Janssen she inspected it closely. A dark smear could be seen on the frame of the door, as if something had brushed against it at speed. From experience, she knew it was dried blood.

Indicating for them to enter in silence, Janssen nodded. With her foot, she pushed the door open. The stress on the hinges from the movement caused them to creak, the sound carrying. Flies were once again accumulating around them in the kitchen. The place smelt worse than it had done before, how that was possible she did not know. Waiting in the kitchen for a moment, they both listened for a sign from the occupant to acknowledge their entrance but nothing was forthcoming. Moving forward into the sitting room, they found it empty. The ticking of the clock sounded like thunder in the still air of the room. A mug lay on its side on the floor next to the sofa. Kneeling down, she touched the carpet nearby. It was damp to the touch. Meeting Janssen's eye, he indicated towards the door in the corner with a flick of the head. She agreed.

The door was closed and Janssen opened it carefully, gingerly doing so with the tip of his fingers in such a way as to not destroy any potential trace evidence. Clearly, he was coming to the same conclusion as her. Something untoward had gone on here and she could feel the sense of trepidation growing with each step. The door opened onto a narrow hallway leading to the front door and another reception room to their right. The stairs ran up off to their left. The passage to the front door was blocked by a mass of bags and clutter. Judging from the condition of its appearance from the outside, she doubted it would even open in any event. Precious little light came in from the small window set high in the door, the only source of natural light to the hall.

The door to the front reception room was pulled to but not fully closed. An odd, yet familiar, smell carried to them. They exchanged a knowing glance with one another. Running her tongue across the inside of her cheek, she braced herself and eased the door open. The door made a shrill sound as it moved. The interior was shrouded in total darkness and they couldn't make out any detail. An abundance of flies circled the room, far more than there should be even in such a rural location. The air was stale and the smell of death was all around them. Placing one hand over her mouth and nose, she took out her mobile and activated the torch function. Scanning the room, they were greeted by something of a macabre scene.

A body lay on the floor, slumped on to its left side with the face angled away from them. Even without moving closer, she knew it was Conn. The mass of blood-soaked matted hair was easily identifiable as his. He was still wearing the same clothes he had worn on their last visit. He lay with his left arm beneath him, his right fully extended away across the floor. He was lying on something, it looked like a rug but was unlike any other she'd seen before with an odd decorative finish she couldn't quite make out. A pool of blood had formed beneath the body, spreading out and seeping into the fibres and heavily staining them. Janssen moved past her and approached the still form of Conn. Dropping to his haunches, he reached over the body and gently felt the neck, searching for a pulse. A brief shake of the head confirmed he was already dead. "He's cold to the touch," Janssen stated. "He's been gone some time."

Crossing the room to the front window, the blackout curtains barred any natural light from penetrating the interior and easing one of them back threw up a great cloud of dust and particles into the air, visible in the sunlight now streaming through. With the benefit of daylight, she counted five candles on the floor she'd failed to notice before. Understandably so, because they were black. The pattern of the rug was visible now. Rather than being woven into the near black material, it was seemingly hand drawn either in white chalk or liquid pen. She couldn't tell but the result looked like a rough sketch. White lines interlocked with one another forming geometric patterns. She concluded the dominant pattern at the core was either a pentagram, or possibly a hexagram. At the centre of the pattern it looked as if two eyes were staring up at her with the bottom of a very angular face disappearing beneath Conn's midriff. Three of the candles appeared to be strategically placed at the points of specific triangles. Two further candles had fallen over, one to either side of Conn's body. Upon closer inspection the three standing candles had burned out, possibly due to the molten wax swamping the wick and extinguishing the flame. Wax pooled on the floor alongside the fallen candles, hardening and becoming one with the material they were set upon. "They must have been inadvertently knocked over, either during a struggle or when

Conn fell to the floor," she theorised aloud. Janssen nodded agreement. "This place was lucky not to go up last night."

Arcs of blood spatter were visible up the wall behind her. From the angle of trajectory, she concluded Conn must have received multiple blows for the blood to have fallen in several different directions of travel. From his position, still lowered onto his haunches, Janssen indicated above them. She angled her head to the ceiling. Here too, a bloody pattern could be seen across it.

"There's no sign of forced entry that I could see," Janssen said, Tamara lowered her gaze back to Conn. She agreed with the assessment. "That means he most likely knew his assailant."

"Or was expecting someone," she suggested. Janssen stood and crossed the room. Inspecting what he found on top of a small cabinet and an occasional table, he called her over. On the table was a pouch of tobacco, a packet of rolling papers with some sections torn from the cardboard flap. A large press and seal plastic bag, containing a significant amount of what was obviously cannabis, lay on the floor next to a lighter and an overturned ashtray. Lowering herself, she looked at the butts strewn across the carpet. They were hand-rolled with DIY cardboard filter tips. All reminiscent of the paraphernalia surrounding recreational drug use.

"This is way more than what is justifiable for personal use," she said, indicating the bag. Janssen, having donned a set of latex gloves knelt to open the cabinet alongside them. Inside he found a set of digital scales and a box containing smaller sandwich bags. Rather than touching what he'd found, he drew her attention to it.

"I reckon it is safe to say Conn was dealing?"

"If it was a dispute over a drug deal, why wouldn't his killer take the drugs?" she said, pointing to the bag on the floor. It was easily worth several hundreds of pounds. "If he was dealing, I dare say we'll find more than just that stashed around here."

"Maybe the killer realised what they'd done and panicked. From what the neighbour said, whoever left here last night did so in a hurry."

"Had the sense to cover their face with a hood though," she said quietly. "This far out, I doubt the killer walked here. I guess it's possible but they parked nearby." It was certainly usual for buyers not to park at a dealer's house. Dealers of recreational drugs were rarely in stock twenty-four seven. More often they would receive a batch and sell it through to those they knew before sourcing fresh product. This resulted in multiple visits by customers in a short period of time, then nothing until a new shipment arrived in the area. Once the call went out, too many visitors at one time risked drawing attention. Hence, customers would park up nearby and send one individual to score while the others waited in the car. "Next door didn't mention multiple arrivals though. Something's not right here."

Tamara scanned the room, searching for anything that looked out of place. Rising and walking back to Conn's body, she took another look at his injuries. The head wound was hard to examine. The thick mass of hair made it difficult to judge the extent of the injury. Observing him now from a different angle, his eyes were open, staring straight ahead. Shining the light of the torch onto Conn's face she noticed the pupil to the left eye was heavily dilated whereas the other was almost pinpoint, possibly down to the nature of the head injury, she wasn't sure. His upper torso was also saturated in blood, implying there were more injuries hidden beneath. Certainly, there was far too much blood visible for it all to be the product of a head wound. It was more likely he'd suffered a stab wound which had pierced a main artery, perhaps several.

"Looks like he suffered a laceration, possibly more than one, below the neckline of his shirt," she advised Janssen. "Do you see a potential weapon anywhere?" Janssen moved away from his vantage point near the window, taking great care where he put his feet. Tamara was well aware they were trampling a crime scene and until it had been processed, they needed to be very careful not to contaminate the scene more than they had already. If they couldn't locate a weapon, they would need to search the gardens as well as the surrounding lane for anything that may have been discarded.

"I can't see one," Janssen said. "I'll check in the kitchen, see whether it's obvious if a blade is missing."

"Good thinking," she said, reassessing Conn's position. It was a good thought. Crimes such as these committed in the heat of the moment, a spontaneous attack, would often see weapons found close to hand belonging to the victim. If the killer brought a weapon with them, it would be indicative of an element of premeditation.

The significance of what Conn was doing before he died intrigued her. The geometric patterns along with candles denoted some kind of ceremony rooted in the occult. *Was he practising some manner of ritual?* If so, he would be unlikely to be expecting multiple visitors. The state of the room suggested he was interrupted in the middle of what he was doing. Alternatively, someone joined him in his practice before the situation deteriorated. She leaned in and tried to look at Conn's hands in greater detail. Expecting to find evidence of a struggle, scuffs or scratches to the knuckles, she was surprised to find nothing of note. Although Conn was a slightly-built figure with very little muscle on his frame, he didn't strike her as the type not to fight back. Investigating further, there was no apparent damage to the right forearm or clothing, the left arm remained concealed beneath the body. Defensive wounds were absent. Everything pointed to either an unexpected attack or the high probability he was caught off guard.

"Tamara, out here!"

Leaving the room, she passed through the sitting room and into the kitchen. Janssen was outside, standing alongside Conn's car, leaning over the foot-high grass at the base of the trees lining the driveway. To reach the threshold of the door and breathe fresh air came as a relief. "What do you have?"

"Most likely the murder weapon." Moving to join him, she watched as he gently moved the grass aside to enable her to get a better look. "Looks like it was discarded as the killer left the property," he said, staring down the length of the driveway to the lane beyond. At his feet, in the grass lay a knife, or at least she thought it was a knife at first glance. Approximately twenty centimetres long, the handle was predominantly black with red trim and appeared to have rubber moulded into a comfort grip. The blade itself was unusual. Perhaps two fifths of the overall length and half-rounded, tapering down to its point. The blade was heavily blood-stained. It had dried and darkened but was clear to identify.

"That's a strange looking knife."

"I don't think it is a knife," Janssen said, kneeling and coming closer. "Look at the grit along the length of the blade. This isn't a tool for cutting with. It's more of a diamond file."

"I think you're right. My father kept something similar in his tools at home," she replied, racking her brains to remember. "It was slimmer but then again, he had different sizes to work different pieces."

"I presume he didn't use it to butcher drug dealers or witches?" Janssen said with a dry smile.

"No, he was good with cars. Loved working with anything mechanical that needed rejuvenating. Beaten up old Land Rovers were his thing. If I'm not mistaken, you would use something like this on concave surfaces."

"Does Conn come across to you as someone who tinkers with old cars?" Janssen asked, looking at the Golf. She shook her head.

"Quite the opposite. According to Niall Bradshaw's manager, Conn was a very good customer of theirs. That doesn't sound like someone who enjoys spending time under the bonnet."

"Seeing as you mentioned it. Bradshaw had an altercation

with Conn at the weekend and now the latter is dead. This is as good as a smoking gun," Janssen indicated the file.

"I'll call in and have CSI on scene to get this squared away as soon as possible. We'd better bring Niall in and see what he has to say for himself. With a bit of luck, we might be able to get his clothes and any other trace evidence before he gets shot of them. Throwing the weapon away like this doesn't suggest he was thinking clearly. Let's face it, he's not a criminal mastermind. Maybe he left fingerprints inside as well."

"Likewise, we'd better obtain a search warrant for his place of work. This will be missing from their inventory," he said, pointing at the file.

"Eric can coordinate that. At least this time we will know what we are looking for. It should be straightforward enough to confirm. I'm intrigued to know what's driving Niall Bradshaw."

"What motive would he have to do this?"

She slowly shook her head. "They were arguing about something. Niall was at work so it's fair to say Conn sought him out. When I spoke with him, Niall was adamant that he was turning his life around and looking to stay clear of trouble."

"This doesn't strike me as *staying clear of trouble*," Janssen countered, looking back at the house with a frown. "Do you think Conn might have had something over him? Our rehashing of the old case and turning up another body triggering a chain reaction of events, maybe?"

"He was passionate about his desire to stay out of prison, I'm quite certain that was genuine. Would he seriously run the risk of killing someone in order not to go back?"

"Just a thought but…" Janssen let the words hang in the air. Tamara pressed him with her expression. "What if Niall had already killed before?"

"Sophie?"

"Yeah. If Conn somehow knew… or at least suspected, then the discovery of her body would have more or less confirmed his suspicions. We know Niall was within her circle, so he had the opportunity. He might be willing to kill to keep the secret."

Tamara caught sight of Robert Beaufort, holding the net curtains aside and staring down at them from an upstairs window next door. The man's phone call proved not to be precipitous after all. "Let's find Niall and ask him. This time he'll have to be a lot more open than he was before."

CHAPTER TWENTY-NINE

PARKING UP ON NORTHGATE, a short walk from the cliff tops of Hunstanton, Tom Janssen switched off the engine. Niall Bradshaw rented a flat in a small block in the parallel St Edmunds Street. Once their requested uniform assistance arrived, they would make the arrest. Although he was certain that himself and Tamara Greave could manage him themselves, the flats had a rear entrance and the support would enable coverage of all angles in case the arrest didn't go to plan. Heavy cloud cover meant the setting sun was obscured from them as the light faded. Turning his thoughts to Bradshaw, he couldn't help but find everything slotting together too neatly. It wouldn't be the first, nor the last time a criminal's actions failed to tick a box for rational thought, though. Tamara must have read something into his expression.

"What is it, Tom? You've been quiet since we left Conn's place." Once the murder scene was delegated to the CSI team to process, there was nothing else for them to do. They'd left and come straight to detain Niall Bradshaw believing him to be the most likely suspect. A murder of this nature wouldn't stay quiet for long, word would spread like wildfire through the community and they wanted to bring Bradshaw in before it became common knowledge. That way, maybe they'd catch him off guard.

"It's probably nothing," he replied, drumming his fingers on the leather-bound steering wheel. "This isn't sitting right with me, that's all."

"Too easy?"

"Far too easy. Have you ever found a suspect so…" he let the question drop. Of course, they'd both found murderers easily enough in previous cases. Most murders were committed by friends, family or acquaintances of the victim. Often spontaneous and carried out by way of seemingly random acts of violence, the path to the culprit was easy to trace. Even so, in this case, he found it unsettling. "Bradshaw must know that we would come for him. You only spoke to him the other day."

"True," she agreed. "Unless what Conn knew could damage him more than the risk of us suspecting him as the killer."

"Yeah," he replied but even to his own ear he sounded unconvinced.

"Eric spoke to Niall's boss. He didn't show up for work this morning, didn't call in either. I'm guessing he was in some kind of a state, either too stressed or showing signs of being in a fight."

"Could be to give him time to dispose of his clothing and other evidence. He will have some idea of our processes… especially since he's been inside for five years in the greatest criminal training centres this country has to offer."

"Let's hope not," Tamara said glancing at him. The street was quiet with little passing traffic. Many of the large stone-built houses were now guest houses or B&Bs and would fill up with clientele at the weekends this close to the end of season with people choosing a short break rather than booking a full week's stay. She stifled a yawn.

"How are you finding the hotel? Sleeping okay?"

She laughed. "I could always sleep better, you know."

"Things on your mind?" he asked, leaning his head back onto the rest and taking a deep breath. He was uncomfortable with waiting around and far happier when on the move.

"You could say that, yes." Her tone suddenly became melancholic which surprised him. He noticed her absently rubbing at the middle fingers of her left hand. Just as Peter Samuels had pointed out to him the other day, she still wasn't wearing her engagement ring.

"Tell me if it's none of my business but…" she looked over to him, seeing his gaze aimed towards her left hand, she withdrew it, dropping it to her side accompanied by a nervous smile.

"I'm not sure what to say… Richard and I are at something of a crossroads. We've reached an impasse, is a good way of describing it."

"Regarding what?" he asked, sensing she might need someone to listen to her.

"What do couples disagree about the most?" Janssen blew out his cheeks. This was a subject he was well versed in.

"In my *personal* experience… money, family…"

"Children?" she asked, meeting his eye. Admittedly, he hadn't come across that one. His own marriage lasted barely three years, although they were together for closer to thirteen. He didn't know what to say, so he kept silent. Tamara turned her gaze towards the sea, just visible between the nearby buildings. "Probably something we should already have talked about before the run up to the big day."

"When is the big day anyway?" he asked, finding his attention drawn to a solitary figure rounding the corner a short distance away and approaching them, hooded and clutching a plastic carrier bag in one hand.

"A couple of months," she said, looking across at him. He acknowledged her before looking back at the approaching man. He appeared to have slowed once he was clear of the trees of

Lincoln Square, an open patch of grassland separating two parallel streets that ran down to the esplanade. He dismissed it as his overactive imagination. "Or... at least it should be... in a couple of months. I'm not sure—"

"I think that's him," Janssen said, cutting her off.

"What?" she said looking down the street. "Is it?"

"I reckon he's clocked us."

"No, he can't have—"

At that moment, the man spun on his heel and sprinted back in the direction he'd come from. Janssen started the car, putting it into first gear and flooring the accelerator. The tyres howled as they moved off, closing the distance between them rapidly. Turning the car onto Lincoln Square North, Bradshaw cut across them forcing him to swerve in order to avoid running him over and nearly collided with an oncoming vehicle. Stopping so abruptly, he stalled the car. Bradshaw passed between the trees of Lincoln Square and was now running across the open ground and putting some distance between them. Janssen restarted the car, blasting his horn in frustration as their route was blocked by the car in front whose driver glared back at him.

"Hang a left at the end of the street. See if you can get ahead and cut him off," he declared, jumping out of the car without waiting for a response and sprinting after their quarry. Bradshaw was nearly at the Cliff Parade and disappeared from sight, glancing behind him briefly as he rounded the corner. Janssen gritted his teeth, increasing his stride as he picked up the pace. As a teenager he'd taken part in athletics trials, sprints being his speciality due to both his powerful physique and length of his stride. A naturally gifted sprinter, he was confident that even with such a head start he would be able to run Bradshaw down, even though he was far from the standard he'd been in his teenage years.

Rounding the corner, he saw Bradshaw crossing to the other side of the road, still glancing over his shoulder as he ran. His gait was awkward, laboured. Janssen judged he'd already closed down a third of the distance between them. Oncoming cars sounded their displeasure at the man running between them, forcing them to brake or stop altogether. Bradshaw ran into one of the cars, striking him on the thigh but he appeared to bounce and continue running. The vehicle in question was stationary and the driver getting out of the car as Janssen ran past. Almost sensing Janssen upon him, Bradshaw ran to the edge of the road and took a blind leap over the fence running to the side of the road. Janssen knew a bowling green lay the other side and the drop was significant.

Reaching the fence himself, he peered over to see Bradshaw making his way across the green, favouring his left leg and practically dragging his right. For a second, Janssen figured he must have twisted his ankle and might give up on his flight but the thought was short lived. Bradshaw, a pained expression on his face, merely loped away. A car screeched to a halt alongside him. It was Tamara. She leaned out of the window as he turned.

"Head down there, take the first right for the promenade," he instructed her, pointing ahead before turning and clambering over the fence. He heard the sound of the engine pick up rather than seeing her leave as he dropped onto the sloping embankment below, lined with bushes and foliage, he struggled not to stumble as he pressed through to the manicured bowling green beyond. Angry voices shouted to him from the direction of the pavilion protesting his presence but he didn't look back, running across the grass and resuming his pursuit. At the far corner, a set of steps descended to the promenade along the sea front. Hunstanton wasn't large but if Bradshaw could make it past the amusement arcade and on towards the fairground, he could very easily disappear into the maze of side streets in the lower town that he wasn't as familiar with. He was determined not to allow that to happen.

Descending the steps to the promenade at speed, people were

forced to take evasive action. He was grateful, such was his momentum there was little chance he could avoid them. There were angry exclamations but Janssen only had eyes for Bradshaw. He was visibly slowing now, barely thirty feet from him and stumbling forward as he tried desperately to escape him. This only inspired Janssen more and he pushed himself harder. His own breathing was ragged and both his legs burned with the build-up of lactic acid from the intensity of the chase. Ahead of them, the slip road down from above opened into the small car park and on cue, Tamara's vehicle came into view, tyres squealing as she brought it to a standstill.

Bradshaw pulled up, presumably having caught sight of her. He turned, saw Janssen approaching and then looked from side to side. To one side was the cliff face, steep and impenetrable, to the other was the sea. He leaned on the sea wall, made up of two-foot-thick concrete, and peered over the edge most likely considering it an avenue of escape. The tide was incoming, already driving against the wall several metres below them. He chose not to slow his advance. Bradshaw's horrified expression as he realised what was about to happen crossed his face a moment before Janssen hammered into him. The two men slammed against the wall before falling to the ground in a heap with Janssen on top. Bradshaw exhaled a shrill shriek as Janssen's body weight forced the air from his lungs. Quickly flipping him over, Janssen pressed him face down with a hand on the back of his head whilst securing an arm behind his back. Tamara appeared alongside him and knelt, reaching for her handcuffs. Horrified onlookers stood nearby with expressions of shock or curiosity.

"I haven't done anything!" Bradshaw shouted before protesting further as his wrists were bound behind him.

"Is that so?" Janssen stated, looking around for the carrier bag he'd been carrying. It was nowhere to be seen. "Then why were you running? Where's the bag, Niall?"

"What bag?"

"Okay," he replied, standing up and taking his weight off of Bradshaw's back. With one hand on the collar at the scruff of his neck and the other on the cuffs, Janssen hauled him to his feet. Bradshaw was still breathing heavily, sweaty, red-faced and full of protest. Looking to Tamara, he flicked his head back along the promenade. "He must have dropped it back there somewhere."

"It was my dinner, that's all!" Bradshaw stated.

"You didn't make it into work today," Tamara told him, inclining her head to one side.

"I felt sick," he replied, seemingly having been able to gather himself.

"You don't look sick."

"What are you arresting me for anyway? I'll have you done for harassment."

"You're not the first to say that," Janssen said, marching him towards the car. "We'll start with littering and take it from there, shall we?"

Reaching their car, a liveried police van came into view driving down the hill. He signalled them and they pulled up alongside him. Handing Bradshaw over to the constables, he watched as he was placed in the cage in the back and the doors closed. Leaving them to transport Bradshaw back to the station, he returned to Tamara and together they set off along the route of the chase to search for the discarded bag. The primary concern was that he'd thrown the bag over the wall and into the sea, greatly reducing their chance of finding it.

"What were you about to say before... in the car?" he asked her, as they picked through the undergrowth to either side of the steps up towards the bowling green.

"Oh... nothing important." She moved away from him, focussing on the search. He wasn't sure her response was truthful. Choosing not to press it, he ascended the last few steps and cast an eye across the bowling green. As he half-expected, there was nothing there. A white carrier bag would have stood out. Several aggrieved looking members of the club softened their positions when he identified what they were looking for, confirming they had neither seen Bradshaw discard anything, nor had they retrieved it themselves. The only conclusion was the one he'd initially countenanced. The bag had been thrown into the sea.

CHAPTER THIRTY

NIALL BRADSHAW SAT QUIETLY as Tamara Greave entered the room, nodding to Tom Janssen who was already seated across from their chief suspect in Conn's murder with his arms folded in front of him. Already fingerprinted and a swab of his DNA taken, his clothes were also removed and sent away for immediate forensic analysis. Robert Beaufort's description of a hooded figure leaving Conn's house loosely chimed with Niall's description. Eric was leading a search of the premises where he worked in the hope of establishing where the murder weapon came from. Entering the interview room, she was confident that any evidence placing Niall at the scene of the murder would force him into a confession. All they were missing was a credible motive.

Niall's white coveralls rustled as he adjusted his seating position, rubbing at an itch on the end of his nose with his right forefinger. His eyes tracked her movements as she pulled a chair out and sat down alongside Janssen, his stare focussed and direct. Placing a thick polythene bag containing the murder weapon on the table, she saw his eyes drift across towards it but he didn't comment on it.

"This is bloody ridiculous," Niall stated, not for the first time since his detention.

"I'm afraid the reality says the opposite," she replied, indicating for Janssen to start the recording. They'd already decided she would lead the interview and Janssen would only speak if he thought it pertinent to do so. They identified themselves, logging the date and time. Niall crossed his arms, shaking his head with incredulity. "Right, let's start from the beginning. Where were you last night?"

Niall took a deep breath, exhaling in a sigh. "At home. All night, alone. Next question."

"You didn't go out at all?" He shook his head slowly. "Funny. We spoke to your neighbours and several of them thought you did. When you're home you have a consistent habit of playing music or having your television on too loud."

"Not loudly enough to make it a crime though. I'm a reformed character." His response bordered on a sneer. Meeting her eye, she waited. Moments later his shoulders dropped and he broke the eye contact. "No! I didn't go out. Like I said earlier, I was ill. I was in my bed before eight."

"Someone matching your description was seen running away from Mike Collyer's flat, you will know him as Conn, late yesterday evening. Conn was found dead this morning."

"Tragic as that is," Niall replied in earnest, "it has nothing to do with me."

"So, we're not going to find your fingerprints inside the house… nor on the murder weapon itself, a metal file commonly found in workshop tool kits?"

"Now, listen here," Niall sat forward in his seat. Tamara held her ground and found barely a foot separating the two of them across the desk. "I wasn't there, I've never been near Docking."

"How did you know he lived in Docking?" Janssen asked, maintaining his fixed expression. Niall sat back and shrugged.

"I know Conn, I'll freely admit that but I didn't have any involvement in his death."

Tamara watched him, despite the confrontational demeanour

she saw something else in him, a vulnerability. No, it was fear. She was almost certain but fear of what? "Tell us about your relationship with him."

"*Relationship*?" he scoffed. "There wasn't one."

"Then how do you know him?"

"From years ago... he was tight with some of the group."

"During your activist days?" she asked. He nodded. "Were you friends?"

"No, no way. Conn was a weirdo, if you ask me. I don't know what the others saw in him."

"Which others?"

Niall looked to the ceiling, Tamara noting his eyes went up and to the right. Remembering what Eric said about accessing memory, she smiled internally. At this moment, Niall was searching for the truth. "River, Sophie... Les... probably a couple of others as well. I can't remember everyone. It was a long time ago. They were all into that rubbish he spouted."

"Rubbish?"

"Yeah, the harnessing of earth's energy and all that guff. We all shared a love of nature and the environment but all the hocus pocus was not my thing at all," Niall explained, reaching for a small plastic cup of water. Lifting it, he sipped the liquid slowly before putting it down again. She thought she saw his hand tremble a little as he released his grip.

"Why did he seek you out last weekend?"

"Did he?" Niall countered.

"You and he had an argument at your work. Something you failed to mention to me when we first spoke." Niall's eyes narrowed, his expression resembling a scowl.

"I didn't see it as relevant."

"Well, it's relevant now he's dead, so can you tell us what it was about?"

Niall put both hands to his face, pressing them against the bridge of his nose and running them across either side of his face, spreading his fingers out through his hair. Looking down at the desk, his hands met once more at the back of his head. There he rubbed the back of his neck before snapping his head upright and drawing a deep breath. "Conn was a real piece of work. You're right, he came to see me. There was nothing wrong with his car. He said a body had been found, in the dunes out by Wells."

"Why would that interest you?"

"He told me it was Sophie."

"How did he know that? We've only just been able to identify her in the last day or so?"

"Something about the jewellery she was wearing..." Niall said, shaking his head, "he was certain it was her. He was convincing."

"Why tell you?"

Niall laughed but it was bitter and without genuine humour. "Because that was Conn, always looking for an angle."

"To what end?"

"Money... what else? Everything he did was geared towards money. This spiritual... guru... personality he created was just that, a choreographed routine. I don't know if he believed all that mumbo jumbo," Niall waved his hands in the air in a circular motion for emphasis, "but it was always about exploitation. He wanted me to give him money. Despite his threats, I had the impression he was pretty desperate."

"What makes you think that?"

Niall shrugged. "I spent five years in prison surrounded by people I didn't know actually existed in this world. You learn a lot about humanity on the inside. I know desperation when I see it... those rules apply in the real world just as much."

"How did he think he could get money from you?" she asked, intrigued.

"As I said, he knew me from before. He knew where I came from, or the others told him, I don't know." Niall sniffed loudly, then ran his tongue across his bottom lip. "I guess he figured where he failed last time, this time would be different."

"Last time?"

"After the fire… at the clinic."

"Go on."

"It was always a source of fascination to Conn how I was able to be at the clinic protesting all the time. Others came and went but me… I was the stereotypical middle-class kid in that my family were well off. I was something of a rebel, not wanting to fit into their harvest suppers and Sunday morning services… you know what I mean?" Tamara could relate. Not to the religion as such but her own upbringing was far removed from the experience of those who struggled. "My family tolerated my passions. One day they must have figured I'd grow out of it, come back into the fold, go off to university… whatever."

"Conn knew all of this?"

Niall nodded emphatically. "Oh, yeah. He saw me as a cash cow, tried to edge his way in using the girls but I saw him coming a mile away. I always knew he was a two-bit player. So," he took a deep breath, "when he came to me and demanded money, threatening to push your lot in my direction for the fire, I laughed in his face." Niall cut a rueful smile. "You should have seen the look on his face when I did. It was a picture. I don't think he was used to that reaction and certainly not coming from a posh boy such as me."

"Are you saying he was attempting to blackmail you? Forgive me if this sounds far-fetched."

"Damn right it does! I thought so too… until you lot knocked on my door," Niall countered, resting the palms of his hands flat on the table in front of him and staring into her eyes. "Even then, I didn't put it together. Not until you found my fingerprints at the scene. Then I knew… he wasn't bluffing."

"You allege that Conn planted evidence at the clinic to frame you for the arson?"

Niall shrugged. "How else did our prints get inside?"

"Maybe because you broke in and set the fire," Janssen concluded, drawing a dark look from the accused.

"I was nowhere near the clinic that night."

"A defence rejected by the investigators and the jury," she said, glancing at her notes. "You failed to produce anything to corroborate that. Nor could any of the others."

"That's because they were at the camp outside. The only people who could corroborate my account were those who were also charged. Every single one of them said I wasn't there."

"We've been here before though, haven't we Niall? What about last weekend?"

Niall blew out his cheeks in a gesture of exasperation. "He alleged I murdered Sophie... or at least, he could make you believe I did. Asked me how I would feel about another stretch, only this time it would be far longer."

"Did you kill Sophie?" Janssen asked.

"No! What possible reason would I have? And don't give me that rubbish about an innocent man has nothing to fear because I lost five years of my life, as well as all contact with my family, despite *being an innocent man.* Conn told me I should think about what happened the last time I knocked him back... I've thought about nothing else since. I couldn't pay him off this time even if I wanted to... and yes, I'm very scared of him."

Tamara tried to gauge his credibility. Despite the implausibility of the tale, there was that passion shining through once again. The simple fact he turned down legal representation got her thinking. Someone with his experience of the system should know he was risking a lot by doing so, with an ex-con suspected of a serious offence, this was practically unheard of. Either he knew they would find nothing to tie him to the murder or... perhaps... he was telling the truth.

"You do realise you are describing an almost perfect motivation for you to kill him, don't you?"

He met her gaze, she figured he was assessing her just as she was him. "Yes, I see that. However, I didn't do it. Unless, of course, he planted evidence at the scene of his own murder."

"Who else has a reason to kill him?"

"I have *no idea*," Niall replied, "but I'll tell you this, if he was murdered then I don't doubt he deserved it and I hope he's sitting in the hell of his own making!"

Tamara reached for the evidence bag and pushed it across the table in front of him. "Recognise this?"

Niall's eyes flicked downwards but only briefly before coming back to hers. "No."

"It was discarded at the murder scene, presumably by the killer. We have useable prints lifted from the handle. But they won't be yours, no?"

"I've never seen that before in my life."

"We have officers combing over your workplace as we speak. If we find a matching set and your prints on this," she indicated the file, "or in Conn's house, you know what that means, don't you?"

"Yeah. That I've been fitted up once again."

"You're still not telling me the truth, though, Niall. Darren Robinson confirmed to us how he supplied you with the information needed to circumvent the security system at his father's clinic. Also, that he was the source of your financial information you alluded to the last time we spoke." Niall relaxed in his seat which was not the reaction she expected.

"Yes, that's true. Darren had a conscience, unlike his father."

"And yet, you maintain you didn't break into the clinic that night."

"I do, yes," he confirmed. "Why would we do that? There was no need. Darren confirmed the business was failing. Another six months and Shaun Robinson would have folded. *Why* would we risk everything to do something *so stupid*? Ask yourself, it makes no sense."

"Then why ask Darren how to get in?"

"That was ages before! We talked about upping the ante, really going for some drastic course of action to make a statement but we ruled it out. We weren't a bunch of nutters... just people with a conscience, trying to make a difference."

"I'll humour you for a moment. Who else knew about this information, about how to get into the building?"

He thought about it for a moment before answering. "Me, obviously. Not all of the group, River, Sophie, Les…" he paused and she had the feeling he was holding back. "Maybe a couple of others. I don't know for certain."

Tamara chanced a sideways glance towards Janssen. She really wanted to know what he thought but his expression was unreadable. He doubted Niall's role in the murder from the outset. What she would give to know exactly what he was thinking now. "What was in the bag you discarded earlier today when we arrested you?" He glared at her. This was his chance. "You want me to believe you, Niall, then you've got to give me something truthful to work with or… let's face it, you'll be going back to prison." He glanced at the machine, recording every word spoken. "Give me something, Niall."

He shook his head in resignation. "Look, it's hard when you get out. Particularly when everyone believes you got someone killed, intentionally or otherwise. Making a fresh start with that around your neck… is hard, you know? You don't earn much changing tyres and exhausts."

"What was in the bag?"

"A bit of recreational…"

"You are talking about drugs, let's be clear about it?" He confirmed it with a slight bob of the head. "I need you to confirm it for the benefit of the recording, Niall."

"Yes!" he stated through gritted teeth. "Nothing else. I don't want to go back to prison. Do you blame me?"

She didn't reply, merely glanced at Janssen indicating to stop the recording. They concluded the interview and she scooped up the murder weapon and left the room. A uniformed constable was despatched to return Niall to the cells while they headed for ops. Eric was waiting for them. Immediately, she knew he was itching to tell them how the search of the garage went.

"The garage was a bust," he said emphatically. "All of their equipment was present and accounted for. What's more, their franchise has a contract to use a particular manufacturers kit and this brand isn't on the approved list." Normally, such information would have made her heart sink but on this occasion the revelation had quite the opposite effect.

"Have we heard back from scenes of crime?" she asked Janssen, who was already at his keyboard. She waited patiently as he went through his emails, recognising multiple lines of red in the inbox. Tom was efficient but, he too, struggled to keep up to date. He opened a link, scanning the contents before turning to face her.

"Niall's prints have not been found at the scene," he inclined his head to one side, "nor were they found on the murder weapon. There is a distinctive set lifted from the handle but they don't match any already in the system." He sounded disappointed. "Dr Williams has counted seventeen individual stab wounds, along with the single blow to the head. In conclusion, she describes it as a frenzied attack. I would argue that makes this either very personal, or carried out by someone with an emotional attachment to the victim."

"Well, that fits Niall to a tee... what did you make of him in interview?"

Janssen's brow furrowed, he appeared to choose his words carefully. "Killers who I've interviewed before react very differently to the way he came across. Niall didn't try to dominate the room, seize control of the conversation. He got emotional you could hear it in the inflections in his tone. Cold killers will often detach, seek to assert their authority and speak in a monotone pitch. If I had to say one way or the other right now, I just don't see it." He met her eye. "I really don't."

Frustrated, Tamara perched herself on the side of a desk thinking through his observations. "If Niall is telling us the truth, about Conn's familiarity with blackmail at least, it stands to reason he makes something of a habit of it."

"Funny you should say that," Eric interrupted her. "I was just going to mention that pathology took Conn's prints and I ran them through the database. The results were really interesting."

"I like interesting, Eric. What do you have?" she asked.

"Well, Mike Collyer is dead for starters."

"I know that, Eric. We found him after all." She cast a sideways glance at Janssen, who smiled.

"Yes, but it turns out the prints taken don't belong to Mike Collyer. I went further back and found he died at the age of three," Eric replied, handing her a sheet of paper. It was a copy of a death certificate. "He was born with leukaemia. Three years later it proved fatal."

"Then who was Conn?"

"Harry Sutcliffe," Eric announced, reading his notes. "A convicted fraudster, burglar and onetime, low end drug dealer. He's served time on three occasions, two for fraud and a short stint for intent to supply. Nothing in the past seven years though. He dropped off the radar."

"And now we know why," she concluded. Eric was hesitant, she sensed it. "Is there more?"

"Yeah... but you're not going to like it. Sutcliffe was a registered informant... here, with Norfolk Constabulary."

She exhaled, seeing Janssen drop his head from the corner of her eye. "You're right, Eric. I don't like that at all."

"What do you want me to do?" the DC asked.

"I want you to pull his file and find out who his handler was." She looked to Janssen. "Something tells me I'm not going to like that either."

The phone rang on Janssen's desk and he answered it. A brief conversation followed. Putting the phone down, he stood up. "Someone's asking for me in the lobby. I'll be right back." She watched him leave. What had looked like the simplest of cases to solve was proving to be altogether something else entirely. For the moment, she was at a loss as to how they should proceed.

CHAPTER THIRTY-ONE

JANSSEN ENTERED the lobby of the police station. Aside from the clerk on the counter, only one other person was present. For a moment, he failed to recognise the welcoming smile of the young woman waiting for him. As soon as she spoke, he remembered.

"Inspector Janssen," she said, offering her hand as he approached.

"Kelly..." he struggled for the surname.

"Donovan," she finished as he shook her hand warmly with an apologetic expression, feeling slightly embarrassed at the gap in his memory. "We have only met the once and it was brief."

"Even so, my apologies. What is it I can do for you? If you're looking for a statement on the inquiry—"

"No, no. It's not that. I have someone I think you need to speak with."

He was intrigued. Her tone was sombre, the smile dissipating into a concerned, serious expression. She glanced around nervously, as if fearful of being overheard. "Can we take a walk?" Gesturing for her to take the lead, they left the station together.

Outside, he needed to shield his eyes from the glare of the

sun. The time spent in the windowless interview room was in stark contrast to the outdoors. He didn't mind. The break was refreshing and much needed. The breeze felt cool on his skin. The journalist walking alongside him was hesitant. Whether it was a result of her inexperience, for it was obvious to him the first time they met she was new to her role, or that she couldn't articulate the words he was unsure. For the moment, he gave her the space she needed sensing it was important.

"I've found this murder case captivating," Kelly said after some time, looking up at him. She was a slightly built young woman, in her mid-twenties he guessed. "The story has been passed onto a senior correspondent... but... I've still been following it." Now he understood her reticence. She was nosing around in a story that was no longer hers.

"Why did you ask to see me?"

"I interned during the holidays in every year of my degree, that's how I landed this job straight out of university."

"You read media?" he asked, making polite conversation to put her at ease.

"No, criminology," she said, moving her hair away from her face, battling against the strength of the breeze. "I wanted to be at the heart of criminal investigations and that meant joining the police or journalism."

"Why choose the latter?"

"The investigative process enthrals me... I'm not so sure about managing drunks on a Saturday night," she grinned. "That's probably why I couldn't let this one pass me by. I might never get this close to a murder inquiry for years."

"Let's hope so," he countered. Her gaze narrowed. "From the victims' point of view." She nodded, appreciating the sentiment. "I presume you're here because you found something. Am I right?"

"Not something... *someone*." She had his full attention, encouraging her to continue with a flick of his eyes. "I wrote my dissertation on the life cycle of a serial killer. This was too tempting an opportunity not to apply my conclusions to it."

"Sounds like an interesting read," Janssen replied, "if a little grim."

"Thirty-four thousand words," she told him. "Much of it will be telling you how to suck eggs, I'm sure. The body unearthed in the storm got me thinking though. Serial killers learn their trade just as the rest of us do. They aren't hatched as a perfect killer, forensically aware and able to commit murders at random."

"No. They build up, both in the level of their crimes as well as developing their MO."

"Exactly. Which is why I thought this might be such a case. After all, to kill a young girl and bury her in such a prominent location, where she wasn't found for years, struck me as a bold enterprise. Far too bold for someone to do straight out of the gate." The view was one he'd already considered himself. Not that he voiced the thought, conscious he was still talking to a journalist. "So, it got me thinking. I visited the archive, looking at as many of the missing persons cases around the time you think she was killed. There were a few. More than I'd anticipated." She met his eye, possibly seeking confirmation. He didn't comment, although they'd done similarly. "There didn't seem to be any major investigation into them at the time."

Janssen shrugged, although he certainly didn't mean to be dismissive of her. "It's a sad fact people go missing all the time. Mostly, that's a decision of their own choosing and, presumably you've been diligent, there was no indication of violence, no body. Precious little to base an investigation on."

"True enough," she conceded. They walked on. Some distance from the station now, they'd taken a route away from the main road and were now on the edge of the fields rolling out towards the coast. Janssen was well aware he would need to get back soon. A man passed by them, walking his dog. Once he was out of earshot, Janssen stopped, turning to face her.

234 J M DALGLIESH

"Are you going to tell me who you found, as well as why I need to speak with them?"

"I'm toying with requesting a *quid pro quo* style arrangement." She chewed her lower lip as she spoke. There had to be a story in this, arguably a big one.

"If it's really worth my while, I'm sure we can come up with something. Who is it you found?"

"Tracy Bartlett." Janssen was momentarily stunned, Kelly read his expression accurately. "And I think you'll want to hear what she has to say."

"How did…" the words dropped away. Despite their searches, Tracy hadn't appeared anywhere and they'd looked.

"There was an interview in the archives with a neighbour of hers, she mentioned family who moved away years before. I started digging. It took some doing. Tracy had an aunt who divorced from the family and returned to her native Lancashire, along with her maiden name. I took a punt."

"You found her?"

"Yes. The aunt was unwell, needed looking after. The timing was somewhat fortuitous you might say. It worked out well for all concerned. Tracy has been there ever since."

"Until you got in touch?"

"At first, she didn't want to know," Kelly explained. "She was aggressive but I guessed it was a front, concealing her fear. I let it drop, gave her a few days. We've been talking most days since last week, building up a relationship, you know?" She looked at him. He thought it was a look seeking acceptance or praise. "When the news of the murder broke yesterday… she called me. I was surprised." They hadn't released Conn's name officially yet but locals had already identified him to the press as often was the case. On this occasion, most likely his neighbour Robert Beaufort. "She wanted to talk. I dare say, she needed to."

"Can you give me her address or contact number?" he asked.

"I can go one better than that, Inspector. Tracy drove down through the night," she said, turning her head to the left and indicating further along the path. A lone female stood a short distance away. Her hands were clasped together in front of her and she looked awkward, out of place. "I convinced her to speak with you. She insisted we do it this way, otherwise she threatened to run again. Only this time, she was adamant we wouldn't find her."

Kelly walked them towards her. To Janssen, she appeared agitated, shifting her weight between her feet. As they approached, her eyes moved furtively in every direction but his and he realised she was vulnerable. He would need to tread carefully.

"Hello, Tracy," he said softly, keeping a respectful distance. Aware of his stature, a physical presence such as his could be a curse at times, as much as it was a gift at others. She was tense, he could see the whites of her knuckles as she stood before him wringing her hands. "My name is Tom. I'm a policeman."

"I know who you are," Tracy all but whispered, allowing herself to meet his eye for a second before glancing away. "Kelly told me you haven't been around here for very long."

He glanced in Kelly's direction, inclining his head off to one side. "I've not worked here for long, it's true. Although, I grew up near here on the coast." He took in the surrounding landscape. She followed his gaze. "Seems a long time ago now, mind you."

"I haven't been back in six years… and it feels like yesterday to me."

"Would you like to walk with me?" he asked, tilting his head to one side. She nodded and they moved off at a gentle pace.

"I'll wait for you here," Kelly said, placing a reassuring hand on Tracy's forearm. The woman replied with a brief nod. Janssen smiled his gratitude.

"I don't know where to begin," Tracy said, stuttering as she inhaled.

"Take your time," he told her. "You can have all the time you need." She smiled weakly in thanks. Her eyes appeared hollow and sunken. Dark rings hung beneath them indicating a lack of sleep more than just from the previous night. Her general appearance and demeanour were such that he saw her as deeply troubled.

"It took a lot for me to come back, you know." She flicked a glance in his direction. "Right now, I wish I hadn't."

"Why did you come back?"

"I had to… years too late, if I'm honest. It is difficult to explain."

"Why not start with how you came to leave."

She laughed. It was rueful. "I left because I made a choice. I decided I wanted to live."

"That sounds…" the words tailed off.

"Melodramatic?"

He was embarrassed to admit it but then he remembered her background, the recorded visit and suspected domestic violence.

"It's okay. I hid it so well for such a long time, I'm not surprised people didn't believe me when I eventually managed to speak of it."

"Your boyfriend?"

"Yes," she replied, holding up her left hand, palm up, and spreading her fingers wide. Or at least, she tried, three of them were twisted awkwardly reminiscent of an arthritic condition. "He broke my fingers once… putting my hand against a door frame and slamming it shut." Janssen winced at her recounting of the memory. "He wouldn't let me go to the hospital… I had to bandage them myself the next day once I woke up from the beating I had to go with it." She caught him looking at her, misinterpreting his expression. "You think I should have called you… or left, don't you?"

He shook his head, genuinely, those were the last thoughts in his head. "If only it were that easy."

"Yes, if only," she agreed. "Looking back, I'm surprised he allowed me to work. Not that I got to keep any of what I earned. I guess he needed the money as he didn't earn much himself."

"How did it come about that you did leave?"

"Oh… I wish I could say it was me finding an inner strength, my courage… but it wasn't." They walked on, with the fields to either side of them they seemed so far away from the realities of the world. The scene was peaceful. Tracy continued, "I met someone through a mutual friend. He was different, kind and gentle. I was a bit messed up as you can imagine. Don't get me wrong, my boyfriend could be charming and funny. It wasn't a totally oppressive existence. I wouldn't have been able to live like that, if it was. I went looking for something and I found the others." She paused, seemingly weighing up her next words carefully. "We were an unusual collection of souls. All of us were in search of a different life. Well, I say *all of us*, but maybe not Sophie."

"Sophie Maddox? Presumably, the others were Lesley Abbott and River Malloy?"

"Yes, a really dysfunctional band we were. Lesley was trying to find her peace with the world having lost her family. River… she was missing something in her life. Her mother was a controlling influence, I could relate, and she didn't have a father around as far as I could tell. She hung off of every one of Sophie's words."

"It was common knowledge they were a couple?"

"Amongst us, absolutely."

"What about Sophie herself? What was she looking for?"

"That, I couldn't tell you. I had a lot of time for her but she didn't let anyone particularly close, not even River. She struck me as the selfish type. If you no longer suited, she would drop you without a word. Just like she did with poor Darren. You know about them?"

"Yes, we know that's how the group knew how to access the clinic. How did you come to have an interest in the occult?"

"You'll probably laugh."

"I assure you I won't." She looked into his eyes. He saw a

sparkle in hers, making them appear more youthful than the rest of her face which seemed older than its years.

"At first, it seemed off the wall. Talking of energy and spirits... but I liked it. Wicca seemed to make sense out of all the chaos... and then there were the girls. The four of us and Conn. He was our spiritual guide, or at least that's what he called himself."

"Is it Conn you were speaking of before?" She shook her head.

"No. Conn was intense, charismatic. To a troubled group of women at any rate. With hindsight, he was dangerous. I should have seen it. If there was anyone who should have been able to see danger, let's face it, it was me! I'm talking about Niall."

"Bradshaw?"

"Yes," she said, her face lighting up. "He was so passionate and caring. Quite the opposite of what I was used to. Lee wasn't the first abusive relationship I was involved in, you see. I don't know how but he knew what I faced, saw through all the lies and excuses for the bruising and no-shows when we all agreed to meet. I think he was always looking out for those who couldn't help themselves. I reckon that's why he led the protests at the clinic. One thing led to another."

"You and he were in a relationship?"

"Yes. I believe he thought he could save me. In a way he did, to be fair."

"How so?"

"Niall wanted to approach Lee, have it out with him but he didn't know Lee like I did. He would have killed him and probably me as well. I managed to make him understand the danger. We had to keep things a secret. No one was to know. It was the only way... maybe one day in the future we could get away from here. Niall wouldn't leave until the job was done at the clinic. After that, we would leave. Start again."

"What happened?"

"Conn happened," she said, exhaling deeply. "He found out.

I don't know how, approached Niall making all kind of demands. He was no better than Lee when it came down to it."

"Conn looked to blackmail you and Niall?"

"Yes. He thought Niall was an easy mark. A liberal rich kid, out to save the world. Something of a soft touch. He was soft, Niall. Don't get me wrong, he had an inner strength to be admired but he was something of a bleeding heart. I shouldn't say that as a negative, without him, I might not be here."

"Niall didn't pay, did he?"

"No, he was certain Conn was all bluff but I knew better. There was much more to that man than he ever let on. When Niall was arrested for the arson at the clinic, I knew... I knew Conn had gone through with his threat."

"The night of the fire at the clinic where were you?" he asked, taking great care to avoid any accusation in his tone.

"I wasn't there, if that's what you are asking? Nor was Niall."

"How can you be certain?"

"Because he was with me," she replied, staring him straight in the eye, unflinching. "It was the arson that spurred me into running. With Niall arrested I realised all that I feared about Conn was true. He was capable of anything. I hid for a day or so, in my car. I drove around places, keeping out of sight. I tried to contact Lesley because she wasn't named in the papers as one of those arrested but I couldn't find her. As a last resort I called Sophie but she'd disappeared as well. I figured she was scared of being arrested and took off. So, I did the same. I knew roughly where my aunt lived. I was desperate. She was all I had and I knew Lee wouldn't find me there. Had I stayed Conn would have seen to me too. Like I told you before, I chose to live."

"So, why have you come back now?"

She took a deep breath before pursing her lips and contemplating her response. Turning to him, he saw tears brimming in her eyes. "I thought I could run away from this, forget about everything and leave it all behind. Even though I was safe, and have been for years now, it's still here." She placed a closed fist at the centre of her chest, her eyes narrowing. "I can still feel the knot every morning when I wake up. When Kelly found me, saying they'd discovered a body in the dunes... I knew it had to be either Sophie or Lesley. I had to come back. I have to make this right."

CHAPTER THIRTY-TWO

SHAUN ROBINSON SAT at his desk scanning through the emails in his inbox. This past week had unsettled him, waking in the early hours every morning with a knot in the centre of his chest. Regardless of how little sleep he'd managed overnight, he found the need to rise in spite of his growing exhaustion. The change in his manner along with keeping odd hours did not escape the attention of his wife, leading to yet more questions. Searching questions that he felt disinclined to answer. At least in the office there was a little respite. The phone on his desk beeped to signify an incoming call from the front desk. His chest tightened as it did every time the phone rang. Hopefully, this would pass.

"Yes, Camille. What is it?"

"I have Detective Inspector Janssen on the line for you."

Why was he calling again, so soon? What could he possibly want? The thoughts came at him in quick succession, repeating themselves over and over. *What should I say?*

"Mr Robinson?" Camille's professional tone cut through, edged with curiosity. Even the receptionist was aware of the change in him. "Should I put him through?"

"Yes... yes, of course. Please do," he silently chastised himself. He never spoke like that. The familiar echo from the lobby changed and he could hear road noise in the background. "Inspector Janssen," he said with a grin, hoping to convey informality, "what can I do for you?"

"I'm sorry to trouble you, I won't keep you long."

"No trouble at all, none at all."

"It's just a courtesy call, really. I thought it only fair to keep you up to speed with developments. We've had something of a development in the case and it ties in with the arson at your clinic six years ago."

"Really, how so?" The surprise in his tone was genuine, although he managed to internalise the sense of alarm.

"You'll understand that I can't give you the specific details of an ongoing inquiry but, bearing in mind the damage it did to your business back then, I figured it only fair to give you the heads up."

"That's great, much appreciated," he sat back in his chair, gently chewing his lower lip as he considered pressing for more detail. "Tell me, and I'll understand if you can't... I thought that was all settled and the culprits were all jailed. Were there others... that no one knew about?"

"As I said, I can't go into the specifics... however, it would appear that the original investigation team weren't aware of a number of factors in play. There appears to have been some manipulation of the evidence. I'm sorry to be so vague."

"That's no problem, Inspector," he said, thinking through the potential permutations. "What does this mean for the original investigation, trial and so on?"

"Too early to say, I'm afraid." The detective was amiable, just as focussed as when they'd spoken before, only this time, he didn't leave him with an underlying sense of dread after each comment. "The developments are more to do with the police investigation rather than anything directly related to your business. I think you should be prepared for the eventuality that this is going to make front page news again. We are preparing for it ourselves. I'm just glad I wasn't around at the time. If I was on the original team, then I'd be... well, I've said too much already. Suffice it to say, arrests are imminent, so I thought you and Darren would want to be aware."

"I appreciate your candour, Inspector. I'll have a word with Darren... the cryptic nature of what you're saying means we'll, no doubt, be on tenterhooks waiting to see what was going on."

"I dare say you will be, Mr Robinson. I'll be in touch in due course once we've finalised exactly what will happen next."

Shaun spun his chair slowly to face the window, looking out across the site and into the trees beyond. The constriction of his chest was such that a sharp pain stabbed at him with every inhalation. "Thank you for the call, Inspector. Very decent of you." The line went dead and he held the earpiece of the receiver to his chin momentarily before slowly placing it down. *What was it they could have found?* The answer didn't come easily to mind. As far as he was aware, the original investigation was watertight. If not, how was nothing said at trial? Reaching back to his desk for his mobile phone, he scrolled through his contacts. With his thumb hanging over the green button, he hesitated before initiating the connection. The call was answered almost immediately with a curt greeting.

"I thought we agreed you wouldn't call this number again."

"Yes, yes, I know but there's been a development." There was almost silence at the other end but he could still hear the familiar rattle of breathing. "They're looking into the arson again." He waited, acutely aware of his growing agitation.

"I don't see how that's the case... I suppose it is possible."

"I thought it was all tied off at your end. An arrest is about to be made. How can this be poss—"

"How exactly did you come by this information?" The tone was accusatory, curious, although bordering on dismissive.

"Janssen just called to let me know. Not the details, you understand."

"Did he?" Nothing more was forthcoming and once again, Shaun found himself listening to the slow rasp coming to his ear while he waited. The moment dragged, so much so that he almost regretted making the call in the first place.

"What should we do?" The trepidation in his voice made him sound pitiful, he hated it. "Do you think we should meet?"

"Yes. I think you're right, we need to talk about this... face to face."

"Where? The club?"

"Yes. Half an hour. Wait outside."

"Should we—" The question was never completed as the line disconnected. Dropping the mobile onto his desk, Shaun scratched at the top of his head while a sense of relief came over him.

Switching off his monitor, he stood up, slipped his mobile into his pocket and put on his blazer. Leaving the office and walking down the hall he passed several members of staff but spoke to none of them. Once in the lobby, he approached Camille on the front desk. She smiled at him warmly, always fastidiously presented, always professional. "Camille, have the rest of the day's appointments rescheduled please."

"Yes, Mr Robinson..." she hesitated.

"What is it?"

"Mr Sheldon, your two o'clock, is already here," she whispered, leaning towards him and indicating to the seating area behind him with her eyes. He glanced over his shoulder, making eye contact with the bespectacled salesman sitting on the other side of the lobby.

"Make something up," he replied with no attempt to ensure he wasn't overheard. Leaving the building, he quickened his pace walking to his car. Unlocking the Jaguar, he took off his blazer and threw it onto the passenger seat before getting in. The engine started and the radio kicked in on his favoured station. A smile came to his face. They could manage this, he was certain. Reversing out of his space, he set off for the golf course. At this hour, the traffic would be light and he was confident of making good time.

A blue Vauxhall caught his eye in the rear-view mirror. It seemed to be matching his speed, maintaining more or less the same distance regardless of whether he accelerated or slowed down. That was unusual. Most of the time, he found himself to be the quickest driver on the roads and very few drivers seemed bothered about stopping distances these days. Taking the next left, a familiar shortcut along a narrow lane to pick up the coast road leading all the way to the golf club this side of Sheringham, he looked for the Vauxhall and was surprised to see it follow. His new found optimism dissipated to be replaced by concern.

The lane was single track, running for a quarter of a mile before opening up and joining the coastal road. Intentionally not indicating his direction, he watched in his mirror as the car approached coming to a stop behind him. Two men were inside. He didn't recognise either. They were sharing a joke about something. Checking in both directions, the way was clear and he pulled out to the right. Accelerating away, he watched the Vauxhall closely as it indicated and turned left, heading in the opposite direction. Smiling at his own foolish paranoia, Shaun increased the volume via the steering wheel controls and eyed the road ahead. A train passed by him on the left, the line running parallel to the road on the approach to Sheringham. Between them and the sea lay the golf course and at the thought of the coming meeting, nerves returned.

Hitting the outskirts of the town, he took the first left and cut across the train track driving down the metalled road and turning right into the club car park. Multiple vehicles were already there but none belonged to anyone he recognised. A couple of people were on the driving range to his right but neither were close by. The weather was good, clear skies and a gentle breeze. The flags lining the entrance road fluttered overhead. The perfect day to play a round. However, golf was currently the furthest thing from his mind. Parking the car some distance from the clubhouse, away from all the other vehicles, he looked around. Checking the time, he realised he was a few minutes early. Turning off the engine and getting out, he leaned against the side of the car and waited. Hearing another car coming along the approach road, he turned expectantly but it was a silver Volvo, not what he was hoping to see. Time passed and continually watching the entrance gates grew irritating.

Looking at his watch for the third time in as many minutes, he paced back and forth. His journey here took just shy of half an hour. *How could it take this long to get across town? It's not like he's an invalid.* He checked the time again. It was now approaching the hour mark. He should have been here by now. Maybe there had been a miscommunication and, all of a sudden, he doubted himself. Was this the agreed location of the meet? Another car. Turning, he was surprised to see a blue Vauxhall crossing the train track between the bungalows sitting either side of the road. *That's coincidental.* The car turned into the gravel-lined car park at a speed far in excess of the signposted ten mile per hour limit and drove towards him. The car stopped and two stone-faced men got out. One was younger and noticeably shorter than the other, and he took the lead.

"Shaun Robinson?" His voice was as light as he was young. "Detective Constable Eric Collet." The officer brandished an identification. He didn't look at it. His stomach felt hollow. His legs numb. Nothing came to mind. It was blank as fear took control. All he managed was a brief nod. "I am arresting you on a charge of perverting the course of justice. You do not need to say anything..." The words failed to register as the other policeman approached him, turning him around to face the car and drawing his hands behind his back. He felt a sharp pain in his wrists as the handcuffs were tightened and he winced.

CHAPTER THIRTY-THREE

TOM JANSSEN GOT out of the silver Volvo and watched Eric making the arrest, Tamara did likewise. It felt fitting that he got to do so. After all, it was his digging that found the connections. In years to come, Eric would be certain to remember this moment. He'd justified the decision to grant his move into CID, coming a long way in a short space of time and proving himself capable in the role. Despite his sense of pride in watching Shaun Robinson's detention, they were far from putting this case to bed.

"Well, you were right about what Shaun would do but did you honestly expect him to hand it to us on a plate?" he asked, turning to Tamara. She smiled, shaking her head.

"No, I didn't."

"I think it was a mistake not to put a car on his house," the bitter edge to his voice gave away the rising levels of apprehension. Tamara seemed not to notice, or ignored it. Either way, it was irritating. "I'll bet he hasn't waited around—"

"Tom, can you leave it?"

Checking his tone, he inclined his head to one side. "Fair enough. I'm sorry, I didn't mean to challenge the decision."

"Yes, you did. That's exactly what you thought," she said.

"Evidently Shaun thought he'd agreed a meeting. That's not happened, so either he's mulling it over back at his house or he's packed a bag."

"Yeah, right. Using our patience against us and making a run for it!"

"Where do you see him going, Tom?" He looked at her. She had that same condescending expression on her face that he often got from Alice. To be fair, that was usually when he'd suggested *she* was in error as well. "And stop doing your chewing thing."

"What *chewing thing*?" he asked, puzzled.

"That thing you do when you're annoyed. You chew, even when you've got nothing in your mouth. It's a dead giveaway that you're pissed off. Hasn't anyone ever told you?"

"No. Thanks for the heads up," he replied, breaking into a grin. Tamara returned it.

"Seriously, if he's done a runner he won't get far." Her phone rang and she answered it. He turned back to see Shaun Robinson being placed in the back of the police car, ready to be shipped back to the station. The man looked almost like he was about to cry. Anyone relying on his silence would be in for a shock. Men like Shaun were powerful in their own world but when taken out of their comfort zone, easily malleable and just as easily broken. Tamara grabbed his attention and he listened to the final exchanges in her conversation. "No, don't do that." She checked her watch. "If it's due to leave at four we'll be there by then. I don't want anyone to tip our hand. Just keep an eye on him please. Discreetly."

"Who was that?" he asked as she thanked the caller before putting her phone away.

"The Border Force. Come on," she instructed, getting back into the car. "He's just bought a one-way ticket to The Netherlands, paid in cash. Anyone would think he knows what we might be doing."

"You tipped them off?" he said, climbing into the car alongside her and pressing the engine start.

"Well, you didn't think I would leave it to chance that we would pick him up, did you?"

"The thought occurred."

"I put it out to the Border Force, particularly focussing on the Eurostar terminals and the airports. If he stays in the UK, then it would only be a matter of time until we pick him up. Once abroad, it would become harder although not impossible. He knows that just as much as we do. The risk would be we might watch the terminals but if we're sloppy, he could slip through. You're going to have to put your foot down."

"Where are we headed?"

"Norwich International Airport. He gambled. He's already passed through security. If we're not there before the flight departs then they'll pull him off the plane. How long will it take us to get there from here?"

"Three quarters of an hour, maybe less if we can get some uniform to run interference for us."

"I'm on to it," she replied, picking up her radio and connecting the control room with their request. Janssen set off, offering a thumbs up to Eric as they passed. The young man looked pleased with himself, unable to shield the elation of his first major collar. He hoped that enthusiasm never waned. Driving back across the train line and joining the main highway, he knew once clear of Sheringham it was a straight run down the A140 to the airport situated on the northern edge of the city. There was every possibility that he, too, would have an expression similar to Eric's when they arrested Peter Samuels. Tamara put the unit down, looking over to him. "Keep an eye out for the flashing lights. A traffic unit is going to pick us up on the outskirts and lead us down."

"Fantastic," he replied. The route was single carriageway, as was most of the road network in Norfolk, and clearing it ahead of them would press home their advantage. "He's not going to roll over, you know."

"Who? Samuels?"

"Yeah. I know the type. He'll make us fight for it every step of the way."

"I don't doubt that. If I was him, though, I wouldn't put much faith in my partner."

"Agreed. Shaun is one of the weak links. If we touch the right pressure points, then I reckon he'll flip."

The traffic car was waiting for them in a layby on the edge of the town and Janssen flashed his lights to signify their approach. The car pulled out ahead of them, flicking on the lights and sirens and accelerating away. Janssen put his foot down and slotted in behind it. This would be a white-knuckle ride and he could feel the adrenalin building.

The two cars pulled up outside the airport terminal half an hour later. Janssen never thought that route could be done in that time frame and he felt on edge as he switched off the engine. For her part, Tamara remained calm and placid throughout the breakneck drive. It was as if she was out for a weekend tour. She caught him looking at her across the roof of the car as she got out.

"Relax, Tom. You made it!" she said, grinning.

"Are you some kind of a master of meditation or something?"

"Speed doesn't scare me," she said, indicating for the uniformed officers to accompany them. They left the cars at the main door and entered the terminal. It wasn't a huge airport. Once beyond security there were limited places in which to kill time. Samuels would be easy to find. Identifying themselves to the nearest officer, they were escorted through the terminal. Glancing at the flight information display, they saw his flight was already boarding. Tamara exchanged words with the staff at the gate and asked about Samuels' whereabouts. He was yet to board.

Ushered through a staff entrance, they arrived at the gates. A group of approximately thirty people were lined up having their passports and boarding cards checked before passing through the double doors and out onto the tarmac. The plane was visible through the windows with passengers making their way up the stairs to board. Janssen scanned the line as they approached. Almost at the back of the queue, he easily spotted the figure of the retired inspector. He glanced at Tamara who gestured for him to proceed. With the two uniformed constables alongside him, they approached the group. Samuels must have heard the approaching footsteps on the polished floor because he turned to glance over his shoulder. If he was surprised to see them, then he didn't show it. Turning to face them, he smiled.

"Tom. What a surprise!" He greeted Janssen warmly.

"Is it, really?" Janssen failed to hide his scepticism.

"Are you gentlemen taking a well-earned break as well?"

"You didn't mention a holiday," he countered.

"I didn't realise I was under obligation to," Samuels hit back.

"The holiday is going to have to wait," Janssen told him, gesturing for the constables to step forward and detain him. "We're placing you under arrest for perverting the course of justice—"

"Preposterous!" The smile dropped, replaced by an air of indignation. He scowled at Tamara as she joined them. "I've done no such thing."

"Good afternoon, Mr Samuels," she said.

"You better have a good explanation for this, young lady."

"Oh, I do. I *really do*," she told him. "We are confident we can build a case against you regarding your handling of the arson at Shaun Robinson's clinic."

"Is that right? What did I do?"

"Falsifying evidence for a start," she replied. Samuels was about to protest but she continued before he was able, "We have a witness who is willing to testify that she was with Niall Bradshaw on the night of the fire. He couldn't possibly have broken into the clinic that night. Furthermore, he was blackmailed by Conn, a registered police informant. But you know all about that already."

"Do I, young lady? The name doesn't ring a bell with me," Samuels said with a shrug.

"You probably know him better as Harry Sutcliffe. After all, you were his handler." Janssen watched as Samuels' eyes narrowed. He was processing events, probably trying to gauge what they knew in order to stay ahead of them.

"Now… yes. Come to think of it, he does sound familiar but I still don't see what this has to do with me."

"Conn not only threatened those people you collared for the arson but I suspect he planted the cans and bottles on the premises which placed their fingerprints at the scene. Either that, or he was close enough to gather that evidence and pass it on to someone else who was closer to the investigation."

"Now, listen here," Samuels' tone lowered and his expression took on a menacing look as he stared directly into Tamara's eyes, "I understand that poor Harry met his demise recently. I think you'll have a hard job garnering testimony from a corpse. To that end, I do hope you have more evidence to produce otherwise my solicitor is going to have a field day with you in court. Although, I doubt it will get that far."

"Green and Gold Holdings," Janssen said. Samuels' head snapped around to face him. For the first time he looked surprised and more than a little concerned. "Care to tell us about that company?"

"I'm not saying anything until I have representation."

"That's okay," Tamara told him. "We expected as much. Just so you know, we are aware you're a director of that company. The only director listed at Companies House. It was very interesting when we found your company invested an eye-watering sum of money in Shaun Robinson's firm shortly before it rebranded itself. One heck of a stroke of business genius to know his business was about to turn around its fortunes. You must have made a killing."

"I have nothing further to add," Samuels said in an almost inaudible whisper.

"Don't worry, there's plenty of time for us to chat," she replied. Janssen could see a barely disguised smile crossing her lips. She was enjoying this moment. The uniformed officers took a firm grip on the retired detective and at Janssen's instruction moved off with him. As Samuels passed her, Tamara leaned in a little closer. *"Not bad for a lesbian, huh?"* Samuels glared at her but didn't speak. They stood together in silence for a moment watching the retired detective being led away.

"Unless Shaun Robinson coughs, we're not going to get him," he said under his breath.

"I know. It's a pity Conn isn't still alive. We could have played the three of them off against each other with almost certainty one of those two would flip on Samuels. We'll still pitch it to the two of them. Let them know there's a deal on the table for the first one who is willing to talk. It might work on Shaun, he's feeble."

"Conn was a career criminal. He would do what was best for himself every time. He's just as weak a link in this chain as Shaun, perhaps more so when you take into account his habitual criminality."

Tamara turned to face him. "What are you saying?"

"We've been asking questions about the arson… about Conn and speaking to all of these guys. What if Samuels sensed we might get wind of what they were up to?"

"And decided to remove the threat from one of those weak links before we could get to them, you mean?" Tamara asked, thinking on his suggestion. At first, Janssen thought the theory too half-baked but the more he considered it, the more it made sense.

"Shaun would be too obvious. Conn on the other hand… he made enemies, moved in dubious circles. Whoever killed Conn knew him. He let the killer into his house and felt confident enough in their company to relax. They were able to get close enough to catch him off guard and strike. I don't see how he would be so complacent if it were Niall Bradshaw, for example. He'd threatened him barely a few days ago."

"I know what you mean," she agreed. "The fact we can't find any evidence Niall was ever in Conn's house, let alone touched or had access to the murder weapon looks good for him."

"A fingerprint comparison should rule Samuels in or out. The problem is, Samuels is way too knowledgeable about our procedures to make that mistake."

"Maybe he used someone else, another character we aren't familiar with who isn't on our radar yet." He was frustrated. Every time they took a large step forward they appeared to come up against yet another obstruction. No one involved in this case appeared capable, or willing, to tell the truth and it was beginning to grate.

"If Samuels helped frame Niall Bradshaw for the arson, we still have to find out who did set it and why. If it was an insurance job with a relaunch of the business in mind, having seen off the threat of the protestors, who did set the blaze? While we're on the subject, we're still no closer to identifying who died in the arson either. I'm beginning to wonder just how much effort was put into finding out. I know it's not technically our case but if we can turn Samuels and Robinson over, prove collaboration and conspiracy, then it will quickly become our priority. It would be nice to have the answers before the next storm from above comes at us. Senior ranks don't like bent coppers, it doesn't read well in the press."

"Maybe it was that simple. All part of that pension plan Samuels was boasting about when we spoke to him at his house. Speaking of the press," he said, thinking of Kelly. "I had to imply some kind of arrangement was possible with a journalist in order to get access to Tracy Bartlett. Without her help, we never would have found her."

Tamara rolled her eyes at him. "We'll work something out but I tell you this, Tom, if she's pretty, you and me are going to have words."

"It was a purely professional agreement," he protested, splaying his hands wide.

"I'll be the judge of that," she said, indicating for them to set off. "Let's get back to the station."

CHAPTER THIRTY-FOUR

TOM JANSSEN SAT IN OPS, turning to see the dispirited faces on both Eric and Tamara as they returned from interviewing Shaun Robinson. Judging from their demeanour, it was quite apparent they were equally successful in their efforts as he'd been with Peter Samuels.

"It went well, then?" he asked, feigning sincerity. Eric shook his head and Tamara frowned.

"It's just as we thought. He's weak but he can afford a decent solicitor," she explained. "We have circumstantial evidence surrounding potential infringements on financial trading but nothing to tie Shaun to a conspiracy, let alone an arson. The strength of the case against the convicted arsonists plays directly to his favour."

Janssen rubbed at his face, attempting to drive away the mental fatigue. "Shaun's prints don't match any of those found at the scene of Conn's murder, neither do Samuels. It was a long shot anyway."

"What about the murder weapon?" she asked. "The file? Anything come back on that?"

"It's clean. Plenty of blood to match it as the murder weapon but no matches in the system for the prints."

"Damn it!" Tamara let her frustration show. "Without a confession or testimony from Conn himself, we're not going to be able to make any of this stick. How did you get on with our dirty copper?"

"Less well than you, by all accounts. He stuck to his guns and said nothing until his solicitor arrived. Then he read out a pre-prepared statement denying each and every allegation before I even managed to put them to him on the record."

"So, we're back to square one?" Eric asked, dejected.

"It looks that way at the moment, I'm afraid."

"What's that you have there?" Tamara asked him, eyeing the paperwork he was reading.

"The detailed forensic analysis from Sophie's excavation in the dunes. I'm trying to find something to tie her to the wider case. We still don't have a motive for her murder and somewhere in all of this is a link, we just haven't found it. She disappeared around the same time as the arson attack, moved in the same circles as Conn, Niall Bradshaw and the other activists and I'm certain they must be linked. Coincidences like this *don't just* happen."

"I couldn't see anything in the post mortem that helps beyond the nature of her injury," Tamara argued. "The body was fully skeletonised and the exposure to salt water killed any trace evidence of DNA on the scraps of her clothing that remained."

"Agreed. I'm revisiting the spectral analysis undertaken on the sheet she was wrapped in when the killer buried her. It's interesting, although I'll admit to having to google some of the science. It was never a strong point of mine at school."

"What's interesting?" Tamara said, coming over and perching herself on the edge of the desk alongside him. He glanced up at her before returning to the papers in front of him.

"The material is a simple cotton, mass produced and gives us nothing to run with. However, there was staining to fibres beyond that which could be attributed to the exposure to the elements, sand and sea water for example. Several sections of the sheet were contaminated by a mixture of silicon dioxide and metal oxides." He glanced back at her before quoting directly from the report, *"These levels could not have resulted from the location of where the body was interred."* He sat back, putting his hands behind his head and interlocking his fingers. "Assuming the killer didn't randomly acquire the material en route to the burial site, which I believe is unlikely, it is more likely to have been present at the scene of the murder."

Tamara nodded. "The killer used whatever was close to hand to wrap the body, making it easier to conceal and transport to the beach."

"Therefore, I suppose the question is *where* could the deposits have come from?"

"Anything else?"

"I was just going to look up the next part. Have you ever heard of a substance called *swarf*? I haven't."

"Yes. It's a generic title used to encompass metal chips as well as other process-specific terms."

"For example?" he asked, impressed by her knowledge.

"Filings, shavings… that type of thing. The by-products of turning and working metal," she said, concentrating hard. "Silicon dioxide is the common constituent of sand but science wasn't my strongest subject at school either—"

Janssen retorted, "You know far more than me. As I understand it, the lab has ruled out the dunes as providing the silicon dioxide in this case."

"If I remember right, silicon dioxide and metal oxide are the common constituents of *slag*, the impurities drawn out of a raw metal ore during the smelting process."

"There aren't any ironworks around here, as far as I know," he said, thinking aloud.

"Not on an industrial scale, no," she agreed, "but we do know someone who has a furnace and works both metal and glass locally. Beatrice Malloy. *Swarf* produced from grinding or turning metal could easily fly off for several metres in any direction. Similarly, *slag residue* needs to be cleaned away. It's messy."

"And you'd want to ensure it didn't get everywhere when you were doing it." A wave of optimism passed through him as he turned his thoughts to Beatrice's odd daughter, River. "River was convicted of the arson but can we be sure she was guilty, seeing as we're confident Niall has an alibi now?" A desk phone rang in the background and Eric, who had half an ear on their conversation, turned to answer it. Tamara looked focussed, piecing the theory together in her mind.

"Niall does but let's not forget River's fingerprints were found inside the building on the window frame at the presumed entry point, whereas Niall and the others were tied to the attack by the beer cans and bottles alone," she said drumming her fingers absently on the desk alongside her.

"We're working on the principle that they were placed there later or provided to Samuels after the fact," Janssen confirmed, looking to the ceiling.

"Exactly, but they couldn't have planted River's prints at the scene. They were catalogued there by CSI. Maybe River Malloy *was* there and the others were telling the truth, they weren't," she theorised. "River didn't confirm or deny their presence. She never spoke a word to the investigators or in her appearance in the dock. Either way, I think we need to pay the Malloys another visit, don't you?"

"Agreed."

"Tom," Eric said, hanging up the receiver, "you have a visitor downstairs."

"We're just on our way out, Eric. Can you deal with them?"

"Sure, I can but I think you're going to want to speak with him directly." Janssen found his curiosity piqued and looked over expectantly. "It's Darren Robinson but he's refusing to speak with anyone apart from you."

A CLEARLY NERVOUS and agitated Darren Robinson stood alone in the lobby of the police station, the officer attending the front desk keeping an eye on him surreptitiously. He glanced towards Janssen as he came through the internal access door, raising a curious eyebrow and inclining his head in the young man's direction. Janssen barely had an opportunity to say an acknowledgement before Darren bounded over, crossing the distance between them at speed.

"Darren, what can I do for you?" he asked. "I can't discuss the reasoning behind your father's detention if that's—"

"No, no. I understand," he replied. His eyes flitted around the space. For a moment, Janssen considered he might be on something such was his apparent state of hypervigilance. "I should have spoken to you about this before but… what with my father… I just… it was all too mental…" the words tailed away. He was talking quickly, his tone raising and lowering at a similar rate, and bordered on incoherent.

"Slow down, Darren. Whatever it is, I'm here to listen." The reassuring words cut through and Darren took a deep breath, steadying himself. "What is it you need to see me about?"

"Before, when you came to the house. You were asking me about Sophie. I told you the truth about her, what I knew… which wasn't much but…"

"*But?*" he pressed.

"The photo you had with you. I wasn't expecting that. It threw me," Darren said. Again, his eyes drifted around the room to focus on anything but Janssen. "I didn't know what to say… I wasn't sure but I am now."

"Take your time." He was careful not to sound annoyed for there was something important coming, he could sense it.

"The picture… not those of Sophie's parents. The other one."

"The party scene?" Darren nodded. "What about it? Did you recognise anyone in it?"

"Yes… my father. Years ago, I worked on a project for my degree. It was my first year, nothing taxing. Merely analysing manmade fibres and their multiple uses." He waved his hands around before him, dismissing the significance of the content. "That doesn't really matter. Anyway, I put together a report and used photographs of clothing taken over the years. I found that shot in a family album. It wasn't particularly important, no one ever noticed that I used it. It's just a random shot. I don't understand the… I don't understand." Janssen took his measure, he was confused, arguably overwhelmed.

"Where was it taken, do you know?"

"Some local festival, I think. Perhaps a harvest supper? I don't really know."

"What about the others, do you recognise any of them?"

Darren shook his head. "I don't think I even realised Dad was in the picture when I used it. After you showed it to me, I went back inside and dug out the old report. It was in a box in the garage with a load of my other uni stuff. Mum never throws anything away, no matter how insignificant it might be. She has boxes of the pictures I drew at my nursery school. Can you believe that?"

Janssen thought about the pile of crayons pictures and random splashes of paint accumulated in Alice's house, artworks created by her daughter Saffy. He could see why a mother would choose to keep as much as possible. It was an old cliché but children grow up fast. "What did you find?"

"The picture was missing. Sophie must have taken it."

"Why would she take that particular photograph?"

It was such an odd thing to do. Darren appeared just as perplexed.

"I have no idea. I mean, I remember her flicking through the stuff in my room back when we used to hang out when my parents weren't around. We were laughing at the fashions over the years and I showed her this report…" He turned and went back to a nearby seat. Rummaging through a small backpack, he produced a document. Bringing it back, he passed it to Janssen. The report was dog-eared at each corner. A result of being stored in a box for the past six years. Janssen flicked through, Darren excitedly pointing out where the picture had been attached. "There!"

Janssen noted the faded section where a picture was clearly missing. There were slits for each corner to be fed through in order to hold it in place, similar to what would be found in a photo album. "She never said anything at the time?"

Darren shrugged. "Not that I recall, no. But she must have taken it. How else could you have found it amongst her things?"

"Do you mind if I hold on to this?" he asked. Darren nodded briefly, looking past him towards the station's interior.

"Will you be charging my father today?" he asked, fear creeping into his voice. Janssen met his eye.

"Too early to say, I'm afraid."

"He wouldn't do it, you know."

"Wouldn't do what?"

"My father wouldn't have set that fire... he's not a killer."

Janssen saw the pain in the boy's eyes. Despite living under his father's intense scrutiny and overbearing nature, he still feared losing him and maybe feared loving a man who could have committed such a terrible crime. That was etched into every line in his pained expression. "I hope not, Darren. I really do."

CHAPTER THIRTY-FIVE

THEY TURNED off the lane and drove through the gates to the Malloy property. Parking the car in front of the main house, Tom Janssen saw Beatrice step out from under the cover of her exterior workshop as she came to see who was visiting. Her expression was fixed and unmoved as she wiped her hands on a dirty cloth before discarding it to one side. Sporting a leather apron, her straw-like hair was pulled away from her forehead and tied at the nape of her neck. Turning away, she retreated from view. He looked at Tamara, raising his eyebrows as he spoke, "That was warm."

"Maybe she's got to know you," she replied with implicit sarcasm. They both got out of the car and crossed the short distance to find Beatrice labouring at her furnace. The door was open and Janssen felt the blast of heat from the fire as Beatrice removed a short length of iron from the flames. The end glowed a light yellow passing to an intense orange a few inches further along. The two detectives kept their distance as she transferred the piece to an anvil. Bending over, she picked up a hammer and began forcefully striking the heated metal. The clang of metal on metal sounded loudly around them.

"Beatrice, we need to speak with you and also River, if she's around," he said, glancing back towards the house for an indication of where the girl might be. Beatrice continued her process, pretending not to have heard him.

"Mrs Malloy!" Tamara addressed her, stern and uncompromising. Beatrice looked up, ceasing her hammering. The two women locked eyes, neither appeared willing to submit to the other's will. "We're not going away until we do." Beatrice glanced between the two of them and put the hammer aside. Picking up the heated metal, still clamped between tongs, she lowered it into a nearby pail of water. The resultant hiss cooled the object and once satisfied, she lifted it out and placed it on a rack to cool. Removing her thick leather gloves, Beatrice placed those on a nearby wooden bench and ran her hands past one another to clear any detritus from her palms.

"Have you not messed with my daughter's head enough already?" she said. "Are you ever going to leave her alone?"

"Once we get the answers we need, certainly," Tamara replied. Beatrice leaned against the work bench, folding her arms across her chest.

"Go on then. Ask your questions." Janssen cast a sideways look at Tamara but she only had eyes for Beatrice. Stepping forward, he held up a photograph to Beatrice. It was the shot removed from Darren Robinson's project work, the one taken at the party and found in Sophie's possession. She stared at it, unflinching. He remembered how she'd lingered on it the first time he showed it to her, several days previously. This time, there was no recognition. "And? What's that supposed to be."

He angled the photo back towards himself momentarily, pointing to those sitting behind the dancing couple in the foreground. Turning it back towards her, he held his forefinger in place. "Well, this was taken back in the late 90s at some local function. The man seated there is Shaun Robinson." Beatrice remained tight lipped. "He's clearly not aware of the camera. He only appears to have eyes for the woman he's talking to. This one here," Janssen indicated to the woman next to Shaun. "The woman in the white dress. You, Beatrice." The two locked eyes, hers narrowing. He waited for a rebuttal but it didn't come.

"What of it?"

"In and of itself, nothing," he replied. "However, it did lead us to wonder why Sophie took such an interest in it. So much so that she took the picture without permission. Why might she do that, do you think?" Beatrice shrugged, breaking eye contact and glancing back towards the house. "We were stumped too. For a while at least. Then we got to thinking about Sophie and why it might be relevant."

"And?" Beatrice asked softly. Janssen thought she wasn't quite as curious as someone might be when coming at something from a position of ignorance.

"You were aware of Sophie's relationship with your daughter, weren't you? The fact they were more than friends."

"Yes," she replied, curt. "They were lovers. So what?"

"You were friendly with the man whose business your daughter campaigned against, even set fire to," Tamara said.

Beatrice glanced in her direction. "It's a small community. Everyone knows everyone else. That's inevitable once you've been here for a few years."

Janssen lowered the photo. "You told us how hard it was to be a single parent, raising your daughter alone. That got me thinking, so I looked into your daughter's history. You never listed her father's name when you registered River after she was born."

"You've got no right," she fumed.

"Oh… yes we have," he countered. "You could clear that up for us now, if you'd like to? You told us how you worked multiple jobs to make ends meet," he said looking around. "This place must require a fair income to keep it running. I don't see how working those jobs could keep you in a house like this around here, not without assistance. We're making a leap of course but Sophie's curiosity says a lot. Did she know? Did she guess, much the same as we have done?"

"She was a horrible, spiteful child," Beatrice sneered. "My River deserved so much better than her. A brat of a teenager who moved from one mark to the next, only ever out for what she could get and I told her as much."

"You argued?" he asked.

Beatrice looked away for a moment, chewing her lower lip. Turning back to him, she scowled as she spoke. "I spoke to her, yes. I told her I wanted her to have nothing to do with River. She was seeing Shaun's son but you knew that, but did you know it was at the same time as she was coercing my daughter into a relationship? Feigning a love affair... convincing my beautiful little girl that she had all the answers. She was a disgrace."

"How did she react to that?"

"You would think she would be angry," Beatrice said, the bitterness subsiding. "But she didn't rise to the insult... she laughed. She laughed in my face! Sophie didn't care, she had no conscience. The world was her plaything and I was just another toy. She thought it hypocritical... my relationship with Shaun. How I always took the moral high ground despite having a bastard child with such a disgusting man."

"How did that come about, the affair?" Tamara asked, moving to Janssen's left. He knew she was placing herself in a strategic position to one side of Beatrice while he remained on the other.

Beatrice shrugged. "Like I said. This is a small community. Sometimes..." her expression took on a faraway look. "Sometimes you make mistakes in life..." she paused, looking past Janssen. He turned and saw River standing behind him a short distance away. By the look on her face, she had been there a while. Beatrice continued, staring directly at her daughter as her expression softened, "And they turn out to grant you the most wonderful gifts imaginable." Her genuine pride was evident. Tears brimmed in her daughter's eyes. "I'm sorry, love. Sorry you had to hear this."

"That night, when you argued, what happened?" Janssen asked.

"We both said our piece… and she left."

"I don't think that's the case, is it," he asserted. "We believe Sophie was killed elsewhere before being buried in the dunes. What's more, she was most likely wrapped in a blanket at that very location… we have evidence that that happened here."

"That's not true!" River barked. All eyes turned on her. Beatrice tried to move towards her daughter but Janssen blocked her path. "That's not how it happened *at all*!"

"Then tell us how it did," Tamara said quietly.

Beatrice appeared pained, the anger and bitterness replaced by compassion for her daughter's plight. River's breathing became ragged. The emotion threatened to overwhelm her. "I was here that night." She looked to her mother. "You didn't know… but I was. I heard you arguing with Sophie. I heard what she said about you and Shaun." Beatrice raised a hand across her mouth as she, too, appeared on the verge of tears.

"Oh, my poor baby," she whispered.

"I met Sophie as she came outside," River continued. "I couldn't believe you would be involved… with… that man and I told her so. She swore it was true… claimed she had some proof." Her eyes were glazed over now, she was speaking in a monotone voice, expressionless and unfocussed. "She told me I had a right to know. That everyone should know where they come from, no matter where that was. I was angry with her… furious… she reached for me, to pull me in for a hug and… and I picked up the first thing I saw and I hit her." Tears streamed now. River's entire body seemed to be gently rocking from side to side. Janssen feared she might keel over at any moment. "She fell." A lucid moment followed as she looked into her mother's eyes, repeating the words, "She fell… she fell and I ran away… and I kept running until I couldn't run anymore."

Janssen exchanged a glance with Tamara and she nodded

almost imperceptibly. "Where did you run to, River?" he asked. Her head rolled and she blinked away tears.

"I ended up at Lesley's. I didn't know where else to go. I was angry at her, at Sophie, my mother... myself for being the daughter of that piece of shit Robinson... angry at him for abandoning me for all those years. I wanted to die..." Beatrice gasped. "I wanted to set fire to the world and watch it burn in the flames around me."

"And that's when you went to the clinic... to put those discarded plans into action," Tamara suggested, referring to what Niall had told her in interview. River looked at her and nodded.

"I didn't care about the consequences anymore. I wanted to hurt Robinson... break him just like he broke me."

"Lesley went with you, didn't she?" Janssen asked.

"Yes. She wanted to stop me... I shouted at her to leave, wished I had never gone to hers in the first place. She thought it was madness," River said, barely above a whisper. "She was right. I should have listened but... it was like I was someone else. It wasn't me doing it anymore. I read about that once in a book I found in the prison library. A dissociative state I think they called it." She looked to him, inclining her head to one side. "Les tried to stop me but I pushed her away and then... then there was fire. It was in front of me and then all around us... in seconds. I froze. I remember part of me wanted to stay, be consumed by it all. That way it would be over. Les was screaming, pulling at me to get me to leave." She stared into space, Janssen thought she was reliving the moment.

"But you did leave," he said.

"Yes, but we were cut off from the way we got in and... it was all really confusing. I think there was an explosion, I can't recall it properly but I was on the floor. We both were. I called to Les but she wasn't moving. I tried to lift her up but she was too heavy, I couldn't manage her. The fire was so hot... so intense." She wept openly, speaking through the tears. "I panicked... I didn't want to but I ran and I left her there." River looked into his eyes. "I left Lesley there to die."

Janssen drew breath, the gaps in their knowledge were being filled piece by piece and he knew there was more. "Tell us how you went about burying Sophie's body." River snapped her attention back to the present, almost as if flicking a switch.

"I didn't!" she stated emphatically. "I swear to you. I wandered around that night, after the fire. I didn't know what to do and in the end I came home."

"What time was that?" he asked.

"Three in the morning, something like that. Sophie wasn't here. She'd left. I figured I'd knocked her unconscious, that's all. I never thought for a moment she was dead." She implored him with her eyes. "I didn't bury her in the dunes. I would never do that to her... despite everything she said, I still loved her. I've no idea who killed her or how she got there. *I didn't do it!*"

CHAPTER THIRTY-SIX

TAMARA GREAVE EYED RIVER CLOSELY. There was something dangerous about the girl but at the same time, she exhibited a vulnerability that drew out compassion from deep inside her. She was a much-troubled soul.

"The problem is, River," she explained, "we know Sophie's body was wrapped here before being transported to the beach. The forensic analysis of the material shows residue from metalworking. I'm certain it's only a matter of time before we will definitively prove it came from here, in this very workshop. If it wasn't you, then how did it happen?"

River fixed her with a stare, appearing to be readying herself for a strong rebuttal. Her lips moved but for a few seconds the words wouldn't come. Instead, her expression softened and her gaze carried to her mother. Tamara followed it. River noticed and became suddenly alert. "I... I was mistaken. I remember now," her eyes darted around, fixing onto nothing in particular before moving up and to the left as she recounted the events of that night. "You're right. I came back and Sophie was still there, where she fell. I wrapped her in cloth and... took her to the beach."

Janssen caught Tamara's eye. She wondered if he also

remembered what Eric said about the involuntary movements of the eye when accessing memory or the creative centres of the brain. He was as sceptical as she was. "How did you get her there?" she asked.

River hesitated. "I dragged her."

"From here?" Tamara failed to mask her doubt. "It's several miles to the coast. Which route did you take?" River stood looking at her, wide eyed. Her body language telegraphed her deceit.

"I... I don't remember. I must have blanked it out."

"And yet, you remember everything else so clearly," Tamara countered. River nodded. "You were unable to pull Lesley Abbott away from the seat of the fire you started at the clinic but you could drag Sophie several miles to the beach and then bury her. What with, your bare hands or did you manage to carry a shovel with you at the same time?

"I... I... don't remember."

"Then see if you can remember how you came to kill Conn?" River was thrown. Standing open-mouthed now, she failed to muster a response. "Because somebody killed him in order to stop him revealing a secret. That was his business, finding out the darkest secrets people wanted to keep hidden and using them to extort money. By all accounts he was quite adept at doing so. When did he come to you? How much did he demand in order to buy his silence?

"He... he... didn't," River stammered, seeking an effective reply.

"That's because you didn't kill him..." Tamara stated, turning to face Beatrice, "did she?" All eyes fell upon Beatrice who stood with her arms at her side, fists clenched. Her body language tense and rigid. "How did he know about what happened to Sophie? Who did you tell?" Tamara asked.

"No! It was me," River pleaded, her desperation evident.

"Enough!" Beatrice snapped. River's tears fell once more. "Enough of this. It has to stop." Stepping forward towards River,

Janssen moved aside on this occasion. Beatrice placed a reassuring hand on her daughter's shoulder and with the other, tilted her chin upwards, forcing her to make eye contact. "I told you I would do anything to make sure you didn't go back to prison. I failed before. I won't this time." Turning back to face Tamara, she smiled weakly. "I guess the past cannot stay buried forever, no matter how hard you try."

"River is Shaun's daughter, you can confirm that," she said. Beatrice nodded.

"We had an affair. It was not a great period in my life. I cannot say I regret doing it because I ended up with my beautiful little girl, who I wouldn't change for the world," she said, touching River's cheek with the outside of her palm. "Shaun was married... his wife pregnant with their child."

"Darren?" Tamara asked.

"Yes. To be fair to him, although he insisted on keeping everything quiet, he never tried to force me into having... well, not carrying the baby to term. And he made regular financial contributions. As you rightly said, this house takes a lot of running and I had very little at the time. I still had to work. It was a struggle. He didn't cover everything and why should he? I can have no complaints about that side of things. I always thought that one day I would tell you," she said to River, "but the time was never right. I know it wasn't fair on you, none of it. Maybe I got it wrong but I did my best."

"You buried Sophie?"

"I did," Beatrice confirmed with a solemn nod. "I found her that night. River had already gone. She was lying just over there, unconscious," she said, pointing to the ground near to where Tamara was standing. "I strangled her. The world would be a better place without someone like Sophie in it. She didn't deserve to be here, *didn't deserve* to be with my daughter. I figured no one would miss her. One more troubled runaway. Who would make much of an effort looking for her? Had the storm not revealed her to the world that's how she would have remained, a forgotten life, as tragic as much as it was wasted."

"How did you get her to Wells?" Tamara pressed, ignoring the callous nature of her explanation.

"In the back of the van," Beatrice said flatly. "I rolled her in one of my old dust sheets and drove her out to the coast. I parked away from the highway and dragged her through the pine forest thinking no one would see me if I went that way. It was in the early hours. There was no one around." She exhaled deeply through her nose, a rueful smile parting her lips. "I saw that necklace she was wearing. I made it for River, gave it to you as a present that Christmas. Do you remember?" she said to her daughter. River smiled weakly.

"Yes, I gave it to Sophie."

"I know. I almost took it back," Beatrice said, the smile fading. "I didn't think she should keep it. In the end, I left it on her for fear that if I took it and someone found it here, at the house, I might be linked to her death." She looked back towards Tamara, taking on a forlorn expression. "The irony of it."

"And what of Conn?" Janssen asked, his eyes scanning the workshop. Tamara wondered if he was searching for a tool to match the murder weapon they found at the scene. She did likewise. "How did he find out? Because he did, didn't he?"

Beatrice nodded slowly. "Although I'm certain no one saw me taking Sophie out to the dunes, I bumped into him on my way back to the van. Heaven knows what he was doing out there in the woods in the middle of the night. He was such a *strange* fellow. What he made of seeing me at the time I don't know but, that morning when her remains were unearthed, he was there. He recognised the necklace... put two and two together."

"So, he was blackmailing you after all?" Tamara asked.

"He tried," Beatrice replied with a humourless chuckle. "I think he thought we had much more than we actually do. I promised him I would pay, obviously. I mean, what else could I do," she shrugged. "Paying him wasn't an option, though. Shaun stopped giving us money years ago. Even after River turned eighteen, he still contributed. All that stopped after the fire... and the court case. I understood."

"You probably could have made him continue in order to keep the secret," Tamara suggested. Beatrice shook her head.

"You may find this difficult to believe but I'm not minded that way. He did right by us... to a certain extent," she explained. "Had Conn come on me for money a couple of years earlier then I may have been able to pay him off. However, my art doesn't sell as well as it used to. I went to Conn's house to speak with him, to try and reason with him. I had no intention of killing him. You should know that. Thinking about the type of man he was even if I had paid him the money he wanted it would never have been enough. He would only have come back for more and more."

Janssen drew her attention towards the rear of the workshop. She followed his gaze and saw a line of tools hanging from an elevated bar fixed on to the far wall. They appeared to be of the same collection, aged, with wooden handles, light brown and well used. Even with a cursory glance it was clear the murder weapon matched.

"You went there with a weapon, Beatrice," Tamara said flatly. "You wore gloves and you parked away from the house. I find it hard to believe you didn't know what was going to happen that night."

Beatrice put a hand to her daughter's cheek, affectionately stroking it and doing her best to smile. River leaned in to her mother's touch. "Think what you must. I only ever sought to protect my daughter and I would change nothing."

Janssen stepped forward, gently drawing Beatrice's hands down and placing them behind her back. He attached the handcuffs and gently encouraged her to walk in the direction of the car. She silently mouthed an apology to River as she was led away. River appeared crestfallen, sinking to the floor and weeping openly. Tamara looked on as Janssen placed the self-confessed killer in the back of the car. Walking away a short distance, she called in to the station, requesting officers to attend. They would need to process the area, looking to scientifically corroborate the story as far as possible.

Observing the crumpled form of River, sitting on the floor while she talked, she wondered what would become of her. Beatrice's claim to have strangled Sophie to death conveniently absolved her daughter of another manslaughter charge. Confident that River was indeed telling the truth, there was no suggestion of premeditation on her part in the attack on Sophie and her attempt to shield her mother from blame was admirable if misguided. Could Beatrice have killed the stricken teenager and then buried her to cover up her murder? It was certainly plausible, however, in her opinion unlikely. It was more likely Beatrice was seeking to do exactly what she just claimed, *to protect the daughter she loved.* To prove either scenario would be difficult. In the event of a confession, Beatrice would most likely get her way and keep her daughter out of prison.

Beatrice would face two counts of murder. *Another life destroyed by the secrets we choose to keep.*

CHAPTER THIRTY-SEVEN

Tamara Greave pulled into the car park. Having only been here once before, she struggled to remember exactly where Janssen moored his boat. The marina was small, four jetties along either side of the riverbank for owners to moor their vessels. Eyeing Janssen's car parked near to the water's edge, she drove over and parked alongside it. Janssen was on deck at the stern kneeling alongside a hatch, seemingly working on the engine. He looked up, noting her approach. It took a moment for him to realise it was her, though. Gripping the side of the car door as well as the passenger seat, she levered herself up to sit on the top of her seat. Janssen couldn't hide his surprise.

"Nice convertible," he said, picking up a rag and wiping his hands while he stepped from the boat onto the bank. Coming closer, he tilted his head and scanned the length of the Austin Healey. "Cars aren't really my thing but... this is in a beautiful condition. Her face split a broad grin as she cast a sweeping glance around the car before opening the door and getting out. The door shut with a reassuring thud, far removed from the modern era of smooth closing mechanisms and lightweight composite alloys.

"Isn't she just? I thought you lived on a canal boat?"

He shook his head, his brow furrowing.

"No canals around here." His gaze shifted, taking in her car. "This is new, right?" he asked, before shaking his head with an embarrassed smile. "I mean, to you. It's a classic."

"It's a Mark III 3000. One of the last ever built," she said, beaming with pride. "Although, judging by the state of the hood I won't be taking it out in the rain anytime soon."

"Where on earth did you find it?" Janssen leaned over, first checking he wouldn't transfer grease to the vehicle from his hands and spied the interior.

"I told you I was going to see Ann Grable, Sophie's former foster mother." He met her eye and nodded that he did. "Well, this was her late husband's hobby. It had been sitting in their garage for the last few years and she saw how enthused I was when I saw it. She made me an offer I couldn't pass up. She took some starting after this amount of time I can tell you."

Janssen stepped back, chewing on his lower lip at the mention of the dead teenager. "How did she take the news?"

"I think it came as something of a relief. The Grables gave themselves a hard time about failing the girl... you can still see the pain in Ann's expression. At least now, she can see that Sophie didn't take off and end up who knows where. Although she was devastated to learn of the circumstances surrounding her death." Janssen bobbed his head in understanding. Returning his focus to the car, he inclined his head to one side.

"So, what are your plans?" he asked her.

"I've been thinking... about the job offer," she was aware of the sensitivities surrounding the subject. They hadn't discussed it since her transfer was first mooted.

"Oh, yeah. What have you decided?"

"I figured... I'd take it," she said glancing to her left as another boat chugged past them into the marina. She held her breath for a moment trying to gauge his reaction. He said nothing, merely continued his inspection of the car. His apparent indifference to her answer irritated her and she lost her patience, perhaps snapping at him more than she meant to. "*What do you think about that?*"

He glanced up at her, seemingly unaware of her frustration with him. He shrugged and then smiled. "I think that's great. It'll be nice to have you around." She was momentarily thrown. That wasn't the reaction she expected, hoped for, yes, but certainly not *expected*. His choice of the word *nice* bothered her greatly, though. It was such a vanilla word that offered no depth to his actual feelings. Although, that was Tom all over. "Really? Are you sure?"

"Yes, of course," he said, backing away from his inspection of her new toy. "After all, I didn't come back to Norfolk for the career move. It was never about that." She was watching him intently and he appeared to notice, becoming uncomfortable all of a sudden. "Really," he added, not wanting to meet her gaze. "It will be great to spend more time with you." She smiled, feeling the tension dissipate from her shoulders only to be replaced by an awkward sensation. Burying her attraction to him for the good of their professional working relationship this past week had been necessary but now, there was nothing to stand in the way.

"I was thinking that you might want to join me in taking this little lovely for a spin," she said, brushing her hand across the front wing, accompanied by an enthusiastic bounce and a warm smile. "You'll know somewhere we could get some lunch and—"

"Tom," a female voice called. They both turned to see a figure appear from below deck. She recognised her as Alice, although they'd only met once in passing some time ago. Tamara felt her heart sink. Alice smiled at her, stepping from the boat onto the bank and crossing the short distance to them standing beside the car. Tamara assessed her. She was curvy and attractive. A brunette, her hair hung below the shoulder and appeared tousled as if she was yet to shower and, judging by the size of it, she was wearing one of Tom's shirts. "Sorry, I didn't realise you had company." She looked to Janssen, evidently seeking an introduction.

"Alice, this is Tamara…" his tone was softer than normal, the voice a pitch higher, "my new boss."

"Hi," Alice said, offering her hand. Tamara took it, returning the smile. "Nice to meet you properly at last. Tom talks about you all the time. I was just thinking about making us an early lunch. We missed breakfast. You're more than welcome to join us."

She could think of nothing worse. The awkwardness of asking Tom out on what she hoped would be a date had been replaced by a wave of embarrassment. Feeling herself flush, she waved away the invite as politely but firmly as she could, fearful that she would see straight through her.

"Another time, then," Alice replied, slipping an arm around Janssen's waist. He too, appeared uncomfortable but Alice was alongside him and couldn't see the mixture of emotions he exhibited. Was it merely embarrassment or was there some guilt thrown in at the same time? She was uncertain. If so, from where did the guilt derive? His feelings towards her, Alice, or both. Wanting to remove herself from the situation, she encouraged Janssen to move aside with her eyes, thereby enabling her to get back into the car.

"Right, I'd best be off," she said as jovially as she could, realising her own voice arguably betrayed her emotions but neither of them seemed to notice. Putting the key in the ignition, she silently prayed for the car to start without a fuss this time. Almost blowing a kiss heavenward as the engine fired up at only the second attempt, she found reverse at the first time of asking and moved off. Alice gave her a friendly wave before leaning into Janssen, raising herself onto her tiptoes and affectionately kissing him on the cheek just as she turned the car around and made to drive away. Returning the wave, she forced a smile.

"That went well, T," she muttered to herself as she reached the junction and waited for a car to pass before she could pull out. Looking in the rear-view mirror, she saw Alice climb back aboard the boat ahead of Janssen. He looked in her direction. For a second she thought their eyes met in the mirror but there was no way he could see that level of detail from this distance. Then he turned away and stepped aboard himself. "Stupid idea anyway," she chided herself, although the words sounded hollow with little genuine feeling. A car horn sounded, snapping her back to the present. Someone else was stationary off to her right, waiting for her to move off so that he could reach the main road himself. Offering an apology by way of a small wave, she pulled away.

The uplifting optimism of the day ahead was tempered only slightly by disappointment. The wind blew her hair across her face and she brushed it aside with her left hand. What she'd seen of the coast road thus far encouraged her to go exploring. The smile returned to her face as she selected fourth, the powerful engine roaring as she picked up speed. The road ahead was hers and hers alone. Thinking on it, that was just how she liked it and she wouldn't have it any other way.

Turn the page for a preview of the next book in the series;

Kill Our Sins
Hidden Norfolk – Book 3

FREE BOOK GIVEAWAY

Visit the author's website at **www.jmdalgliesh.com** and sign up to the VIP Club and be first to receive news and previews of forthcoming works.

Here you can download a FREE eBook novella exclusive to club members;

Life & Death - A Hidden Norfolk novella

Never miss a new release.

No spam, ever, guaranteed. You can unsubscribe at any time.

Enjoy this book? You could make a real difference.

Because reviews are critical to the success of an author's career, if you have enjoyed this novel, please do me a massive favour by entering one onto Amazon.

Type the following link into your internet search bar to go to the Amazon page and leave a review;

http://mybook.to/Bury_Your_Past

If you prefer not to follow the link please visit the Amazon sales page where you purchased the title in order to leave a review.

Reviews increase visibility. Your help in leaving one would make a massive difference to this author.
Thank you for taking the time to read my work.

KILL OUR SINS - PREVIEW
HIDDEN NORFOLK - BOOK 3

A FAMILIAR FEELING, the tightness in the chest, returned as the car headlights illuminated the brick pillars set to either side of the driveway's entrance. The metal gates hung open. Granting them a cursory glance as she passed by, they looked like they hadn't been closed in years. One hung low, embedded in the ground with the vegetation growing through it. A sign, cable-tied to the bars, indicated danger and advised the public to keep out. It too had seen better days, no doubt put there years previously.

The drive wound its way up towards an imposing building, standing almost in silhouette as the first shafts of daylight threatened to crest the horizon at any moment. Bringing the car to a stop a hundred feet or so away from the building, she sat there, staring at it unblinking, her fingers flexing on the steering wheel as she sought to control her breathing. The only audible sounds came from the fans circulating warm air to the cabin along with the car's engine, quietly ticking over in the background.

Was she ready? She would never be ready.

No light was visible from the interior of the building. It was long since abandoned. The windows boarded up. The once well-tended gardens left to run wild. Parking the car before the main entrance, she switched the engine off and the cabin lit up. Getting out, she braced against the cold, shivering as the breeze blew across her. The overnight skies were clear and the slate grey of the pre-dawn light illuminated the heavy frost underfoot.

A solitary call from a crow broke the silence.

Opening the door to the rear seats, she retrieved her coat and pulled it on, hurrying to fasten it up. Pushing the door closed, it did so with a loud *thunk*, the sound carrying in the crisp air. She looked around. There was no need for concern. There was no one around to hear.

No one ever heard.

Set within three acres of grounds, the building was wholly encompassed by farmland, in its heyday its status unparalleled. A masterpiece of the Victorian Arts and Crafts movement. But that was a bygone age. Now it remained empty, bordering on derelict. Forgotten by the world, unwanted.

The sound of another car approaching came to ear and she turned. The beam from the headlights could be seen first, flickering through the hedgerow lining the main road before it slowed and took the turn onto the drive. Moments later, the car briefly came into view as it cleared the trees before the lights fell on her. The beams were dazzling and she raised a hand to shield her eyes. Glancing at her watch, she waited patiently. A strange feeling passed through her as the car came to a stop and the driver got out, nervous anticipation mixed with a sense of relief. A passing sense of self-doubt flashed through her mind and she dismissed it almost as soon as it manifested. This was the time.

It had to be.

———

Kill Our Sins
Hidden Norfolk – Book 3

———

ALSO BY J M DALGLIESH

The Hidden Norfolk Series

One Lost Soul

Bury Your Past

Kill Our Sins

Tell No Tales

Hear No Evil

Life and Death*

*FREE eBook - A Hidden Norfolk novella

The Dark Yorkshire Series

Divided House

Blacklight

The Dogs in the Street

Blood Money

Fear the Past

The Sixth Precept

Box Sets

Dark Yorkshire Books 1-3

Dark Yorkshire Books 4-6

Audiobooks

The entire Dark Yorkshire series is available in audio format, read by the award-winning Greg Patmore.

Divided House

Blacklight

The Dogs in the street

Blood Money

Fear the Past

The Sixth Precept

Audiobook Box Sets

Dark Yorkshire Books 1-3

Dark Yorkshire Books 4-6

*Hidden Norfolk audiobooks arriving 2020

Printed in Great Britain
by Amazon